Mulligan's Reach

Jennie Orbell

*Best Wishes
Jennie Orbell*

Published in 2013 by FeedARead.com Publishing –
Arts Council funded

Copyright © Jennie Orbell.

The author or authors assert their moral right under the Copyright, Designs and Patents Act, 1988, to be identified as the author or authors of this work.

All Rights reserved. No part of this publication may be reproduced, copied, stored in a retrieval system, or transmitted, in any form or by any means, without the prior written consent of the copyright holder, nor be otherwise circulated in any form of binding or cover other than that in which it is published and without a similar condition being imposed on the subsequent purchaser.

A CIP catalogue record for this title is available from the British Library.

For Mum, who remains my inspiration.

Prologue

The wind caught his frantic cries, bowling them pitilessly against grey rock, smashing them into oblivion. Twice he stumbled and fell, and twice he rose, throwing his gaunt body against the flattening wind, until, finally, he reached the edge of the precipice. Cut off by grey, swelling sea stood his wife, her face ghostly in the pale moonlight. At her breast, the baby sobbed.

He screamed at her to jump but the wind swooped again, lifting his cries and hurling them undelivered into the sea. She fell to her knees, cradling the whimpering baby, pulling the drenched shawl around its fragile body. He called again, begging her to jump, and this time the wind ignored him, letting his voice reach her. She rose to her feet and stepped towards him, stiltedly, afraid of what lay ahead and terrified of what lay behind her. Again, he called, pleading with her to jump the divide, promising he'd catch her.

She cried out, her voice broken and desperate. She would try. Try to jump the swirling undercurrents that gaped beneath her like the waiting mouths of a pack of ravenous wolves.

He stood on the edge of the platform and stretched out a hand.

Kitty Mulligan leapt for her life, the baby, Asak, clutched tightly to her breast. Legs kicked. An arm flailed. A hand reached out. Fingers touched. Then they were gone and the murderous sea closed over them.

Isla dived into the rushing water.

Present Day
Chapter 1

Alex McBride stood on the beach, watching as the paint-blistered charter boat floated towards her like a ghostly apparition through the afternoon heat shimmer.

She narrowed her brown eyes against the glare, focusing hard on the man standing at the bow. Even at a distance he stood tall and steady. She didn't want a man on the island. After Peter, she wouldn't be too upset if she never saw a man under the age of fifty again, let alone, have to put one up as a house guest. Fifty was a safe age; a nicely rounded kind of age; an age when a man's deceitful, commitment-lacking ways should be over and if Jodie had used her common sense, this wouldn't be happening. Three weeks ago, they had learned that their stud horse, Mac, was useless. Lab results had proved conclusively that his sperm count was not only abnormally low, but slow as well. Alex had ranted, blaming Jodie, demanding to know why, as a vet, she hadn't run the appropriate tests *before* Alex had paid out three-quarters of a million pounds for the horse. Jodie had shouldered the blame and promised she would come up with something. This *something* was now approaching the island in the form of an old university friend of hers, Kane Mitchell, who, according to Jodie, just conveniently happened to be in Queensland with his stallion. For 'old times sake' Kane Mitchell was prepared to bring his stallion over and let Jodie use him to cover their mares. The rest of the information had been rather sketchy. Jodie had mentioned Mitchell was travelling with his kid and that they came from Amarillo, Texas, which by all accounts made him the original 'rootin' tootin' cowboy.' Jodie had been up half the night baking cakes, making up beds and generally trying to creep back into Alex's good books, something that Jodie always, somehow, managed to do.

Briefly, the boat changed direction, avoiding the narrow stretch of shallow coral reef and headed towards the landing ramp. It had seen better days, never being intended to be used for off-loading horses and Alex hoped that it would last long enough to get the visiting stallion on to the island. As the boat nudged its way in and berthed against the ramp, Jodie joined Alex on the beach.

Like a gold medal athlete descending from the parallel bars, the tall man leapt from the boat and landed with a perfect bend of both knees. Alex let apprehensive eyes run over him, studying, evaluating. He was better looking than Jodie's brief description had led her to believe and younger too – much younger. He was sturdy, without being overweight, with thatched, honey-coloured hair that curled to his collar. His eyes were the colour of a Norfolk sea on a winter's afternoon: deep, grey and stormy. His face was unshaven, his nose a little on the large side and his mouth ordinary. Fine lines fanned from the sides of his eyes suggesting he smiled a lot. That was good. He would need a sense of humour if he intended to stay. Alex took the large hand he offered. 'Mr Mitchell,' she said politely. 'How nice of you to come and bale us out in our hour of need, as it were. I'm Jodie's friend and business partner, Alex McBride.'

Jodie stepped up, confusion all over her elfin face and was about to explain that *this*, unless he'd had extensive surgery, a voice-box replacement and had shrunk by at least three inches, *wasn't* Kane Mitchell, when the man said quickly, 'I'm Jack, Miss McBride, not Kane. Kane's bringing the horse.'

Alex frowned, 'Not Kane?'

'No.'

There was little room for further conversation as just then a chestnut horse, the size of a small mountain, careered forward from the back of the boat. There wasn't much time for Alex to do a bit of mental arithmetic, but if this man, Jack, was Kane Mitchell's son then that must make Kane Mitchell well into his fifties – probably even older. Maybe her earlier fears were going to prove unfounded. Jodie hadn't said that he was a mature student when she knew him.

'I think you had better stand well back, Miss McBride,' Jack said politely, as the chestnut horse, snorting and plunging, dragged its handler to the edge of the boat. Then it reared, teetering on its hind legs, punching the hot, dead air like a champion boxer intent on flattening anything that got in its way.

'Blimey,' Jodie squeaked, edging her small body behind the man and linking her fingers into his belt loops. 'Is *that* the thing that's going to serve our mares?'

Jack nodded, grinning, his vision fixed on the rearing horse. 'Don't take too much notice. The journey's freaked him out a bit. We hit a bit of choppy water back there. He'll be fine when he's on dry land.'

'Perhaps I should help?' Alex said, instinctively moving forward along the ramp, only to feel a restraining hand circle her waist.

'I don't think that would be advisable, Miss McBride. Best leave it to Kane; he knows what he's doing.'

Alex moved away from his grip as Jodie sidled up to stand behind her. Again the stallion reared, its rapier-like legs cleaving through the air before it slammed back down and charged towards the ramp. Almost there, it appeared to change its mind and, with an action that took everyone by surprise, dropped its head between its knees and ran backwards, cannoning across the boat.

Captain 'Plug' Towers - so called because the locals reckoned he always had his sticky, fat fingers bunged into something – edged nervously to the side of his beloved boat, *Donna.* Plug Towers understood boats perfectly, right down to the last rusting nut and bolt, but not lunatic horses. He wouldn't lose any sleep if he never had to transport one again. The trouble was it paid well. He'd made a tidy sum out of this little circus. Plug wiped a greasy hand across two days' stubble, surveying the manic scene through grey eyes screwed up against the sun. His sun-bleached hair stood erect, gelled by days of salt spray and sea breezes. He took another step towards the side of the boat as the horse continued reversing in his direction, slamming huge hooves against the deck, one after the other, in a rapid tattoo.

'Bloody hell, cobber!' he cussed loudly, in a broad Australian tongue, plastering his squat body against the peeling paintwork. 'Is that thing safe?'

As a direct response, Nightwalker slammed on the brakes, kicked out a piece of Plug's rigging with one lethal blow from a hind hoof and sent splinters flying in all directions.

'Streuth! Watch me boat, mate!' Plug shouted, waving his arms at the approaching horse as it continued backing towards him.

Alex, Jodie and Jack watched in wide-eyed, mouth-opening horror as again, the stallion ducked his head to the deck, gained control and, towing his handler the remaining distance across the boat, pinned Plug up tight against the side. His face had disappeared somewhere in the darkest depths of the horse's voluminous tail, up against its anus. No one could quite decipher the muffled expletives coming from the horse's backside.

Unfortunately, Nightwalker chose that precise moment to raise his tail and defecate. The little man was freed from his hairy, stinking prison as the horse took off again, unaware that Plug had ever been there. Spluttering and spitting profusely, he ripped his shirt from his body, threw it with force onto the deck and screamed, 'Some pommy bastard is gonna pay big dollars for this! I'm covered in shit!'

Kane Mitchell had remained cool throughout the entire episode. Now, the man and horse were stepping off the boat and onto the rickety ramp. This creaked a severe warning as the horse halted and surveyed its new surroundings before executing a perfect arabesque with one back leg, removing any remaining tension. It raised its lathered head and whinnied, its burnished coat reverberating over its ribcage. From the barn, Mac challenged back. The stallion flicked his ears, snorted and tiptoed along the ramp, calmer now, wanting to be on *terra firma* as soon as possible.

Kane Mitchell's steadying tones reached Alex. As the man and horse drew level, he raised his free hand and touched his hat.

'Ma'am,' he said, short and to the point, in a voice so sugary it could probably have set jam.

Alex lifted her head. With the sun behind him, it was difficult to make out his features. She raised a hand to shield her eyes and said, 'Well done, Mr Mitchell. I thought for a minute there you were going to lose him. You did very well to keep hold of him.'

The cowboy removed his hat and bowed theatrically, sweeping the hat before him in a full-stretch semi-circle. 'Why, thank you, Ma'am.'

Alex winced. He seemed a bit short on vocabulary. *And* she was getting a headache from staring into the sun. He seemed to appreciate this and handing the horse over to Jack, turned. As she lowered her hand, he came into view - perfectly. The man that stood before her was no crusty old cowboy; not crusty, not old, and definitely *not* the father of the man standing chatting to Jodie. The latter, Alex noticed, was making no attempt to come forward and acknowledge the arrival of her *'friend from way back'*, the old buddy she'd known for *'donkeys years.'*

Kane Mitchell was the full set - tall, dark and handsome. He looked like a Hollywood film star, the old–fashioned type that always saved the day and always got the pretty girl. Even his clothes looked as if they adored him, clinging like diluted paint to his hard, muscled body.

As Alex's widening eyes met his, a warning bell clanged in her head. The message was loud and clear. *Send him away Alex. He's trouble. Trouble! Are you listening? Send him far away, NOW!*

Penetrating, amber eyes bore into her face, familiarising every detail instantly, like the split-second snapping of a camera lens. She almost felt as if in that briefest of intimate moments he had captured and taken her soul.

'If it's all the same with you, Ma'am -' he said, touching the brim of his hat, '- I'd like to get him sorted?' He nodded at the horse.

Alex nodded back, sure that her voice, if she tried to use it, would betray her calm, unruffled exterior.

Jodie chose that moment to breeze up, grinning nervously, hands clasped behind her back. 'You've, er, met Kane, then?' she said unnecessarily, not daring to risk a glance in Alex's direction, who had little choice but to stand with gritted teeth and narrowed eyes watching.

Kane opened his arms and stood waiting for Jodie to fill them. 'Hi!' she squealed, throwing her arms around his waist and hugging him hard. He swung her into the air as easily as a feather, his hard, chiselled face breaking into a smile. 'So, how's little Jodie, then? Keeping OK by the look of it?' He settled her back on her feet, his hand lingering under her elbow while she found her balance.

Jodie gushed, 'Yes. Yes. I'm fine ... Oh, it's so good to see you again after all this time. How long has it been? Ten? Eleven years? Goodness, doesn't the time just fly by? It looks like it's been good to you?' She cast a brief, nervous glance at Alex. 'Just as ... er, good looking as ever.'

Kane made a show of shaking his head in denial but he needn't have bothered. He was beautiful. He knew it. Why deny it? Jodie was really going to pay for this. First, the irresponsible handling of the stallion's purchase and now this.

Plug Towers crept up behind them, picking dried horse dung out of his hair, still quietly cussing. 'Any chance of gittin' cleaned up before I leave? Only, that critter -' he pointed towards the horse who stared back innocently through wide, unblinking eyes, '- just shit on me head!'

'Sure,' Alex said, eyeing Kane and Jack who were at least having the decency to turn their backs before laughing. 'Follow us. I think Mr Mitchell and his *son* want to get the horse settled in anyway, so shall we go?'

Kane pushed back the brim of his hat and scratched his head. He looked to Jack, then Jodie, then Alex. 'Son!'

Alex shrugged. 'Jodie, here -' she glared at Jodie with a deathly stare, daring her to deny it, '- Jodie here said you were bringing your kid with you, Mr Mitchell.'

Kane mock-punched Jodie on the shoulder. 'As easily confused as ever, eh, Jodie? I said I was bringing my *kid brother*.' He nodded at Jack. 'He's a year younger than me.'

'Oh,' Jodie whispered, turning the colour of pickled beetroot. 'Sorry. The phone cut out after you said kid. I just thought …'

'Never mind. No harm done, eh?' Kane said, putting an arm around Jodie and squeezing hard until she started to choke.

That's right. Squeeze the air out of her treacherous body, Mr Mitchell. Because it will save me a job, later, Alex thought, and then, something else came to mind that caused her to discreetly smile. Jodie had been up half the night finishing off the icing on the *kid's* 'welcome-to-the-island' cake. She'd scoured cupboards and drawers until she'd found six yellow candles – a nice, neutral colour because she hadn't known if the child was a boy or a girl - which she'd arranged neatly around the edge. *How cute!*

'I'll bet you're all hungry and thirsty, aren't you, after your journey?' Alex asked sweetly. 'If you go and sort out the horse, Jodie will put the kettle on and we can all have a nice cup of tea and a piece of Jack's 'welcome-to-the-island' cake.'

All eyes turned quizzically towards Jodie.

Alex almost suggested to Plug Towers that he use the horse pool to clean up in rather than her main bathroom, after all it did seem more appropriate. She'd had to walk upwind of him as the group made its way back towards the house, dropping off Jodie and the two men on the way at the box where they were going to stable the visiting stallion. It would have to be kept well out of the way of Mac or a range war would ensue. The island might be four miles wide and five miles long but that was still too small for two territorial stallions.

Plug Towers stood in the middle of the bathroom and admired the décor, nodding, rubbing a hand across his whiskery beard. This was Alex's favourite room in the house, decorated from ceiling to floor in pure brilliant white. The walls reflected the sun for most of the day, adding a warm, natural ochre tint, a unique shade provided by nature. Bright green palms and cordylines dotted around the vast room gave the only splashes of colour. That was one of the nice things about the Australian climate. You could grow houseplants the size of small trees.

'You going to be all right, Mr Towers?' she enquired.

'Sure, Missy.'

He started to peel off his clothes and Alex exited fast and waited in the hallway, prowling up and down, waiting and listening for him to finish.

When, twenty minutes later the lock turned and the door opened, Alex pushed past him having prepared herself mentally for the devastation awaiting her. 'Need the loo,' she lied, locking the door almost before the poor man had stepped through it. Her mouth fell open. The bathroom was immaculate. The shower cubicle had been rinsed and sprayed with shower-shine. The bath mat hung, folded neatly over the towel rail. The towel he'd used had been placed in the dirty washing bin and he had even flushed the toilet, even though he hadn't used it and, removed the two dead leaves from the six-foot-high cheese plant. Alex had seen it all now – a tidy man! She ran a finger along the glass shelf – nothing. She was pretty sure he'd dusted as well. She closed the bathroom door and stepped out into the hallway. A strong aroma of newly percolated coffee drifted from the kitchen.

Plug looked up sheepishly from the coffee pot as she walked in. 'Hope you don't mind, Missy, but I could do with a strong cup of coffee after that little charade down on the jetty,' he said, through a perfumed cloud of shower gel and deodorant. 'I've made a pot of tea for the others. It don't look like they're back from settling in that lunatic horse yet. What's your poison? Tea or coffee?'

'Coffee smells good.' She had to smile.

'What?' Plug said, pouring cream into two mugs.

Alex waved her hand. 'Oh, it's just a bit of a surprise. You know … the bathroom and coffee and stuff …'

Plug watched her under heavy brows. 'You think because I smell like a pig I should act and live like one.'

'No!' Alex said quickly. 'I didn't mean …'

Plug grinned. 'Nah, don't go taking any notice of me. I'm only joking with you. Bit of a surprise, is it, to find a bloke that can clean up after himself?'

Alex nodded and took the coffee he offered. She sipped it before saying, 'Just didn't see you as the domesticated sort some how.'

'You don't have much choice in the matter when you live alone. It's no good whingeing and whining, you just have to get on with it. It's a bummer, but fair dinkum.'

She didn't really understand his bizarre language. It was going to take considerably longer than three months to get her very English head around words like 'dinkum' and 'bummer'. 'Have you always lived on your own, Mr Towers?' she asked, taking another sip of his excellent coffee.

His face collapsed, as if he had trouble getting his smile the right way up. 'Nah, I married when I was eighteen - the only sheila I ever fancied, then, or since. We had thirty-seven years together and never a bad word. The big C got her five years ago. One day she was there, bright as a button, making plans for us to go on holiday together, then, two weeks later my old love was laid out on a mortuary slab, cold as Christmas.' He took a gulp of his coffee and swallowed hard. 'If you'd told me my whole world would be lying there like that, I'd have said you were barmy. I hope you never have to see anything like that, Missy. It ain't nice.

Alex knew it wasn't nice. She'd seen her parents after the accident, five and a half months ago now. The mortuary technician had solemnly opened up the two identical drawers and out had popped her mother and father. Shazam! They'd looked like wax- work dummies, something you might pay decent money to see in Madame Tussauds. They'd had paper identity tags hanging motionlessly from their big toes. Her mother's toes were still painted with that vivid, garish colour, so vulgar against her porcelain-white flesh that Alex had muttered, 'Obviously, *not* one of the colours you always said you wouldn't be seen dead wearing, Mother?' She hadn't cried, not then and not at the funeral. What had there been to cry about? They'd been virtual strangers. The first and last thing her mother had ever truly done for her was to evict her from her womb, naked and covered in gore, and drop her into the arms of the waiting hospital staff. Her mother had then spent the best part of Alex's life dropping her into the hands of someone - theoretically or literally. Nannies took that special place that should have belonged to her mother. They had flowed across her lonely, confused life like sea-bound rivers. Here one day, gone the next. No one stayed, everyone left.

'It really ain't nice,' Plug concluded.

Alex forced another sip of coffee down. For some reason it now tasted bitter. 'So, you've been alone for these past five years?'

'Yeah.' He forced a grin back onto his face. 'Don't reckon I'll find another sheila now. I had the best. Reckon you can't improve on that, can you?'

'No, I guess not. Do you have any family, children?'

'Nah. No family. You could say we weren't blessed. Betsy had to have her womb took out.'

Alex saw the miseries of days past etched into the lines of his worn, weathered face. They weren't so noticeable when he smiled.

'You know what? You flit from day to day thinking it's forever, that you've all the time in the world, but you ain't, Missy. In the blinking of an old sea-dog's eye, it's gone. I held my Betsy's hand when she was dying and do you know what she said?'

Alex shook her head, not trusting her voice. A lump had formed in her throat.

'She said, "Arthur, my old love, let the world laugh at you. If it spreads a little happiness and sunshine, you can take it. Your shoulders are broad." I reckon people have been laughing at me ever since. Betsy would be proud of her '*old fool*' if she could see me now.'

'She can see you,' Alex said thickly. 'Something that strong couldn't be finished by death. She's there – somewhere.'

Plug rubbed a hand across his eyes. 'Yep. You could be right, Missy. I hope so. I still miss the darned woman, even now.' He raised both hands and scratched his head. 'Life goes on though, don't it?' The moment was gone. Plug Towers had wallowed enough in self-pity. Abruptly, he did a complete U-turn. 'You've got this house cleaned up ace. It was a right old rat-sewer when your dad had it.'

'You knew my father!' Alex halted the coffee cup halfway to her mouth.

'Sure. I was always popping him across the water. Dunno why? He could have flown his own 'copter here if he'd wanted to, instead of leaving it on the mainland. I reckon he just liked putting business my way.'

Alex found that easy to believe. Robert McBride may have had no time for his only child, but he'd always been generous with money. No one could ever have accused him of being tight-fisted, not even her money-grabbing, wrapped-up-in-her-own-life, mother. 'If he spent so much time here, why was the place falling down? He couldn't possibly have lived in it in *that* state; it only had half a roof and no east wall. The previous owners had let it go to pot.'

Plug's face dropped. 'Hmm. Well. Least said about that little lot the better. There are those that say the previous owners sucked the heart out of the house. Bled it dry, until it was just a shell. The Mulligans were a strange brood.'

'Strange as in enigmatic?' Alex suggested, throwing the cold coffee out of her mug and pouring another for herself and Plug.

'No! Strange as in down and out weird.'

'Why do you say that?' Alex asked, tilting her head to read Plug's face.

'Oh, don't take any notice of me, Missy. I don't get out enough. I find everything weird.'

Alex couldn't be sure, but it seemed to her that Plug was prevaricating. Before she could push it, he said, 'Your dad didn't stay here in the house; that's why it remained in that diabolical state. I reckon he had plans to do it up, but it just never happened.' He dropped his gaze into the bottom of his coffee mug and said, 'I reckon he would have got round to it if he'd lived. He only had the place a couple of months.'

Alex couldn't believe that a total stranger knew more about her father than she did. 'So, if he didn't stay here, where did he stay? Please don't tell me he camped out. My father was a strict, five-star luxury hotel, kind of man. He would rather die than be caught without a clean shirt, a neatly ironed crease down his Y- fronts and a choice of three Armani suits. No, anything less than pure luxury was rather *infra dig* as far as my father was concerned.'

'Strange, ain't it? I didn't see him like that at all.'

'Hmm,' Alex said distractedly. 'So, where *did* he stay?'

Plug shifted in his chair, looking very much like a little boy about to squeal on his best friend. He looked furtively around the empty kitchen and then over his left shoulder. When he seemed sure no one was about to witness his indiscretion he said in a low voice, 'I used to drop him off up by The Reach, with just a backpack, and he'd take off up the beach and into the trees. He gave me a call when he wanted me to pick him up. Sometimes it would be two days, sometimes three. On one occasion, I started to get a bit worried, 'cause I didn't hear from him for a whole week. And then when I picked him up, he looked real rough, like he hadn't eaten or washed, that kind of thing.' He paused briefly and nodded. In his head he was somewhere else. When he caught Alex peering at him he added, 'Anyways, like I said, I don't know anymore than that.'

Alex considered this. It wasn't much, but it was still more than she'd ever known. In fact, not even her mother had known about the island. After the death of her parents, the old family firm of solicitors, Bowbridge and Bowbridge, had got in touch to say there was a matter outstanding with regard to her father's will and would she, as a matter of great urgency, arrange to visit their rooms in Kensington. Once there, Anthony Bowbridge senior had informed her of her father's assets. Alex had been stunned into silence. She had never realised just how insular and secretive her father had been. He had owned an island, but he had told no one. A few days later it was Bowbridge's turn for stunned silence when Alex returned to his office and informed him that she had no intention of selling

Mulligan's Reach and was, in fact, preparing to move her horses and best friend, Jodie Lower, to the island and start a stud farm. He'd almost choked on his Earl Grey tea when she'd informed him that she intended having the house extensively extended and repaired, the surrounding land re-seeded and fenced and would be leaving for the other side of the world almost immediately. He'd fluffed up his ample chest and passed a few disparaging words about the total unsuitability of the place for two young women. Alex had told him it was none of his damn business.

'I don't know where that lot have got to,' Plug said, jolting Alex back. 'That lunatic horse has probably killed one of them. Be a long day before I have another lunatic critter on my Donna.' He sucked his teeth and shook his head.

She took the mugs, rinsed and up-ended them on the draining board. She wasn't finished with Plug yet. 'Could you show me where you took my father?'

'Well, like I said. I've never been there, so, I wouldn't really know where I was going, would I?' Plug said, crossing his arms evasively.

Undeterred, she said logically, 'My father had to go *somewhere*, didn't he? Even if you don't know where he ended up, you could show me where he started out.'

Plug still looked a bit like a cornered rat as he shifted uneasily in his chair. 'Well yeah, I reckon I could do that. But it's only an opening into the undergrowth. There's no gate or path or anything.'

Alex smiled. 'Well that's a start, isn't it? You know what they say – the longest journey begins with the first small step.'

'And that inner terrain ain't so pleasant … heat … flies … more heat … more flies,' Plug rambled, rubbing at his chin, choosing to ignore Alex's optimism.

'I don't mind any of those things,' she lied, crossing her fingers behind her back. She hated flies. The island seemed like a natural breeding ground for the horrid things. When she and Jodie had first arrived on the island they'd turned the horses out in the mornings, but they'd soon learnt that the heat and the flies were unbearable during the day. Black, biting swarms attacked the mares, until they took to galloping, running off precious condition, in a futile attempt to outrace them. Now they kept the horses stabled during the day and turned them out in the cool of the night.

'So you'll take me there?' Alex continued.

'Well.' He unfolded his arms. 'Sure. OK. But I ain't sure where *there* is...so I ain't promising anything.'

Show me a man who would, Alex thought, and even then, there was a million to one chance he'd be lying through his back teeth. She flashed Plug a beseeching smile and said, 'I'd really like to know why my father would want to go traipsing into the heart of the island and it isn't likely that he's going to tell me now, is it? If you can't help me no one can.'

Plug's face cruised into a sheepish grin. 'Yeah, fair dinkum. You're on. But it's getting a bit late, savvo, to be going gallivanting, especially as we don't know where we're going gallivanting to.'

Alex considered this. 'Fine. Stay the night and we can take off at the crack of dawn.'

Plug blushed, but looked pleased. 'I don't want you putting yourself out. It's not like you know me and don't forget them two cowboys. Have you got enough room?'

'Plenty of room. Loads, in fact. We'll be glad to have you.'

Plug rubbed at his chin and grinned. 'OK. If you're sure and I won't be in the way?'

Alex didn't answer immediately. She was still trying to come to terms with her last comment - *We'll be glad to have you.* Why had she suddenly turned the house into *The Inn Of The Sixth Happiness* and why had she painlessly metamorphosed into Ingrid Bergman? She abhorred people living in her house, getting close, getting under her skin, and now, because of Jodie's lack of thought and stupidity, the occupants had swelled to five: two English women, two American cowboys and an Australian boat captain.

Chapter 2

Alex slept fitfully that night. A blustery wind had sprung up, blowing in off the sea. It rattled the wooden shutters against their frames, the noise, like a constant, irritating drumbeat, played by someone with little sense of rhythm.

She threw herself on to her back, watching the feathery, dancing patterns silhouetted on the walls by the full moon. She turned onto her left side and plumped up her pillow. Why couldn't she get to sleep? Why? Was it because there was a man on the island - three men? No, not three men. Arthur Towers was no problem and the younger Mitchell brother was no threat, but the other one, the Hollywood film star type ...

Alex had felt a huge rush of relief when Jack had turned out to be an adult. The thought of Jodie's friend coming to the island with a child had filled her with an uneasy feeling, an anxiety almost. Yes, that was it - the child.

You might have had a man and a baby.

'Shut up,' she hissed, her mouth quivering against the soft silk of the duvet. She didn't need this - not now. Six years was long enough to have got over it. If it still hurt now, she only had herself to blame. She just hadn't tried hard enough.

Yes, but you really wanted Peter, didn't you? You believed him ... like the gullible fool you are.

'Like the gullible fool I *was*,' she corrected the nagging voice in her brain, pulling the cover over her head. 'I'm not like that now and I don't want to be reminded of it.' The voice was quiet. 'I don't want to be reminded of it,' she repeated under the duvet. But it was too late. She could see Peter's face, there beside her on the pillow: his sun- bleached hair falling over his forehead, his blue eyes hidden behind closed lids, lashes long, resting against his freckled cheeks. How easy it had been to love him, and if her period had come on time she may have gone along thinking, believing, that Peter was for real, that he really did love her. But, her period hadn't come late. It hadn't come at all. She'd watched, mesmerised as the line in the little glass tube turned a delicate shade of blue.

Within two hours of breaking the news to Peter, he'd flown out of the country on a one-way ticket to Guatemala. He'd exited so fast he hadn't even taken his revolting collection of Ella Fitzgerald C.D's from Alex's flat. She'd patiently loaded every one into the dishwasher, programmed it to heavily soiled – something she felt she could definitely relate to - and switched it on.

Peter had broken her heart. He'd destroyed her faith in mankind and, when in time her heart had knitted together and superficially healed, her faith in mankind had remained destroyed. No man would make that journey to her heart a second time. She'd destroy him first. A tear slid down her hot cheek and was angrily scrubbed away. 'Stop crying you *stupid*, *pathetic* woman.' She wiped away the remaining tears on the duvet before burying her face in the pillow, trying to block out the painful memories. It had no effect. It didn't matter how hard she tried, he was always in her head. Like a malignant tumour, waiting patiently in the background, ready to touch the rawest, most tender nerve and send her into a tailspin of loathing and self-pity.

Eventually, through sheer exhaustion, Alex drifted off, slipping gently down into a safe, tranquil harbour where Peter couldn't follow. She dreamt of miniature tadpole sperm with sad little faces, swimming round and round, each holding on tightly to the tail of the one in front, like elephants in a circus ring. One by one they stopped swimming, breaking the chain, falling away into oblivion, dead ... all dead.

Alex awoke with her heart thudding in her chest. Something was wrong - what? The wind still crashed against the house. It was virtually impossible to hear anything else over the din of its relentless drumming. She strained her ears, lifting her head off the pillow, her eyes flitting around the room. Was there something in the room - someone? Shadows still danced, faster now. A pot on the veranda thudded over and smashed, then nothing, except the wind. Except ... she *could* hear something. She sat up. There! There it was again – a faint distant bleating, like a newborn lamb bereft of its mother. No, not a lamb. A kitten? No, not a kitten either. She listened. That was it! Suddenly it registered. It was a baby. The pitiful squealing of a lost, abandoned baby.

Alex flung the duvet off her body with such force it landed in a heap on the floor. She almost fell over it in the semi-darkness as she bolted across the room. She wrenched open the bedroom door, her hand frantically searching along the wall, desperate to find the light switch. As her fingers found it and closed on it, a hand touched hers. The light flooded into the hall as she screamed, 'JODIE!'

Jodie cast her a brief, bewildered look before rushing down the hallway with Alex fast on her heels, babbling, 'Did you hear it as well, Jodie? Did you hear the baby? What's a baby doing out there?'

Jodie was dragging on her overcoat, hurriedly pushing an arm into a sleeve that was inside out and wouldn't permit entry. 'Baby? What baby? It's not a baby, Alex. It's Mac!'

'Mac?' Alex said, struggling to help Jodie into her coat. 'Mac? My Mac? Are you sure?'

Jodie managed to get her coat on, her hand shooting out through the sleeve and grabbing a flashlight. She hurried out into the night with Alex fast on her heels, still babbling, 'Are you sure it's Mac, Jodie, are you sure? Because it really sounded like a baby to me. A lost and frightened baby.'

Jodie negotiated a broken terracotta urn that had once housed a five-foot fern. The plant was nowhere to be seen, blown away into oblivion. Other plants had conceded to the wind remaining subserviently bent, like frail old men crouched over gnarled walking sticks.

Jodie stepped over the urn and broke into a jog, her small frame almost lifting in the gusts. Alex followed in her wake.

'I'm not a *hundred* percent sure it's Mac,' Jodie shouted over her shoulder. 'But I *am* sure it's not a baby.'

Alex put on a spurt, the wind snapping at the thin cotton of her nightdress, depositing it around her ears before snapping it back down, plastering it against her bare legs like a second skin. They reached the barn door together. It *was* the stallion. Now there was no mistaking the terrified, high-pitched squeals coming from the other side of the door. Jodie tugged at the door but it refused to budge. Alex grabbed it further up and they pulled together. It opened slightly before the wind snatched it from their hands and flung it back viciously against its frame, almost trapping Jodie's hand.

Alex took a kick at the door, temper, frustration and lack of sleep finally taking their toll. 'What are we doing in this God forsaken place anyway, Jodie? What in God's name do we know about Australia except that it's full of foreigners, boomerangs and billabongs?'

'When I say pull, pull,' Jodie bellowed into Alex's right ear, ignoring the outburst. 'Just wait for the wind to subside!'

'Is it going to?'

'*PULL!*'

Together they grappled with the door and this time it opened. Alex was through it and charging down the centre of the barn even before Jodie had turned on the lights. Her bare feet made little slapping noises on the herringbone-patterned floor. She reached the stallion's box, situated at the far side of the barn, away from the other horses, just as the lights came on. It only took a second for her eyes to become accustomed to the light. Mac stood at the back of his box, eyes wild, head tossing, snorting and prancing as if the floor was on fire and he couldn't put his feet down. Alex slipped the bolt on his door and was almost through it when he reared menacingly and plunged towards her, teeth bared, eyes bulging.

'Don't you dare go in!' Jodie screamed, having arrived at the box as half a ton of frenzied horseflesh lunged against the door. 'Get out of the way, Alex! The mad devil will kill you!'

Alex ignored her and pushing against the door, in a voice as smooth as silk, whispered, 'Whoa. Steady my old love. Steady now.' She stepped inside the box.

'Alex!'

She turned her head slightly in Jodie's direction, her concentration slipping from the horse as he reared, swung on the spot and let fly with his hind legs, like scimitars slicing through butter.

'That's it!' Jodie yelped. 'I'm fetching a sedative.'

'*NO!* I don't want him knocked out and 'ga-ga' for the next two days. Give him a chance to calm down.'

'I don't think he's going to calm down, Alex. I'll fetch Kane, he'll know what to do.'

Alex swung towards Jodie. 'You will *not* fetch Kane! I'll deal with my horses, my way. It's enough that he's here in the first place … thanks to you.'

Jodie held up her hands in submission. 'Fine, whatever you say.'

Alex continued her approach steadily, a step at a time. Mac watched her moving towards him, involuntary muscles twitching, nostrils flushed salmon red. He tossed his head and snorted a warning. 'There, there,' Alex crooned, reaching his sweat-soaked shoulder. 'So, you have slow sperm. It's not the end of the world is it? The nasty lady vet isn't going to send you back. I won't let her. You're *my* big boy and you're staying with me. Don't go worrying about another stallion on the island. You won't have to see him and he'll be gone soon, along with his Hollywood film star owner.'

From the sidelines, Jodie shook her head, knowing that Alex's little speech was meant for her. The quiet, calming tone was for the horse but the words were aimed purely at Jodie. She maintained her distance, watching as Alex carefully slipped a head collar up over his nose and fastened it behind his ears. She wouldn't have been able to do that. It was a common fallacy that vets were good with all animals. Sometimes it was the chemistry, the science of it all that appealed as much as the animals themselves. Alex just about had the horse under control as Jodie edged up to the door. 'He's got himself into a right old state,' she said, running her eyes over his quivering body. He looks like he's just run the Grand National – twice! He's going to need walking round a bit to cool off after this little tantrum.' She didn't know why she was telling Alex something she already knew.

'Tantrum? Tantrum? Is that what you seriously think this is? Don't be ridiculous, Jodie. Something has upset him and it has to be something close by.' She nodded towards the other horses. 'They're all OK.'

Jodie shrugged. 'It's probably just him. He's obviously become unhinged with Kane's horse being on the …'

Jodie stopped talking as in that split second three things happened. The shavings at the back of the box moved, parted, and the stallion barged forward lifting Alex, still hanging on to the head collar, clean off her feet.

'Get out of the way!' Alex screamed as they hurtled towards the door scattering shavings like a snowplough. 'And open the door before we end up wearing it!'

Jodie shot back the catch as Mac careered through the door, dragging Alex with him, and took off towards the other horses. Obviously, he thought there was safety in numbers. When he got to Holly's box, he stopped. The chestnut filly whickered before leaning over her door and nuzzling his shoulder. Alex left him there and tore back. Jodie was already in the box, pitchfork in hand, stabbing at the wall of shavings. Something moved and hissed.

Alex backed off. 'I can only think of one thing that slithers like that and hisses like that and, believe me, it's all yours.'

Jodie had made a deep hole in the bank of shavings and there, exposed and looking even more annoyed than it sounded, squirmed a brown and green snake. Alex shuddered. 'Urgh! How did *that* get in here?'

'Is this it?' Jodie said, incredulously. 'Is *this* it? That great stropping horse went berserk over this?'

Alex risked another tiny look before turning away in revulsion. She'd never rated snakes. 'Urgh! It's horrible. Of course, that's it! Of course it scared the hell out of him. It would me.'

Jodie turned to look at Alex, an incredulous expression on her face. 'You are one very strange person. You can take your life in your hands with that crazy horse but you're scared to freaking point about a snake?'

Alex was shaking now. 'Is this really the time to be analysing me! For God's sake Jodie, get rid of it!'

Jodie turned away with a shake of her head and focused her attention back onto the snake. She prodded it with the pitchfork and it struck out causing her to jump clear.

'Jodie! Stop antagonising the bloody thing, just catch it!'

As it made to slither back into the dense cover of the shavings, Jodie scooped it up with the pitchfork, deftly imprisoning it like a piece of half-cooked spaghetti. With the snake furiously spitting, she yelled, 'Coming through!' and took off, sprinting down the aisle with her sensible waterproof coat flapping in the after draught. Mac saw her coming, tossed his head and careered off down to the other end of the barn, only to be set upon by their black, manic mare, Do As I Say.

'It's really not your day, is it, Mac?' Jodie shouted over her shoulder as she dashed out into the gusting night with the snake slowly slipping inch by inch.

'And *DON'T* kill it!' Alex shouted in Jodie's wake.

If the wind hadn't taken away Jodie's words as she sprinted into the darkness, Alex would have heard her say, 'Unbelievable Alex McBride. Unbelievable.'

Chapter 3

'Ready? Shall we make tracks?' Alex asked brightly, grabbing an apple and ramming on her baseball cap. Despite being up half the night, settling Mac, and only getting a few hours sleep, she felt surprisingly awake and refreshed.

Plug Towers grinned at her through newly brushed teeth. 'My old Betsy used to say, "Are you ready, Arthur? Shall we make waves?"'

Alex laughed.

'You'll have to watch that,' Plug said mischievously. 'Laughing in the mornings ... it could become a habit.'

When she forced a serious face, he said, 'Is that all you're having for breakfast?' He nodded at the apple in Alex's hand. 'That ain't enough for a growing girl.'

'I'll be fine, Arthur. But ... thank you ... for your concern.' She didn't know when she'd decided to call him Arthur but it sounder nicer than Plug - softer. There was something about this man. It was nothing palpable. It was something akin to the feeling she'd had when she'd met Jodie - an instant, invisible bond, an indefinable realisation that this person was *meant* to be a visitor in her life. It was like a gentle, warm undercurrent of being at peace and ease, as if you'd known the person all of your life – or, in another.

'I'm going to bring this tucker,' Plug announced, waving two Mars Bars and two huge chunks of Jack's '*Welcome*' cake. 'Then, if we get a bit peckish, we can have them.' He'd already had his breakfast, having risen, showered, shaved, made his bed and tidied his room, all before the sun had come up. He'd devoured two bowls of Cornflakes, a bacon and egg sandwich, three slices of marmalade toast and two cups of coffee. Alex wondered if he might have the odd nematode squirming around in his ample gut. When she raised a questioning eyebrow he said, 'Yep, I'm ready. Let's make waves.'

The battered Land Rover revved into life on the first turn of the key sending smoke signals belching from the vibrating exhaust. Alex's parents had given it to her for her twentieth birthday. It had arrived at her party along with a card that explained they were terribly sorry but they wouldn't be able to make the party after all as something had come up. Alex slipped it into gear, pulled off the hard standing and, flooring the accelerator, tore off up the beach.

'Bit quicker than old Donna, ain't it?' Plug shouted over the noise of the engine and the wind rushing through his newly washed, grey-peppered hair.

'Just a bit!' she shouted back, ramming an old C.D of Andrea Bocelli into the C.D player. 'How far?'

'Bout half a mile, up by The Reach!' Plug yelled, through ear splitting strains of *Canto Della Terra.* He added, 'I like this Andrew bloke. Great vision – considering he's blind.'

The vehicle sped along on the firm sand at the waters edge, diminishing the half-mile in minutes. Mulligan's Reach came into view, stretching across their path like a long sleeping dragon, a daunting peninsular of black rock running out to sea. Sea terns lifted grudgingly from their craggy roosts, gentle undercurrents holding them motionless in the cloudless sky as if they had been painted on canvas. Their piercing screams were perfectly audible in the warm off-sea breeze as the Land Rover slowed, wheeled to the left and cut up the beach with The Reach shadowing them.

'Gives me the willies, this place,' Plug said, as the pace slowed when they hit soft, dry sand. He looked a bit pale, like he was about to part with his gargantuan breakfast.

Alex ejected the C.D. 'What place?'

He nodded back over his shoulder towards The Reach.

'Why?'

He waved his hand dismissively.

As the sand petered out, they came to a halt. 'Now where?' Alex asked, scanning the thick bank of vegetation. 'I can't see a way in.'

Plug scratched at his head and pulled a face. 'Don't reckon there is a way in.' He pulled himself up in his seat, peering hard into the greenery. 'I reckon you best just point it and hope for the best.'

Alex peered at him. 'Point it where?'

Plug raised a hand and extended a finger indicating an area that looked slightly less dense. 'There. Try to push your way in there.'

Alex struggled with the gearbox before shooting forward, causing them both to duck low as the Land Rover banked and almost climbed a tree. 'Jeez!'

Plug clung desperately to the doorframe as Alex managed to get the vehicle onto some sort of well-disguised track and ploughed on noisily with the engine screaming in first gear. 'Sorry about the racket,' Alex shouted to be heard, 'but I can't get up any speed.'

Plug waved a hand. 'Don't worry about speed, Missy, just let's try to stay alive!'

She swerved violently, narrowly avoiding a rotting tree-stump. 'Are you sure this is the right way, Arthur, only it doesn't look like anyone has been through here for centuries?'

'It soon grows over when there's nothing to stop it; it's nature's way. Don't pick it and it heals up. And I told you last night, I ain't ever been, so I don't know.'

Alex left the questions and gave her full concentration on trying to keep the vehicle moving through the dense vegetation. A few metres on, a narrow path appeared, winding through lofty palms and ferns; some towered so high their tops weren't visible. Shafts of light speared the tall canopy, casting dusty shadows in hues of green and grey. Debris showered down, ripped from the overhang, landing on their heads. Plug scooped it up and tossed it over the window frame. 'You never know what's living in all this green stuff!' he shouted. 'Best to be on the safe side!'

Alex took her eyes from the path to cast him a horrified look and in that second the off-side wheel collided with a fallen tree, the kick-back spinning the steering wheel in her hand almost breaking her wrist. Reaction made her release the wheel as a pain shot up her arm and the Land Rover nose-dived off the track and into the undergrowth. Plug stood up, elbowing his way through branches and fern fronds, ripping them from the windscreen. Alex flexed her wrist and swore.

'I said it weren't no picnic, didn't I?' Plug said, sitting back down and taking hold of Alex's wrist to examine it. 'It ain't broken. But you're gonna get a good bruise. Do you want me to drive?'

Alex shook her head, swore under her breath, and rammed the gear lever into reverse. 'I lost concentration for a minute. I won't do it again.'

Plug scratched at his head.

Alex revved the Land Rover hard until the undergrowth was thick with blue-black smoke. Then, she released the brake and it shot backwards out of the bushes and hit a tree.

Jodie slid the needle into the stallion's vein and slowly released the sedative. Better sooner than later had been her thought. So, with Alex out of the way on a sight-seeing trip with Plug Towers, it gave her the perfect opportunity to try to right matters. There was no use keeping the stallion entire, not now - not now that she'd screwed up. Mac swayed a bit before his legs buckled and Kane Mitchell said calmly, 'He's going down, Jodie, stand clear.'

As soon as Mac hit the floor, Kane and Jack moved in. They looped ropes round his fetlocks, pulling him into such a position that Jodie could get to where she needed to be. Quickly and thoroughly she swabbed the area before making an incision.

Jack flinched, screwing up his eyes.

'Brings out the chicken in every male I've ever known,' Jodie said, deftly tying off the first testicle. 'I've seen grown men turn to jelly', she teased.

'Not surprising really, is it?' Kane said, exchanging a sympathetic look with his brother. 'I hope you don't sleepwalk, Jodie. I'd hate to find you standing over my bed with a scalpel and a swab in your little mitts.'

Jodie grinned, sliced through the stalk and threw the testicle on the floor before quickly tying off the second and performing a carbon copy. Competently she sutured the incision, pumped the reversing drug into the horse, then filled a separate syringe with anti-biotic and pumped that in.

Kane and Jack released the ropes just as Mac rolled slowly onto his side.

'Poor sod,' Jack said with feeling. 'He never knew what hit him.'

'Okey dokey, that's it!' Jodie said. 'All done.'

Sweat trickled down between Alex's breasts as she sat with her back against a gum tree, waiting for Plug to return. He'd drifted off along the track, 'for a bit of a scout around,' when they'd had to stop to give the engine a chance to cool down. The temperature gauge had been way up in the red as the engine struggled with the hot, still air of the inner terrain. Alex closed her eyes and leant her head back against the bark of the tree. What was she doing? Did it really matter where her father had gone to? It wouldn't make any difference to anything now, would it? And at this rate, they'd end up walking back and she'd look a complete fool. What kind of idiot gets a Land Rover stuck? She should have got rid of it years ago, useless thing. That was one of her problems, misplaced loyalty.

She snatched up a fern frond and frantically fanned her sweating face. Lord, it was hot! She supposed she should take comfort in the fact that she wasn't the only member of the McBride's 'with a screw loose.' Oh no. Silas McBride, according to family history, had 'pulled a blinder.' Back in the late eighteen hundreds, 1869 to be precise, at the tender age of sixteen and three-quarters he'd flown the relative luxury of the family nest and worked his passage to Australia. Once on Australian dirt, he'd started a sheep farm from a few hundred acres of scrub and wilderness and a year later married an Aboriginal beauty. Together, they worked the land and set about raising their own tribe of half-breed Aborigines, fifteen, if the family grapevine had been correct. It seemed Silas could only father boys and so he just kept on trying until finally his fifteenth child was a girl. Unfortunately his girl-child, whom he sired at the age of seventy-five, had been only a year old when The Aboriginals' Ordinance of 1918 came into being. This law allowed the state to remove children from Aboriginal mothers if it was suspected that the father was not an Aborigine. To avoid this, Silas's wife's tribe had taken the children far into the outback, where no white man, however good his tracking abilities, would ever be capable of finding them. It was strongly suspected that old Silas got to see them on a regular basis. When, at the age of ninety-five, Silas passed away, his wife's tribe disposed of him as one of their own and, duly, the McBride family tree was happily pruned of one diseased branch and normality, or near normality, returned to the clan. Alex must have inherited a rogue gene from way back. What other reason could there be for coming to a country that had been called, 'a primitive and Godless land?'

She opened her eyes and glanced at her watch. Midday! No wonder she felt sick; she hadn't eaten anything since last night and then it had only been a quick sandwich in her room. Plug had gone to sort out *Donna*. To make sure she was anchored, or birthed, or whatever it was boat captains did with boats. And Jodie had entertained her friend from *way back*. Alex could have joined in but she didn't want to. It was going to be safer if she stayed well away from Kane Mitchell. The brief interlude on the beach when he'd arrived had warned her of *that* much and it was only a stupid idiot who didn't listen to their own gut warnings. She had been guilty, in the past, of letting people in under her radar but not this time. Mitchell had set off all the warning bells. No, distance was good. Distance was very good.

She pulled herself to her feet and walked over to the Land Rover. At least the horrible burning smell had gone now. She felt like kicking it - stupid thing. It was totally unreliable. Men and machines were exactly the same: unreliable and useless. She started to move old feed sacks, chocolate wrappers and Coke cans, looking for the food that Plug had insisted on bringing with them, when a hand closed on her shoulder.

She swung round to find Plug grinning from ear to ear.

'I've found a track, over there, just by that fallen tree. I reckon it's wide enough to get this thing down.'

'Lead on,' she said, abandoning the hunt for the food and jumping into the driving seat. As Plug climbed in she turned the key, revved the engine and pulled away, following the finger he pointed towards a track off to the left. Once on the track the going was easier. The vegetation thinned out in patches, with areas of fern and sky- bound gum trees, then sparser, shorter trees that Alex couldn't identify. Off to the right the forest thickened but the track still ran through it. Here it was darker. Tall gum trees bolted for the sky, blocking out the light like giant, greeny-blue umbrellas.

The track petered out and they were again battling through trees and overhanging branches that thudded and crashed against the bonnet and the windscreen. The way ahead was starting to look impassable when, without warning, the canopy broke and they shot out into a lush, green, flat area. A flock of sulphur-crested cockatoos startled, whirling away in a flash of vivid colour, rising up into the gangly trees. Alex cut the engine and they sat in silence, taking it in.

Vivid red and orange banksias filled the air with a rich, sweet perfume. A small stream trickled through the clearing, straddled by fallen trees, covered with bracket fungi hanging on for grim death. Across the stream and peeping through abundant ferns stood a cabin. It was in the latter stages of dilapidation. Vines crept possessively up the front wall, claiming their right, engulfing the only small window. The whole thing looked like a scene from a fairy tale. Alex could almost hear little manic voices coming from the winding vines saying, *'You're mine, all mine,'* as they crept stealthily onwards and upwards, smothering any remaining life out of the shack.

She turned and stared at Plug who was now grinning like a Cheshire cat. 'Well done!' She flung her arms around him and planted a kiss on his sweaty cheek. 'Well done, Arthur. I can't believe we've found it. This has got to be it, hasn't it?'

'I reckon it has, Missy. I sure reckon it is.'

Alex leapt from the Land Rover and ran towards the stream.

'Watch out for tigers!' Plug shouted, climbing from the Land Rover and jogging to catch her up, his stomach wobbling over his waistband.

Alex stopped, teetering on the fallen tree, swaying back and forth. 'I hope that's a joke Arthur. I know we have everything on this island that creeps and crawls but, tigers?'

He caught her up, breathing hard, his face extra pink from the heat and the sudden exertion. Plug Towers wasn't built for jogging. 'No, I don't mean those great big striped, cat things. I mean tiger *snakes*. Tigers and taipans. They're both buggers but them tigers will attack anything and they can be lethal.'

Alex grabbed his arm. 'I don't like snakes. We found one last night in Mac's box. Urgh! It was awful! No idea how it got there.'

He glanced around. 'Well, just let's take it steady. Stay together, yeah? There's safety in numbers. Can't say I like them much myself, but it ain't something I come into contact with too often in my line of work. Box jellies, sharks and urchins, yeah – but not snakes. Come on, let's do it.'

Taking Alex by the hand, he grinned toothily and stepped off the log.

Kane stood watching the grey stallion. It still looked a bit dopey but at least it was up on its feet and pulling hay strands from its rack. It would be feeling a lot better by the morning when the last of the sedative had worn off. He let his experienced eye run over the horse. It was a shame Jodie had had to geld it. It was a good looking, powerful horse, the type he liked, not unlike his own horse if you disregarded the colour. He walked across the barn to look at the other horses, his tan boots clicking on the tiles, nodding as he passed each box. Someone had a feeling for a good horse; it was probably the Mc Bride woman, Alex. He couldn't imagine Jodie having much to do with the buying side of things. As he remembered, she didn't know a good horse from a bad one. She was fine with the veterinary bit but she wasn't a 'horsey' person. She didn't have the eye. That was something you were born with, you couldn't adopt it, not in his opinion. There was nothing here he wouldn't have wanted to own, except for maybe the big chestnut that stood tucked into the corner of its box, eyeing him suspiciously. Chestnuts could be a pain in the butt, especially if they happened to be chestnut *and* female as well. This one looked like it would spook at its own shadow. He stood back a little to read the nameplate on the stable door. *Hot Holly*. He nodded, 'Yeah, that's about right,' he said, before moving away and continuing down the barn until he reached the box with the black mare. He glanced at the brass nameplate. *Do As I Say*. He whistled quietly and she turned to look at him and when he spoke, she tiptoed up to the door. He lifted a hand and she allowed him to touch her neck. 'Well, aren't you a little darlin', Dais?' he whispered, and Dais nodded her head up and down as if she understood his accent perfectly and couldn't agree more. Kane laughed. 'And real smart as well. I think you and me are going to be friends.' And that pleased Kane, as did the fact that Jodie's plea for help had arrived just as the contract with Sherman Wily expired. If it hadn't been for that phone call he'd be on the way back to Amarillo by now. And anything that delayed making *that* journey had to be for the better.

Alex and Plug found the door and pushed hard until reluctantly it creaked open exposing the inside of the hut. The putrid smell of the place was the first thing to register and Alex had to clamp her hand over her mouth to stop herself from retching. The damp, rotting walls and roof were overrun with insects at every stage of larval development. Spiders scurried across the roof, confused by the sudden shaft of daylight flooding into their previously dark, dank world. Over in the corner, a heap of what looked very much like human excrement festered. Around it, small animal bones, white and smooth, littered the floor. Under the window, someone had placed a small camping table and chair. Alex found the stench unbearable. She turned to go when Plug, who was obviously made of sterner stuff and had been rummaging around by the window, produced something, holding it up above his head, before indicating the door with a jerk of his head. Alex tumbled outside and hands on hips lowered her head taking deep breaths, frantic to get the putrid smell out of her nostrils. She felt Plug's hand in the small of her back as he steered her towards the stream. His face showed deep concern as he said quietly, 'You OK?'

Alex nodded. She wasn't sure but she wasn't going to admit that to Plug. She didn't want him to think she was a pathetic female incapable of even coping with a bad smell.

'Look, I've found a book,' Plug said, turning a motley-coloured leather-covered book in his hand. 'It's called, *Trees*.'

Alex took her hand from her mouth and swallowed before taking in a deep breath and letting it out slowly.

'You sure you're ok?' Plug asked again, placing a hand on her shoulder. 'You do look a bit crooked.'

If that meant she looked like she was about to throw up, she'd have to agree with him. That's exactly what she did, turning away from Plug just in time before she retched and brought up a half digested apple.

Plug pulled a clean handkerchief from his pocket and shook it, like he was waving it at a charging bull. He held it out. 'Here, use this.' As she took it, he added, 'There's no need to be so brave all the time, you know. You are allowed to feel things.'

No she wasn't. That wasn't the way it worked - not now. She pushed the hankie into the pocket of her jeans and said with a forced smile, 'Thank you. I'll launder it and let you have it back.'

'Whatever,' Plug said, turning his gaze slowly back to the book, turning pages.

Alex looked over his shoulder, watching as he flicked from page to page. 'I thought you said it was about trees.'

Plug pursed his lips and nodded. 'It is. Not these bloody great green things. Trees as in Genealogy. It's titled, *Family Trees.*'

Alex shrugged. 'I don't understand. Family Trees?'

'Perhaps there's nothing *to* understand,' Plug said, halting briefly before flicking on through the dog-eared pages.

'You're not suggesting, are you, that my father came here, that he battled through that...that jungle back there, to get to this hell-hole, to sit in a foul, stinking shack and study Genealogy? Get real!'

Plug slammed the book shut and spun to face her. 'I think it's time we got back. We can study this -' he waved at the book, '- when we get back.' Without giving her time for objection, he placed a hand beneath her elbow, steering her away from the place and back to the Land Rover. Continuing the initiative, he nominated himself as driver, climbed in and started the engine. Alex sat hunched against the doorframe, clutching the book in hands that were suddenly cold, despite the sweltering heat. It had been a mistake to come here. She should never have insisted on Plug looking for this place. He hadn't wanted to, she'd pushed him into it. And what had been achieved by discovering her father had spent some of his final days camped out in a stinking shack in the middle of nowhere, reading a book, that as far as she was concerned was of no interest to him whatsoever? Of course, she knew *why* she'd done it, why she'd talked Plug into making the nightmarish journey. A part of her still wanted to understand the man that had been an enigma to her throughout her life. It was crazy really. She'd never known him when he was alive. What induced her to believe that she could get to know him now he was dead? She slapped at a fly as it settled on her arm and fixed her stony gaze on the pathway ahead.

She saw Plug glance across at her from time to time as he battled with the vehicle to keep it on the track, but she felt too wretched to acknowledge his concern. She was only too aware that she had snapped at him back there. How damn ungrateful did that make her appear?

At least it was easier going back; the track had already been forged on the way there. As they hit the beach and burst out into the late afternoon sunshine, she saw Plug glance at The Reach. He said nothing. She closed her eyes and didn't open them until the tyres hit the yard.

Chapter 4

'*Your* father? Camp out?' Jodie said with barely contained giggles. 'Do me a favour, Alex. I think you've got hold of the wrong end of the stick.'

Alex sat slumped at the kitchen table while Jodie prepared supper. Plug had seen her back into the house and then left. He had a charter in the morning and needed to be away on the afternoon tide. She'd hugged him and apologised and he had grinned and said, 'No Worries.'

'Why would he want to be in a place like that?' 'I mean, come on, does it compute? Would my father have done a thing like that?'

Jodie salted the broccoli before saying, 'No, he wouldn't … at least … not without a reason.'

'A reason? What reason could there be? Unless it's that he lost his mind … and his sense of smell! Honestly Jodie that place was the pits.'

'What place was the pits?' a deep voice drawled.

Jodie and Alex turned together. Kane and Jack stood in the doorway. Judging by the look and smell of them, they'd both just showered and changed after turning out the horses.

Alex lowered her eyes as the two men pulled out chairs and sat down, Kane facing her and Jack by his side.

'Alex found a shack today in the inner terrain and it looks like her father was camping out there,' Jodie explained.

Kane exchanged a look with his brother before saying, 'Why would he want to do that?'

Alex's eyes slid across the table, paused briefly at the black cotton fabric of Kane Mitchell's designer shirt, then slowly, button by button, inch by inch, climbed up his chest, until they came to rest on his chiselled face. She dipped into his eyes, and then quickly out, before they captured her as they had, when he'd arrived.

'I've no idea why he would want to do that,' she said flatly.

'How do you know it was your father?' Jack offered.

Alex looked at Jodie. 'It had to be. Who else could it be?'

Kane played with the cutlery set out on the table, spinning the fork around with his index finger. He seemed quite engrossed, then he looked up and said with a serious expression. 'What do you know about this island?'

Alex pulled a face. 'What do you mean, what do I know about the island? What *is* there to know about the island? It's an island.'

Kane pinned her with a look that would turn cream. 'I meant, what do you know of the *history* of the island?'

'Why would I know anything of the history of the island? What's to know? I suppose I'm right in thinking that it's always been here, right. Well, that's its history as far as I'm concerned, Mr Mitchell.'

Kane picked up his knife and set it straight with the fork he'd been absently spinning. She thought for a minute he was going to lean across the table and stab her with it. He didn't look like the kind of man who supported free speech, especially if it came from the mouth of a woman.

'I'm only trying to make polite conversation,' Kane said, allowing his face to smile a bit. His amber eyes frisked her face attempting to capture hers but she wasn't falling for that a second time and dragged her eyes away to a spot just above the kitchen clock.

'Well, that isn't necessary, Mr Mitchell,' she said coldly, addressing the wall. 'I appreciate the help you are offering by coming to the island to help Jodie out of the massive mess she's made but there's no need to *try* to be polite. I think if politeness doesn't come naturally perhaps you shouldn't have to try?'

Jodie, open-mouthed, ready to defend firstly herself and secondly Kane, dropped the saucepan lid. By the time she'd retrieved it from under the table, with Jack's help, Alex had stood up, pushed her chair under the table and left the room. As she walked slowly down the hallway and to her room she could hear Jodie making apologies for her, saying, what a shock Alex had had finding the place where her father had decided to throw all matters sanitary down the drain. And that Alex had always had a secret desire to be closer to her father. And that the mere subject always put her back up.

She closed her bedroom door and leant against it. Why did Jodie feel the need to make excuses for Alex's behaviour? Why did she feel the urge to do that? Well, it didn't take a genius to figure that out, did it? Obviously she'd been drawn into Mitchell's spell, probably something she had in common with every woman he came across. She'd fallen for his drop-dead gorgeous looks, blatant charm and charisma. *Oh, Lord, did she actually just allow her brain to put that thought together?*

She slumped into the chair beneath the window, closing her eyes against the soft breeze that billowed the thin, weightless curtains, bringing with it the smell of the sea. It had been her first encounter with Jodie's cowboy mate and she'd let her insecurities rise in the face of testosterone. Idiot! It was going to take at least six-months to serve the five mares. She could hardly spend all that time avoiding him, could she? Maybe she should consider a holiday? Where? Why? She lived on a tropical island for God's sake, how much more could you wish for? And why the overwhelming desire to have to avoid him anyway? He was only a man. *Yes a man with drop-dead gorgeous looks, blatant charm and charisma.* She closed her eyes and dropped her head into her hands. No! She really had to stop this. There were plenty of men out there like Kane Mitchell. He was nothing special. Just a nice-on-the-surface, visitor, who, in a short space of time would be gone - just like everyone else that came into her life. Circumstance had brought him here and circumstance would take him away. His stallion would serve the mares and then, with a little more time, she would find a suitable replacement for Mac. Perhaps that's what she should have done in the first place and not made Jodie pay so highly for her mistake? Jodie had messed up but Alex had forced her to right the situation. Perhaps Alex was as much to blame as Jodie?

She swung herself up out of the chair. It was too late now. Things would have to stay exactly as they were for the time being. Kane Mitchell was no problem and he certainly didn't appear to be stupid. After her short, sharp altercation with him in the kitchen, she doubted he would be actively seeking her out to be best mates in the near or distant future. All things considered she had probably played her cards dead right. As far as Kane Mitchell was concerned the best form of defence would have to be attack. Yes. Sorted. Suddenly she felt ravenously hungry. She'd still not eaten and, parting with the apple she'd had for breakfast, now seemed light years ago. She may have come to terms with Kane Mitchell in her head but walking back into the kitchen, sitting down and consuming an evening meal with him filled her with as much pleasure as sticking pins in her eyes. There was still food in the Land Rover. Plug had put it there.

Gently, quietly, she lifted the sash window until the opening was large enough for her to climb through and stepped stealthily out onto the veranda. She sprinted across the yard, cornered the barn, reached the Land Rover, tugged open the door and started rummaging through weeks of debris. She found the squashed cake and melting Mars Bar and peeled them from the wrapper. This was going to be one massive sugar rush but she was fast reaching the point where anything looked good. She took a mouthful, closing her eyes in unadulterated bliss as she chewed and swallowed. The effect was immediate, staving off her hunger pains and lifting her spirits. She cast the wrapper over her shoulder to join the rest of the rubbish and wiped a hand across her mouth. A familiar voice whispered in her head. *'Alex dear, please don't bolt your food…and, oh my goodness, darling, please, not your hand. Use your napkin.'*

'Oh, *SHUT UP*, Mother!'

She turned to look at the field at the side of the house, where the horses, already turned out for the night, grazed contentedly. That's all she needed to end the day on a positive note, a brisk ride out along the beach on her favourite horse.

It took her twenty minutes to catch Holly, who, after only having been turned out an hour previously, flatly refused to be caught. It wasn't until her belly got the better of her and she succumbed to the last lump of squishy Mars Bar, that Alex managed to slip the bridle on. She threw the saddle up onto the filly's back, tightened the girth and after taking her baseball cap from her back pocket, ramming it down on her short hair, climbed up. She closed her heels against the horse's ribs and it jogged forward. They passed the house and left wheeled onto the beach and the inviting, endless stretch of white sand that lay before them.

Holly, keen as ever, jogged along snatching at the bit, tossing her head, almost legging herself up as she splayed out legs in all directions. Alex sat into her and they broke into a canter. Now the horse's action was perfect as they covered the beach in a gentle, rocking–horse motion, heading down towards the firmer sand at the water's edge. Cool, salt flavoured air washed over Alex's face, refreshing, rejuvenating, deleting any remaining thoughts of Kane Mitchell and as she rode, her smile returned.

She unleashed Holly and they flew along, splashing through the tide-lap, gobbling up the distance in moments. They rounded the headland and came back to a walk as The Reach stretched obtrusively across their path. With the tide out and the sun slipping from the evening sky, it looked grey, ominous, a jagged, ever-present scar. Gulls bickered for roosting places, several lifting, winging out to sea, screaming abuse at having been disturbed. Alex reined in and watched.

This was a strange place, the only area of rock on an otherwise flat island. It began a few metres from the green inner terrain, puckering beneath the surface, like something once buried in the hope that it may be forgotten, and broke half way to the beach. Once through the sand it rose dramatically and bolted towards the sea like a terrified water creature fleeing for its life back to the sanctuary of the water. At the point where the outgoing tide remained, The Reach broke; dropping away to nothing for two and a half metres, then it rose steeply and ran out to sea, disappearing beneath the reef. Alex shivered in the cast shade and when Holly started to jog impatiently, Alex turned her up the beach and rode on at a trot until they reached the soft sand. Slowing to a shuffling walk, they came to another halt on the perimeter of the inner terrain. Tyre tracks, where she and Plug had pushed through into the undergrowth that morning, remained, but the flattened vegetation had already sprung back, jealously guarding the pathway to the island's heart. The saddle creaked as she stood in the stirrups, gaining a little height to peer into the thicket. The air that morning had been oppressive, sweltering, but it felt much cooler now, creeping out through the trees, bringing with it a detectable odour of damp, crushed vegetation.

Without warning, Holly suddenly reared, throwing Alex up her neck, clinging on to the mare's mane while it spun, ran backwards and collided with a gum tree. Then it shot forward scraping Alex roughly against the tree trunk before stumbling and righting itself. Wide-eyed and shaking it teetered, snorting, blowing visible breath into the undergrowth. Alex dragged her body back into the saddle and found her stirrups, looking frantically from left to right and straight ahead, flummoxed at what was spooking the horse. Holly was definitely a spooky type but not this spooky. There was only one thing known to Alex that really freaked out the horse and that was the noise of the Land Rover. Again, there was no logical reason why that should be; it was just one of the horse's strange quirks.

There was nothing to see, Alex was sure of it. She leant forward and stroked the horse on its neck but Holly was having none of it. With Alex un-balanced and half way out of the saddle, the filly spun, dropped her head, grabbed the bit and bolted for home. For a dozen strides Alex tried to get her balance, succeeding as Holly slowed temporarily, judging her stride before taking off to leap a fallen tree. Alex regained her position as the horse took off, flying upward for what seemed like forever before landing and continuing its manic dash. The ground flashed beneath them in a white blur, sand spraying in their wake like a flat out motorboat. As the house loomed ahead, Alex made a final attempt to stop the mare, standing in the stirrups, bracing against the speed and took a tug, reeling in the horse like an angler hauling in the big one. It was pointless.

The mare swung right-handed off the beach, tore past the house kicking up a dust storm and continued bolting towards the field gate. Alex's heart turned and sank. Standing by the field gate, admiring the view and the grazing horses stood Kane Mitchell. If he didn't move within the next two seconds, he was going to be trampled underfoot. As if in slow motion, he turned towards the approaching drum of hoof beats. Alex saw the look of surprise on his otherwise blank face as he observed and assessed the situation and, as Holly slammed on the brakes and began to skid, he calmly stepped aside.

Alex teetered while gravity decided her fate, then, with a horrible thud, she hit the ground. If she'd had a choice it would have been that the fall rendered her unconscious because then she wouldn't have opened her eyes and found her self staring at the cowboy's well-oiled, leather tan boots.

Slowly, moving each limb in turn to establish if anything was broken, she rolled onto all fours, her head hanging loosely between her arms, her breath coming in short, sharp rasps.

He made no attempt to help her to her feet. 'Can't say as I'm familiar with that position, Miss McBride and I've studied them all.' He tilted his head, and then shook it. 'No. It's a new one on me.'

'Very funny. And there I was thinking you didn't have a sense of humour,' Alex said sarcastically, attempting to raise her spinning head. 'And you could at least try removing your size eleven boots from out of my face.'

Obligingly he took a step backwards bringing his kneecaps and his painted-on jeans into Alex's field of vision. 'Could you get *right* out of my way!' she snapped. 'I realise you are more than happy having a woman grovelling at your feet, but … '

'On the contrary, I find nothing more off-putting than a woman who throws herself at me. I'd much rather there was a fair chase.'

'I wouldn't have thought you could afford to be that choosey …'

His hands grabbed her shoulders and wrenched her to her feet.

'Don't move me, you idiot, I could be badly injured,' she hissed into his face.

He looked down at her as if she was an insect, his eyes scrutinising every skin-cell on her hot, flushed face. 'Couldn't we all?' he said cryptically, his breath fanning her face.

Alex opened her mouth to ask him what he meant by that, but he'd touched a finger to his forehead in a mock salute, turned and walked away before she had the chance. She watched his tall, lithe frame ambling away and in that moment decided, quite uncharitably, that she would make his stay on the island as horrible and as unwelcoming as was humanly possible. 'Idiot!' she spat under her breath. She turned and took hold of the sweating mare's reins, broken in the fall, and turning her in circles examined her for any injuries. A trickle of blood oozed over the heel of her near fore where she'd over-reached. It was nothing serious but it needed attention. Just as she was about to lead the horse back to the barn, Jodie rushed up.

'Kane said the horse bolted with you and you fell off … Christ, you look awful.'

'I *feel* awful,' Alex said bluntly. She didn't see much point in pretending otherwise. She was a competent rider. Being bolted with and falling off horses wasn't something that was familiar to her. Something had really spooked the horse up by The Reach but Alex had seen nothing. Perhaps the horse had imagined it?

'What on earth got into its stupid head anyway?' Jodie asked, bending to examine the wound. Holly flinched and ran sideways. 'This is one ridiculous horse, Alex, you shouldn't be riding it.'

'I'll be the judge of what I choose to ride, Jodie, not you.'

Jodie straightened up. 'If you take her back to the barn I'll dress that wound. There's no point me trying to get her back there, she'll only freak out. Do that, then go and run a bath. You need a good soak, bring out the bruises.'

The house was quiet when Alex walked in. The smell of roast beef still lingered in the kitchen but it was spic-and-span, the dishes had been washed and the kitchen table set for morning. Jodie was unbelievably domesticated when she wanted to be. There was never much for Alex to do in the way of cooking or cleaning. Jodie was a little star really. Alex hadn't meant to snap at her but losing control of the horse and the altercation with the Mitchell man had reversed her mood and any one or any thing that got in the way of the backlash generally came off the worse.

She rummaged around in the fridge, slicing a couple of lean chunks from the left over roast and using her left hand as a plate, laid them across it, adding a piece of cheese and a stick of celery. She closed the fridge door with her booted foot and left the kitchen. In the hallway, she could hear voices coming from one of the guest rooms. Jack Mitchell had taken the en-suite room opposite hers and next to Jodie's. His brother had set up his equipment in the room next to Alex. His equipment being, two rifles, three saddles – just why he needed three saddles for one horse was a mystery – a C.D player, a C.D collection of around a hundred discs and two travelling leather trunks full of his designer jeans, chaps, shirts, etc.

As Alex tiptoed down the hall the voices got nearer and clearer. They were coming from Kane's room. He was talking to his brother. She stopped at the doorway and leant against the wall. She was eavesdropping and she knew it. But she didn't care. This was her island, her house and her guest bedroom. She considered she had a right to know what was being discussed. She tilted her head and listened. Kane was speaking.

'She took a real hard fall. The horse is a total fruitcake of course, should have been put down at birth. Landed right at my feet in a heap. Not everyday that sort of thing happens.'

Jack guffawed, 'Talk about pennies from heaven!'

For a moment no one spoke, then Jack added quietly, 'Bit quirky though, that one. Got a bit of baggage I reckon. Didn't you say you knew her ex?'

Alex stiffened.

'Yeah. The man's a total moron,' Kane said lowering his voice. 'Jodie made me promise not to bring it up. Opens up wounds barely healed, so she says. Apparently, there was a baby. The jerk ran out on her … '

Alex could listen no longer. She tore along the hall, slammed into the bathroom and hurled the door shut. It closed with a bang that shook the house. How dare Jodie be so free with Alex's private life? How dare she?

Alex threw the food into the bin, yanked off her boots and dragged her clothes from her aching body, leaving them where they fell. She flung open the shower door and stepped in; standing beneath the cool jet of water, letting it beat down on her face.

Damn Jodie. And damn Peter. And damn Kane Mitchell.

Her hands fell to her stomach. Flat. Perfectly flat and empty. It had swelled to a nice little bump, in those first few weeks of pregnancy. She'd been able to link her fingers beneath it, cradle it in her hands, rock her baby. And then …

Blood everywhere: smeared across the toilet seat, splattering the white Italian floor tiles, escaping down her legs, trickling between her toes. Excruciating pain, ripping her in two, doubling her body over, making her sob between the knife-sharp spasms. Everywhere red, and somewhere in the middle of it all… her baby.

Alex let out a rush of breath and grabbed at the wall. Thinking like this would do no good at all. It hadn't in the past and it wouldn't now. Taking another deep breath, which caught in her throat and turned into a sob, she stepped out of the shower.

Chapter 5

Jodie had a plan. It had materialised sometime in the early hours of the morning after she'd laid awake fretting half the night about the bad atmosphere around the place and the fact that Alex really appeared to be struggling with Kane and his brother being on the island. She knew why Alex was finding it so difficult. She was scared.

As plans went, it wasn't earth shattering but she figured it didn't need to be. It just needed to be effective to have the required result. And the required result was to get Alex and Kane on better terms. So, the next morning she was ready, waiting, and cooking breakfast when Alex, still looking like a volcano about to erupt, walked in. She waited until she'd sat at the table, sprinkled cornflakes into a bowl and then went for it.

'I've offered to show Jack around the island today,' she said, a lot calmer than she felt. 'He's taking Kane's horse and I thought I could take Mississippi. She's nice and calm, isn't she? She won't throw me.'

Alex wasn't listening. She had other things on her mind, like how to dispose of a fifteen-stone-plus body without it being traced back to her.

'All of the island,' Jodie added, folding a tea towel for the third time and placing it on the side.

Alex supposed she could always borrow one of his rifles and …

'We'll be gone all day … and all night! We'll be camping out.'

Alex looked up from pouring milk into her cereal bowl. 'What?'

Jodie snatched the tea towel up, twisting it in her hands like a comfort blanket. 'All the island and I'm not coming back.'

Alex halted the spoon half way to her mouth. 'What! Never?'

'What?'

'You say you're never coming back.'

Jodie pulled a face of sheer exasperation. 'Of course I'm coming back. Eventually, well, tomorrow morning actually. It's just, I'm staying out tonight.'

Alex lowered the spoon. 'Just lets get this straight, Jodie. You and 'Jack-the-lad' are going walkabout and leaving me with that, COWBOY? I don't think so!'

Jodie decided to go for broke. 'I've already told Jack I'll take him now. You wouldn't want him to think that you were acting like my mother, telling me I can't go, would you?'

Alex watched Jodie through narrowed eyes. 'You should have checked with me first, Jodie.'

Jodie threw the tea towel on the table and slumped down. 'Listen, Alex, I shouldn't have to check with you first, at all. You said when we came to this island that it was on a fifty-fifty basis …'

'*That* was regarding the business, the stud, as you very well know. It has nothing to do with me wet-nursing that cowboy crony of yours. He's *your* friend, take him with you.'

Jodie bit her lip and picked up the tea towel again, re-folding it, giving her time to think. She was clutching at the proverbial straw now and she knew it. 'I can't leave
 you on your own. You'll be off riding that lunatic horse again and who knows what mess you'll get yourself into.'

'Holly is not a lunatic horse. Something scared her up at The Reach and she couldn't handle it, that's all.'

Jodie let out a deep whoosh of breath. 'Why do you do that? Why do you always find a reason in that horses favour. It's a liability.'

Alex pushed the cereal away across the table. 'You know we'll have to agree to differ on that one, Jodie, so I wouldn't bother pursuing it. You're on much safer ground pushing this plan of yours to leave me on my own with 'Wyatt Twerp'.'

Jodie stared open mouthed.

'Just go, Jodie. Take them both with you. I'll be fine here on my own.'

'I can't leave you on your own, Alex. So I'll just have to tell Jack I can't go.'

'Because of me?'

Jodie's lip trembled. 'I don't see why you have to be so awful about Kane. After all, he is letting us use his stallion.'

Alex refused to look at Jodie's stricken face. 'At a price, I should imagine.'

'He hasn't actually mentioned money,' Jodie said.

'Maybe he's expecting payment of another kind. It wouldn't be unheard of for a man like him, would it? I just hope *you* can meet his demands when the bill comes in.'

Jodie had almost twisted a hole in the tea towel, she'd put it through so much anguish. 'So, is that your final word? I can't go unless I take Kane with me?'

Alex looked up into Jodie's pouting face. 'Sometimes Jodie Lower, I hate you.'

Jodie grinned. 'I know. And sometimes I hate you. But not always and it doesn't last, does it?'

Alex held up her hands in submission. 'Go. Take Jack and leave the other one. I'm sure if I try hard enough I can manage to avoid him for twenty-four hours.'

Jodie beamed. 'Yes I'm sure you can.' Under her breath, she added, 'At least you can try.'

Alex was out of the house before Jodie and Jack's dust had settled, dressed in a bright orange bikini and overshirt and walking the half-mile along the beach to The Reach. Kane had gone out in the Land Rover a short time before Jodie and Jack took off on their so-called fifteen-mile *tour* of the island perimeter. It was a pointless exercise as far as Alex was concerned. Leaving her alone with Kane Mitchell would produce nothing. She didn't have the slightest intention of becoming any better acquainted with the man. Oh, she knew Jodie's little plan. She could read her like an open book. Jodie wasn't the dubious, scheming type and for that Alex loved the woman. What you saw was what you got.

The water felt like gossamer as Alex dived from the rock platform into its mirrored crystal depths. Around her, shoals of gloriously coloured, miniature fish flitted away, then, after realising Alex wasn't part of the local food chain, returned to watch her, their comical striped faces agog.

She surfaced slowly and, turning onto her back, floated with the tide. A ray glided past, a silent silver ghost, its long arms tickling against her leg. She dived again and surfaced before climbing out onto The Reach. The hot rock toasted her feet as she climbed on all fours to a flat ledge, where she sat, knees bent up to her chest, her arms folded around her knees. She turned to watch as a flock of brightly coloured birds broke noisily from the undergrowth, at the point at which she and Plug had gone in, and fluttered away along the beach squawking. She watched them until they disappeared from her sight and then she closed her eyes and turned her freckled face to the sun. This was one of the most beautiful places on earth. She truly didn't deserve this. How could one person own a part of paradise, a tiny slice of heaven? Perhaps she did deserve it. Maybe she'd paid her karma. She'd survived the misery, the loneliness of parents who were never there; parents who bestowed upon her the world but not the love. She'd survived a broken heart, a lost child. At least Peter had let her see that she could *physically* love. And hadn't she been deliriously happy about the baby? Yes, she'd paid. And now? Now, thanks to Mulligan's Reach and a person like Jodie in her life, she would be happy.

She stretched out on the rock, carefully avoiding the needle-sharp edges and closed her eyes. Within moments, she was asleep.

Jodie grimaced and hauled on the reins.

'Don't hold it on such a short rein,' Jack offered with a broad smile. 'It takes two to fight. If you don't, the horse won't. Just relax and sit into it.'

Easier said than done. Jodie found it hard to relax when the wild plunging creature beneath her was trying to buck her off and *this* was the calmest horse they owned. If this little plan to get Alex and Kane on better terms didn't work then all this pain and imminent sore-backside would be for nothing. She loosened off the reins as Jack suggested, pulling a face as the horse seemed to respond and fell into an easy, unhurried walk at the side of Jack's horse. 'You were saying?' Jodie said, a bit happier now that her insides had settled back to roughly where they should be.

Jack nodded. 'Yeah. I was saying … Mum bought Nightwalker's dam, Fly-by-Night, for Kane. The mare had won some big races as a two year old but just into her third season, she broke down rendering her useless for racing. So mum snapped her up at a really good price and gave her to Kane.' Jack cast her a quick glance. 'I think mum thought Kane would stick around the ranch … if he had something to stick around for.'

'Didn't he, then? Stick around?'

'Yes and no. Kane had his future perfectly mapped out. Go to England … don't ask me why he chose England over the U.S.A. because I don't know … get into Vet School, qualify, come home, breed horses and run the ranch. All the eggs in one big basket.'

'And?' Jodie said.

'And then real life kicked in, dealt him a swift uppercut and he dropped the basket.'

'Meaning?' Jodie said, fumbling with the reins and losing them as the horse stumbled.

'Meaning, that while he was in England, mum had a cancer scare so Kane quit his studies and came home to look after her.'

Jodie frowned. She knew Kane had quit the course but she'd never known why. 'But, weren't you there, Jack? Couldn't Kane have finished the course?'

Jack laughed. 'You're joking. Kane considered it *his* position to be there for her. We'd lost dad quite suddenly, heart attack, a couple of years previously, so Kane was head of the family, so to speak. And not only that, he adored mum. He came home and saw her through the seemingly endless months of lousy, painful treatment. After a year, they said she was in regression and life went back to something like normality. She pleaded with Kane to continue his studies but it was like talking to a brick wall. Nothing got through. He refused to leave her and around that time, Fly-by-Night dropped her first foal ... this lump.' Jack slapped the stallion's neck affectionately.

'The mare ruptured her uterus foaling and we couldn't get a vet out in time and she died. It looked like this old lad was going much the same way, except that Kane wouldn't let it. He sat with it day and night until it pulled through. Shortly after that, mum had a bad fall and *that* was the beginning of the end. The cancer was back. It was in her bones. They could do nothing else for her. We've got a pretty big spread in Amarillo: cattle, grain, the lot and I reckon, at that time, Kane would have sold the ranch and his soul as well, if money could have helped.' Jack pulled a bottle of water from his backpack and took a swallow, then he turned to look at Jodie. 'I don't think Kane has truly loved anything more than he loved mum.'

Jodie watched as he halted the bottle halfway to his lips and frowning, added, 'Well, no, that's not quite true. I think Ellie was on a par.'

Jodie's faced creased into a frown. 'Ellie?'

Alex smiled, stretched out her limbs and opened her eyes. She couldn't lounge around here all day. She'd go back now, make some lunch, take it into the study and have a look at the book Plug had found in that disgusting shack. She climbed carefully down the rock face, turning as her feet touched soft sand and jumped back, startled. Standing before her, blocking out the sun stood Kane Mitchell. He was frowning, passing her orange shirt that she'd left at the base of the rock from one hand to the other. A fragment of sleeve fell to the sand. They both watched it as the first incoming ripples lapped over it, turning it, sucking it briefly back to sea before carrying it a little way up the beach. For a moment, mesmerized, they continued watching. Then as Kane unfurled his fingers, the shirt fell from his hand in tatters. Alex stared at it, floating on the water. It was shredded, completely ruined. Her eyes slid back to Kane. 'What have you done?' she said, eyes huge, her voice as tiny as a whisper. 'What have you done?'

Kane tilted his head, as if trying to catch the words. 'Done? What do you mean, what have I done?' He tilted his head in the opposite direction. 'You don't think I did this, do you?' He kicked at a floating fragment, catching it, booting it out to sea.

Alex was nodding. She hadn't intended to. She was on automatic pilot. 'Yes! Yes, I do think you did it. Unless I'm very much mistaken, there *is* only you that could have done it. Do you think it shredded itself? Do you think a ... *baboon* or something came out of the trees and did it? You, *Mr Mitchell*, are the only ape around here.'

If looks could kill, Kane would have been dead, buried and worm bait.

He glared back, jaw set. 'Don't be so paranoid ... '

'PARONOID! How dare you accuse me of being paranoid? You're the one with the unhealthy fetish for origami.'

'Listen,' he said, through gritted teeth. 'I didn't rip your shirt. I've never had to resort to ripping women's clothing before and I don't intend to start now, not even - ' he added in a dangerously quiet voice, '- not even if it would give you pleasure to think that it was me.'

Alex struck him squarely in his chest. 'Get away from me! And the very second your job is done here, send me the bill and get off my island.'

He bent, scooping up the remains of the drenched shirt and in a clenched fist, the size of which could have knocked her over the twenty-five miles of ocean and back to the mainland, held it beneath her jutting chin. 'I didn't, repeat, didn't do this,' he said, fighting to keep his voice level. 'Now whether or not you believe me is entirely up to you. Frankly, I don't give a damn …'

'Oh, please. Spare me the Rhett Butler impression,' she cut in, snatching the shirt from his hands. 'Just get the job done and get off the island. Do you hear me?'

'Be damned hard not to with you acting like a fishwife.'

'Fishwife? Fishwife? Right! That's it. Give me the keys to the Land Rover. You can walk back, I don't know what you think gave you the right to take my Land Rover in the first place.' She held out her hand. It was shaking.

He snorted derisively. 'Stop acting like a spoilt brat.'

'It's *not* an act. I *am* a spoilt brat. Didn't Jodie tell you? Didn't she explain in extended graphic detail how I've always had everything I've ever wanted? How remiss of her. She told you everything else!'

Kane Mitchell wasn't the type of man you could scream at face to face. He closed his eyes against the blast. When all appeared quiet, he opened them. 'Get in the Land Rover. We'll go back together.'

Alex would rather have walked barefoot over burning coals and was more than happy to inform him of such to his beautiful, arrogant face. As she opened her mouth, he snatched hold of her hand and stormed off, dragging her, kicking up sand, up the beach behind him. He didn't stop until he'd thrown her inside the Land Rover, slammed the door and driven off back toward the house. She didn't utter a word, impossible to anyway with the world rushing by at a rate of knots. He drove like he was qualifying for a Grand Prix front grid position. Something else about the man she found totally objectionable – he was a rotten driver.

As he skidded onto the hard standing and slammed on the brakes, she sprang out, didn't waste time shutting the door and ran for the house, knowing that his eyes were glued on her backside, bouncing in the skimpy orange thong.

Jodie pulled the blanket tighter around her shoulders and wafted an insect from her nose. It was getting dark. Funny how the sea sounded different, scary almost, as the light drained from the island. Her plan to get Kane and Alex on a better footing required instant success because sitting here propped up against a hard leather saddle with her knees bent up to her chin wasn't her idea of fun or luxury. She'd already emptied half a can of insect repellent on mosquitoes with the persistence of pneumatic drills. Jack didn't seem bothered by the irritating swarms. He'd settled the horses and cooked up something surprisingly edible on a small campfire before first unrolling Jodie's bed and then his own. He'd advised her to get in it, working on the principle of 'first come first served', and that way she wouldn't find a snake or a lizard dozing in it when she turned in. She couldn't confess to being too worried regarding the island's fauna or flora – it was the people on the island that concerned her most. Jodie had always been a people person. There were very few people she didn't get on with, which, considering her profession was probably a good thing.

She missed her parents. They'd been lovely when she'd broken the news to them that she, their only daughter, was packing up, quitting a brilliant job in a practice that had offered her a partnership to stay, and was going to live on the other side of the world with a woman they had serious doubts about. Jodie had invited herself to Sunday lunch and somewhere between the roast beef and apple charlotte had announced her intentions. Her mother had hidden her disappointment behind a façade of interest, asking relevant questions regarding the island etc. Her father on the other hand had glazed over, rubbing at his grey eyes behind his gold-rimmed specs', saying how much they would miss her but that they understood - chance of a lifetime and all that nonsense. It was a hard wrench. Jodie's childhood had been perfect, an exact opposite to Alex's. Jodie's parents had always been there for her - taking part, pushing her forward, encouraging her through school and later, university. They were nice, caring parents. Her mother chose to work three afternoons a week at the local cottage hospital, just to keep her finger on the pulse, she said, and to have something to chat about with her bridge and W.I friends who were always popping round for coffee and an update on local gossip. Her father was something in government. He never made it very clear just what he did exactly. For years, Jodie told her friends that her father was a secret agent and that he worked for the S.A.S.

They'd made her promise to call at least twice a week, and that was the only condition they burdened her with. Yes, she missed them.

Jack settled next to Jodie, snapped back a ring pull and handed her a beer. She accepted it and took a sip, regarding Jack over the rim, watching as he turned up his collar against the night and shuffled down into the sand. Earlier on in the day, he'd been about to tell her about someone called Ellie but at the time, he'd hesitated, suggesting that they moved on and so Jodie had left it. Now she wondered if she should broach the subject. She took another sip of beer, then said, 'Jack, earlier today you mentioned someone called Ellie? You said Kane had never loved anyone as much as he loved his mum, except maybe for Ellie.'

He took a double gulp of beer, screwing up his eyes as he swallowed. 'Yeah,' he said, nodding, his brows creasing in thought. 'Ellie.'

The name seemed to hang over the sand until the lap of the tide swallowed it and took it away.

Jack drained half a can of beer and it appeared he wasn't going to expand, then, he said simply, 'Ellie and Kane were childhood sweethearts. Everyone who knew them just naturally assumed they would marry one day and they did, a week before mum died.'

'Kane's married!'

'*Was* married. Kane *was* married.'

Jodie knew nothing about this. Kane married?

Jack drained his can, indented it in the sand and snapped open a second before saying, 'Mum wanted them to go straight off after the wedding but neither of them would agree to it, not with mum being so …you know, near to the end. So they disobeyed the last wishes of a dying woman and stayed. Mum died the following week and the funeral was a week after that, a real big affair, half the township came. Mum was much respected you see. She was a strong, honest woman …

what you saw was what you got and people liked her for it. Anyway, after the funeral Ellie took some of the local kids from the choir back into town and that was fine but on the way back to the ranch her Chevy' spun out of control, came off the high top road and she was killed.' Jack up-ended his beer and drained it.

Jodie stared at him. 'Killed? On the same day that you and Kane buried your mother?'

Jack bowed his head and nodded.

'But ... but ... that's so ...'

'Bloody unfair?' Jack offered, looking up at Jodie. There was enough daylight left to pick out the sorrow in his grey eyes. 'You wouldn't believe it, would you? Mum and Ellie, both gone in the space of two weeks ... everything Kane ever loved. That's why he's so besotted with that great chestnut streak.' He nodded at Nightwalker who was in the act of equine foreplay, nuzzling at Mississippi, who appeared not the slightest bit interested and stood calmly with her gaze focused into the inner terrain. 'I think Kane looks on the stallion as his last link with mum and Ellie.'

'How do you get over something like that?' Jodie said, seriously shocked. 'I mean, how *did* he get over it.'

'Dunno if he has, really. There was a time, in the early days, when I feared for his sanity. He just seemed to drift away. And when he eventually came back, it was like a part of him was missing, as if he'd left it some place ... lost it.'

'But he's OK now, isn't he?' Jodie said, peering at Jack. 'I mean, he's recovered hasn't he?'

Jack let out a deep breath, shrugged and snapped open two more beers. 'Mostly. But he's been hammered by some heavy blows. Don't think he'll ever risk loving any thing else in *this* lifetime. He couldn't stand the loss. The next blow could be the one that floors him. The one he won't be able to rise up from.' Jack turned his face away.

Jodie said nothing, granting Jack the privacy to deal with his memories and ghosts. She barely knew him. But she liked him. She liked his easy ways, his honest face and the way his eyes creased at the edges when he grinned. He had a gentle, unruffled air about him, a reassuring rock-like sturdiness. It all made sense now. Kane's *tour de Australia,* his eagerness to bring the horse over to the island. A friendly, helpful gesture, yes, but more than that. Kane didn't want to go home to Amarillo because all that was waiting for him there were sad, bitter memories and dead people. And then, suddenly it hit her. Kane and Alex were both the same: both horribly wounded, scarred people, fighting demons, imagined and real; each unable to allow another human being too close, should it all end, as it had in the past, with pain and consequent loss. Cold apprehension tickled Jodie's spine and she pulled the blanket tighter. She'd made a mistake. Leaving Alex and Kane alone together was a bad error of judgement. Neither of them needed that. Neither of them was ready for it.

Chapter 6

Alex lay on her bed, slowly turning the pages in the book that she and Plug had found. Nothing made sense. On several pages, someone, her father she presumed, had made little pencil marks but they meant nothing to her. Perhaps there was more. She held the book up by its spine and shook it - nothing. Perhaps there had been more at the shack. Maybe in her revulsion she'd missed something. It was damn infuriating. Her gut feeling told her that she was missing something, but what? She turned back to page one, her eyes flicking quickly over the page. It was all so confusing and the racket coming from the bedroom next door wasn't helping. Kane Mitchell had been playing his depressing music for the last two hours and what was more, it was the same boring, wrist-slitting tracks over and over again. What was it with country music? Why did it have to be so damn depressing? Lord, it almost had *her* running to the kitchen for a knife. If he didn't turn it off soon she'd go and give him a piece of her mind. She turned to page two trying to take it in, page three, four, five. Still the music groaned on.

An hour later, when Dolly Parton was into her eighth encore of *I Will Always Love You,* Alex knew she could take no more. It was eleven-thirty, time when all good little cowboys should kick off their boots, hang up their lassos and go to sleep. She climbed off her bed and pulled on her jeans and sweater; there was no way she would be strutting around him in her nightdress, the memory of his paralysing eyes boring into her earlier that day was still vivid. As Dolly started up again, Alex opened her bedroom door. The man had obviously gone to sleep listening to this garbage. If she was lucky she could disembowel his C.D. player and be back in her room without him even knowing she'd been in there.

At his door she halted, carefully peering around the doorframe. His room was immaculate: clothes put away, his bed neatly made and, surprisingly, empty. On the bedside table stood a half full bottle of Jim Beam and a used glass. Alex walked into the room. The C.D. player had been programmed to repeat. Alex flicked a button and the room fell into silence. She glanced again at her watch - eleven-thirty-two. Where was he? *Does it matter? Who cares?* She cast a last look around the room, closing the door behind her as she left.

Alex sprang up in bed. She held her breath trying to pinpoint what it was that had woken her. There was nothing. No, that couldn't be right; she'd heard something. *Something* had woken her. Her eyes scanned the dark perimeters of the room. Was there something in here? Was *he* in here? No. There was nothing in the room. Even in the dark, she knew there was nothing in the room. She peered at the bedside clock. Two-forty-nine a.m. For a moment, she lay there, not moving, listening to the sound of silence. Then, throwing off the duvet, she climbed out of bed. Whatever had woken her needed checking out.

She dragged on a pair of jeans and slipped a vest over her head. Something was wrong. She didn't know what. But something was *very* wrong. Quietly she lifted the sash window and, as she stepped out onto the veranda, a horse whinnied. 'Oh dear God,' she said to no one. 'Please don't let this be another snake-in-the-box situation, not without Jodie here.'

She ran across the yard, struggled with the barn door and stepped inside. At the far end Mac stood quietly, turning to look at her. No problem here. She closed the door and set off for the house pasture, jogging the short distance. At the gate she stopped and watched the horses, silhouetted against the lightening morning sky. Another hour and the sun would be up. Everything looked fine. The horses grazed peacefully, ripping up grass, snorting to blow their nostrils clear of the dust they disturbed. She counted their outlines. One. Two. Three. She climbed up onto the fence to get a better look and counted again. One. Two. Three. She could only make out three horses. Mac was stabled; Jodie had taken Missy; that left four horses. She strained her eyes, screwing them up against the velvet darkness and emitted a low whistle. Their heads shot up. In profile, instantly, she knew which horse was missing - Holly. At that precise moment of realisation, a far away squeal drifted towards her. Turning into the direction of the sound, she found herself looking out towards the beach. What was Holly doing out on the beach? She rattled the gate. It was still shut fast. Horses didn't let themselves out of fields and close the gate behind them. There was only one thing for it. She had to go out there, onto the dark beach, with the tide coming in and find the damn horse.

She ran to the barn, grabbed a bridle and ran back to the field, sweating and breathless in spite of the wind whipping at her bare arms. She had to catch one of the horses. No point trying to catch Holly from the Land Rover, she'd never manage to get it within a hair's breadth of the mare.

After five minutes she managed to catch Flying who looked down her long hooked nose as if to say, 'Are you nuts? It's the middle of the night.' Climbing up onto the fence again, Alex vaulted across onto the mare's back, landing painfully on its prominent spine. Pressing her heels against its ribcage, they took off towards the beach, thundering past the house.

On the beach, Alex reined the mare in and listened. Except for the tumbling sea and the constant wind, all was quiet. 'Come on, Holly, give me a clue,' she said aloud, peering in one direction down the beach and then the other while Flying tossed her head, side-stepping and spooking at the white-crested waves rolling in out of the darkness. Without warning she spun, her back legs sinking into shifting sand like a corkscrew twisting through cork. Alex had to move on, even though she had no idea where she was moving on to. She turned again into the wind hoping that it might bring with it the sound of the horse but there was nothing.

And then she heard it. Carrying towards her, over the sound of the sea came the high-pitched scream. Alex froze. It wasn't just the sound of a lost horse. It was the sound of a terrified, desperate horse. But now at least she had her bearings. Now she knew where she was heading.

She sent the mare on at a fast canter, following the edge of the sea, leaping and plunging over each breaking wave, landing in a splattering of sand and water. Ahead of them, Holly called again. Gripping the mare as tight as a vice, Alex leaned forward over its neck and loosened the reins. Flying responded instantly and within five strides they were flat out and hurtling blindly into the dark.

As they rounded the headland, Holly's distressed squeals were clearly audible, reverberating on the wind, like a magnet pulling Alex closer. The remains of the pale moon slid out from behind high cloud, casting a low, white light across the beach, leading the way to the grey rocks of The Reach as it rose before them blocking the path. Alex took a pull and hung on as Flying came to a skidding halt. Shielding her eyes, Alex scanned the beach. It was still impossible to see much, even with the help from the moon. The sea here was much rougher, chopped up and irritated by the rocks, it rained down in a constant shower of sea-spray. Flying started to spook again, jogging away from the water, edging into the shadow of the rocks. There was no way through. The tide was so advanced that the furthest point had been cut off by a metre of rushing sea. There was nothing for it. Alex would have to turn up the beach and go round.

Just as she turned Flying, Holly called. Alex spun round hanging on to the mare's mane so that she didn't slip off its sweat-soaked back. The sound had come from the sea. But that wasn't possible. Holly couldn't be in the sea. Shielding her eyes against the spray, she let her gaze flit along the top of The Reach, following each rise and fall, squinting hard until suddenly - there she was, on the farthest point, cut off by the incoming tide.

She leapt from the mare's back and hit the ground running, keeping her sights firmly on the horse, silhouetted against the remains of the evening sky. She reached the base of the rock and started to haul herself up. Half way to the top, realisation kicked in. How was she going to get across the sea flowing between the rocks? It was too wide to jump. She'd have to go into the water but then she'd run the risk of being swept away. She stopped. She needed a rope, something to throw across the water, something to latch on to the rock on which Holly stood. She'd have to go back and get the bridle from Flying, that was the nearest thing to a rope without going all the way back to the house. That might be too late.

She slipped back onto the beach and ran to Flying, who, seeing Alex appearing out of the gloom ran backwards into the sea, freaked, lunged forward and hitting Alex full on, knocked her to the ground. Alex threw out a hand and by a chance of fate caught the swinging reins before Flying charged off up the beach. Alex scrambled to her feet, undid the throat-lash, ripped the bridle off and tore back to the rocks.

Pulling herself up the steep rise she made her way to the top, stopping only to reassure herself that Holly was still there. Twice she stumbled against jutting rock, falling to her knees, rising, her hands stretched out before her like a blind man trying to find his way over unfamiliar territory. A few more steps and for the first time Holly came clearly into sight.

Alex stopped dead. The horse stood with its back against the sea, shaking violently with cold or fear, or even both, water coursing from its back, its mane and tail plastered like rats tails against its quivering flesh. 'Don't panic Alex,' she muttered. 'Just ... don't ... panic!' Her hand crept up to her left shoulder. She closed her eyes and suddenly, she was six years old again and it was Christmas. Her parents, who still actually liked each other back then, were out in Hong Kong. They'd called home to say that they weren't going to make it back for Christmas, the airport was fogged in but Alex, being insecure, vulnerable and only almost six, thought it was because she wasn't special enough. Nanny Martha had sat her on her knee in front of the huge Christmas tree and told her that she *was* special and that she would *always* be special, and that all special people had an angel on their shoulder and that if she ever felt lost or lonely or scared she was to reach out and touch her shoulder and her angel would feel the touch and be there for her. Alex believed it implicitly. She never told any one about her angel but whenever she needed strength, like, when she lost Peter's baby, she spoke to it. And what was more, it always listened. She didn't ask for everything, that would be wrong. Some things you just had to work out for yourself. Her angel was there, on her shoulder for special times, times when she *really* needed help – like now. 'If you're there, I need you,' she whispered.

Holly squealed, jolting Alex, focusing her attention back on the dire situation. Without giving it another moment for sanity to kick in, she cast out the bridle, aiming high for a jutting point of rock. The bit latched over it first time and held.

Alex jumped into the water, the sudden, cold rush of it sweeping her through the channel like insignificant flotsam until the bridle snapped taut and held. Hauling against it she pulled herself slowly across the divide and nearer to the platform. Her hands found a grip on the rock and breathing hard, she dragged herself up out of the water.

Holly whickered a relieved welcome as Alex staggered towards her chanting senseless words, hoping that her fear didn't tell in the tone. As the first wave crept across the platform, washing over the horse's feet, it panicked, rearing high above Alex. As it came down, Alex grabbed its mane and hung on, preventing it from rearing again.

It was at this point that Alex realised she had no idea how she was going to get the horse off The Reach. If they stayed much longer, they would be knocked off by the incoming tide and hurled against the rocks. That wouldn't be good. In fact, it would probably kill them both.

She turned towards the edge of The Reach still hanging on to the horse, whose every instinct still told it to rear above the problem, but then, this had never been a very sane horse, not even on a good day.

A huge wave broke, hitting Holly sideways on, forcing her to her knees. Frantically she struggled back to her feet only to be knocked straight back down by the following wave. This time she didn't get up and the water flooded in over her back. Alex had no way of knowing how long the horse had been stranded out here but judging by its huge, white rimmed eyes, it was fast coming to the end of its tolerance level.

This wasn't a multiple-choice situation. There was only one way out of there and frankly, Alex really didn't want to spend too long thinking about it.

With the horse still on its knees, Alex stretched a leg over its back, hung on and kicked. Holly scrambled and splashed through the water for her footing, throwing Alex half way up her neck. She took several more unsteady steps, before finding her feet.

Alex leant forward and with one outstretched hand managed to grab the horse's nose and kicking and flapping like a novice rider, managed to steer it towards the sea. Holly slowly succumbed and inch-by-inch tiptoed nervously nearer to the edge until they were standing looking out on nothing except dark rushing sea. Beyond that, somewhere in the semi-darkness, lay the beach and safety.

Alex took a deep breath, glanced behind her at the next incoming wave that was about to hit them and shut her eyes. This was it!

With her heart thudding away like a jackhammer, she kicked the filly in the ribs. It took off in a blind leap of faith, jumping for its life into the darkness as the wave closed over them.

It hit like a speeding juggernaut, the force of it so powerful that it sucked them down for what seemed like an eternity, before Holly kicked out with thrashing legs and they started to rise. They broke the surface together, the horse, disorientated, striking out, swimming a complete circle before finding its bearings and turning towards the beach. Alex swam by its side, the heavy swell lifting them in its body until the next wave broke, imprisoning the horse in its roll, dragging it under. It disappeared for a full twenty seconds before it resurfaced, ears pinned back flat against its skull, its upper lip raised high off its teeth trying to keep the water out of its nostrils. It looked like it was grinning. But Alex doubted it. This time the mare had lost its bearings and started heading out to sea. Alex spun round in the water. There was no way she could chase after it, but, then again, she hadn't come this far to lose it now.

She struck out after it, hurling her body against the incoming sea – five, six, seven strokes. Then Holly was there. She'd turned again and was heading back. The next wave broke over them and they were dragged under in a mish-mash of legs and arms, thrown together in the rapid undercurrent. A front hoof splayed into Alex's chest knocking the breath from her body, bowling her under the belly of the horse. Alex couldn't breath. She was trapped in a cage of flailing legs. Water filled her head. It felt like it would burst. With a swift backwards thrust the horse kicked her free. She surfaced coughing and choking. Sucking in a lungful of air, she watched the next wave rear up above them. As it crashed down, she closed her eyes. When she opened them, the horse had gone.

'NO!'

The booming of the waves took the scream away. She threw her body across the water, spinning, searching, horrified. Where was she? She had to be somewhere. Without wasting the time to take a breath, she dived, touching the seabed, peering through the gloom and swirling undertow. She couldn't see anything. She kicked out and rose to the surface, popping up like a cork, gasping, her lungs raw. She was about to dive again when Holly resurfaced almost beneath her. She grabbed a handful of mane, twisting it tightly around her hand. If the filly went down again, it was taking her with it. Laboriously they headed towards the beach with Alex almost dragging the horse, as it grew weaker with every stride. Alex tightened her hold as the next wave folded suffocatingly over them and dragged them down to the reef.

They hit the sharp coral upside down before the turbulence spun them full circle and hurled them back towards the surface. Holly lashed out frantically towards the light, dragging Alex with her, bubbles trailing from their mouths and nostrils as they rose slowly up and up.

They broke the surface together. Alex couldn't breath. She was trying but the air just wouldn't, couldn't get into her body fast enough. A glance at Holly told Alex she had fared no better. She grabbed the horse's head, pushing its nostrils clear of the water. Surely, they couldn't be that far from the beach now, could they, they'd been in the water for ages. Alex turned to look behind them, her eyes widening at the sight that met her. This was it. This was the one that had her name on it. They weren't going to survive *this* one. As the wave reared up above them, Alex grabbed onto Holly and closed her eyes.

Above the sound of the sea came a whooshing noise and a rope slapped onto the surface of the water in a perfect circle around the horse's head and tightened. Before the wave hit, they were whisked from its path and dragged like two novice water skiers across the bumpy sea.

Alex clung on, half drowned, as they buffeted against the waves and it wasn't until her knees buckled as they hit sand and she collapsed in a heap at the side of the horse, that she realised Kane Mitchell was on the other end of the rope and that he had just saved their lives.

She was wrenched to her feet in one upward jerk and shaken until her teeth rattled.

'You stupid bloody woman. What in God's name do you think you were doing, trying to kill yourself?' He shook her like a limp rag doll until any remaining breath was jolted from her body and she dropped to her knees in the breaking surf. Again, he grabbed her and yanked her to her feet. 'Answer me, God damn you! Christ, I've seen it all now.'

She staggered away from him on legs that had turned to jelly, choking up salt water and the remains of her supper, while he dragged his eyes away from her and turned them onto the horse. He bent to examine it, checking its mandible pulse, taking in the sight of the bubbles popping from its gaping mouth. He winced at a slash in its neck, pumping out blood, staining the white sand crimson. Taking a skinning knife from his trouser pocket he moved towards its neck.

Alex screamed, 'NO!' and dragging herself to her feet, lunged at him, beating against his chest with clenched fists. 'Don't you dare touch that horse. Haven't you done enough damage already?'

He brushed her aside as if she was nothing more than an irritating insect, before reaching down, placing the blade underneath the lasso and cutting it. He turned to look at her, shaking his head, cussing. 'Stupid bloody woman.'

Alex ignored him and dropped to her knees, gently raising the horse's head, cradling it in her arms. It felt as heavy as lead. Kane knelt beside her and felt again for its pulse. He turned towards her. His face was so close she could see a tiny nerve twitching in his left cheek, see the amber flecking in his eyes, the hard line of his mouth. He reached out and touched her shoulder, his hand lingering as he said soberly, 'Come on, Alex. Let's get you back to the house.'

She watched the words coming out of his mouth, heard them, but they made no sense. 'Back to the house? Why would I want to go back to the house?'

Kane squeezed her shoulder. 'Because the filly's dying. I'll take you back to the house and come back here and sort it.'

Alex stared at him incomprehensibly. Come back and sort it? Sort it? What did that mean? Did he mean he intended fetching drugs, blankets, the horse trailer, Jodie, what? She watched the expression on his face and suddenly she knew what he meant. He meant he would take her back to the house, fetch his gun from his room, come back here and put a bullet through Holly's head. Alex grabbed his arm, roughly pulling his hand away from her shoulder.

'You will *not* sort it,' she hissed into his face, jutting out her jaw. 'She is *not* dying. I won't *let* her die, do you understand?'

Gently he touched her cheek, turning her face towards the horse. 'Look at her, Alex. She's taken too much of a battering, she needs putting out of her misery. There's nothing you can do here.'

She swung her head away from the sight of the horse and glared at him. Suddenly it all made sense. His unexplained disappearance last night. The repetitive wrist-slashing music blasting away in his empty room until almost midnight. Now she knew exactly where he'd been, out here, stranding a defenceless creature in the middle of the Pacific Ocean. 'She does not need putting out of her misery, you pessimistic bastard. Much as it grieves you, you're going to have to accept that your little trick has backfired. You have failed,' she snarled.

His look passed right through her. 'What the hell, is *that* supposed to mean?'

'It means that your sick, horrible joke backfired. *You* put my horse out there didn't you?'

Silently he turned his head to look out across the waves and towards the rocks, watching the incoming rollers smashing against the impenetrable mass. His voice faltered as he said, 'You don't *seriously* think I put your horse out there, do you?'

'I don't *think* you did it. I *know* you did it.'

He turned back to look at her. 'In that case I think you should consider cutting back on your medication.'

'Don't try injecting humour. It won't work. *You* shredded my shirt. *You* put the horse out there and *you* are going to pay for it.' She stood up, towering over him briefly, before he too, got to his feet and dwarfed her.

His finger poked into her left shoulder sending her sprawling backwards 'I did *not* rip your shirt and I did *not* put your bloody horse out on the rocks, either,' he said, through perfect, gritted teeth, prodding his finger into her repeatedly with each stride, backing her along the edge of the tide. 'I can't see any reason to do such a thing and I don't seriously believe you can either, not unless you really are cuckoo.'

Over his shoulder, the horse tried to raise its head. She broke away from him and ran, stumbling, to its side, dropping to her knees as its head rolled back onto the wet sand. This wouldn't do. The horse was freezing to death lying here in the tide lap. She stood up, swaying, holding her head. She couldn't go passing out now. She had to get Holly out of the sea. She snatched the lasso up from where he'd left it in the sand and with fingers that were still half paralysed tried to form a knot. It fell away in her hands they were shaking so badly.

'Give it to me,' he growled, snatching it from her fingers. 'I don't know what you're trying to prove by prolonging its suffering. God only knows how much water it has in its lungs.' He fastened one end securely around the horse's pasterns and the other end to the Land Rover's winch, which he turned on. Alex supported Holly's head as the rope shortened, pulling her slowly out of the water until she was lying on dry sand. Then Kane released the ropes and crouching by the mare's side, laid his head on her cold chest, listening for the slightest improvement in its shallow, irregular breathing. There was none. If anything, her breathing had worsened. There was a definite rattle now and tiny bubbles still popped from her pale nostrils. He straightened up and looked at Alex. 'This isn't fair; you need to do something *now*. It's time to let her go.'

Alex opened her mouth but no words came. Yes, she needed to do something. But hell would freeze over before she would allow him to put a bullet in Holly's brain. Jodie had always maintained that where there was life there was hope. And there *was* still life. And therefore, there was still hope.

Suddenly Alex was running across the sand to the Land Rover, jumping in and turning the key. It burst into life, emitting the obligatory belch of blue-black smoke from its rattling exhaust, before Alex floored the accelerator and swung its nose towards the horse. Kane had to leap out of the way to avoid being flattened as she sped past him, braked violently and spun the vehicle to a halt, just centimetres away from the horse's head. He watched, shaking his head as she revved the engine until it screamed like a deranged banshee and black smoke signals puthered up into the early morning sky. Then she leant on the horn and screamed, 'Get up, Holly, you miserable piece of horseshit! Get up! MOVE IT!'

It was Kane that moved. Wrenching open the door, he made a snatch for the keys.

Alex was faster. She lashed out at his hand and screamed, 'Leave it!'

'What the hell are you doing, woman? Don't you know when you're beaten?'

She glared at him from a frozen, determined face. 'Don't you?'

He made another lunge for the keys and she lashed out again, grabbing his hand, holding it, her nails digging into his flesh. 'I am *not* going home without this horse.'

They glared at each other, delving into each other's eyes, seeking the slightest weakness and finding none.

Kane spoke first, his voice low, the tone sincere. 'I didn't put your horse out on The Reach. If I had, why would I be here trying to save you? I'm just sorry I didn't get here sooner and then the outcome might have been better.'

Alex released his arm but continued to watch him. 'If you didn't do it, who did? I think the chances of Holly getting herself out there on her own are pretty impossible, don't you?'

'Yeah, I do. But that doesn't mean I did it.'

She was shaking now, her teeth starting to chatter like a demented monkey.

He slipped off his jacket and placed it around her shoulders. Her immediate response was to hurl it off and chuck it into the sea, or better still, return the favour and shred it into tatters and throw it back in his face, but she was so cold and with the warmth of his body still in it, it felt too good.

'If you didn't do it,' Alex said - realising she needed his help and that he was more likely to give it if she temporarily shelved the hostility and the suspicions - 'prove it, by helping me.'

'How?' he said, simply.

'Get in here, rev it, and don't stop until I tell you to.'

He frowned. 'Why?'

'Because Holly's terrified of this Land Rover. I don't know why. She always has been and if anything can get her up, this will.'

He stared at her, shaking his head. It was clear he thought she was mad.

Alex stepped out of the Land Rover and looked at him questioningly, tilting her head. 'Well?'

He shrugged and still shaking his head in disbelief, climbed in.

'Now rev it and don't stop,' Alex repeated, disappearing in front of the Land Rover.

Five minutes passed before Kane climbed out and walked slowly round to the front. Alex sprang up. 'I told you to keep revving it, didn't I? Go back.'

Kane looked down at the horse and winced. 'Alex, she's dead.'

'She is *not* dead!'

'Alex.'

'Shut up!'

'Alex.'

'No!' She fell back into the sand at the side of the horse's still body and with both fists pounded on its ribcage. 'Get up Holly. Don't you dare die on me. Do you hear? Get up.' She turned her eyes back on Kane. 'Well! Are you helping me or not?'

He backed off, holding up his hands in submission and climbed back into the Land Rover. He revved it for a further five minutes before it spluttered and ran out of diesel. He got out and walked round the Land Rover. 'It's out of gas,' he said. 'Sorry.'

Alex looked up at him, eyes brimming with tears, face still as white as snow. 'It doesn't matter. We won't be needing it anymore.'

'I'm sorry,' Kane repeated, sounding like he really meant it.

A smile trickled its way across Alex's face and settled in her bright, wet eyes. 'Don't be. Just stand back, Mr Mitchell. The Phoenix is about to rise from the ashes.' Alex watched his face as the horse, which looked as if it had been put through a mangle, stretched out its front legs one at a time and pushing with every last ounce of strength, wobbled to its feet. It stood swaying in front of Alex, who, without taking her eyes off Kane, planted a kiss in the middle of its forehead and whispered, 'My clever, clever girl.'

Chapter 7

'I think we all need to sit down and sort this thing out,' Jodie said diplomatically. 'I'm sure there has to be a very logical reason for what's happened.' She poured coffee into four mugs, handed one to Kane and Alex, who sat at the table and passed one to Jack, who stood cross-legged, leaning against the corner of the work surface. 'Now, let's go over it again, shall we?'

Alex dropped her head into her hands, resting both elbows on the table. It didn't matter how many times they had this autopsy, the outcome was always going to be the same.

'You say you woke up because you heard Holly,' Jodie continued. 'You were asleep. The horse woke you and you went to see what was wrong.'

Alex nodded and muttered, 'Yes, something like that.'

'Well, was it like that or not?' Jodie asked, peering over the top of her coffee mug. 'Because what I'm trying to do here, Alex, is get to the bottom of why I came home to find one of our brood mares almost dead and you not looking much better.'

Alex slumped back into her chair.

'Well?'

'I say *something like that,* because when I woke, I didn't know *what* it was that had woken me. It was like the night we found that snake in Mac's box; something woke me, but I don't know what exactly. And without a reason, I knew something was wrong, somewhere.'

'And, without telling Kane, you just took off into the night?' Jodie's voice rose.

'*Yes!* Without telling Kane I just took off into the night,' Alex snapped, her voice equalling Jodie's in pitch. 'Why would I tell Kane anyway? Who is he? Just a cowboy mate of yours who happens to have a horse with a dick that works!'

Jack choked on his coffee, spluttering and coughing so badly that his eyes started to water and Jodie had to go over and thump him on the back until he held up a hand and nodded, signifying that he was OK and she could stop thumping the life out of him.

Jodie turned her attention back to the table. 'I think that's a little ungrateful, don't you, Alex?'

'No, Jodie! I do not think it's a little ungrateful. I think it's the truth and, I also think that you should drop the 'Perry Mason' act and listen to what I'm saying. I woke up; I climbed out of the window … '

'You climbed out of the window?' Jodie repeated, her eyes disappearing under her fringe. 'Why did you climb out of the window? What was wrong with using the door, like any normal person?'

'Ah!' Kane said, speaking for the first time. 'You've put your finger right on it there, Jodie. She didn't use the door like a *normal* person, because she *isn't* a normal person. Anyone that takes off into the night, bareback, climbs a small mountain, jumps a lunatic horse off a plateau into the Pacific Ocean, is *not* a normal person.'

Alex rounded on him, eyes blazing. 'And leading a horse out onto The Reach and certain death *is* the action of a normal person, I suppose?'

Jodie cut in. 'Stop it! Why do you think Kane put the horse out there, Alex? What does he have to achieve by doing such a ridiculous thing?'

'I haven't figured that out yet,' Alex answered.

'And what is there to be achieved by ripping each other to pieces, either?' Jodie added.

'As opposed to my shirt, you mean,' Alex said coldly, still glaring at Kane.

Jodie turned up her palms, silently asking for answers. 'What's that supposed to mean?'

Jack, who so far, other than his coughing fit hadn't said anything, picked up his mug and walked over to the table and, pulling out a chair, sat opposite Alex. He glanced across at his brother before pointing a finger at Alex. 'You ought to be a bit more grateful to the man who saved your life.'

'Saved my life?' Alex shrilled. 'Saved my life? Why, Jack, do you think he saved my life? It was because his sick joke went belly-up. Killing me wasn't on his agenda. He just wanted to KILL MY HORSE!'

Jodie brought her small fist down on the table, silencing everyone. 'Right,' she said, waving her hands slowly up and down. 'Let's just calm this whole thing down.' She looked at Kane. 'How come you were up at The Reach, Kane. You weren't just passing by, were you?'

Kane threw the spoon down on the table and, looking up at Jodie, said, 'No, I wasn't just passing by. I'd been up half the night, I couldn't sleep and then when I *was* finally dropping off I heard the sound of a horse galloping past the house. I got up and checked the horses in the field, found two missing and went looking. Pretty simple really, not exactly rocket science.'

'So, you knew Alex was out there,' Jodie said.

Kane shook his head. 'No. Not at first. Not until I'd tracked the horse to The Reach and then I saw her. By that time, she was clambering up onto its back and attempting to get it off The Reach and into the water. I couldn't believe my eyes. What kind of an idiot risks their life like that for a horse?'

'And you wouldn't?' Jack said.

For a moment, Kane didn't answer. Then he said sheepishly, 'Depends on the horse.'

'Yeah, right,' Jack said, nodding, not believing a word.

'And what's all this about you -' Jodie indicated Kane with a flick of her head, '- ripping up Alex's shirt?'

'She thinks I shredded her beach shirt. She fell asleep sunbathing, after her swim, when you and Jack took off round the island yesterday. When she woke the shirt had been shredded.' He picked up his coffee mug and, poising it half way to his mouth, added, 'She probably did it herself, in her sleep, and forgot all about it.'

Alex's heart skipped a beat and plummeted.

She shot a look at Jodie. Jodie stared back, knowing instantly what the look meant, what Alex was thinking. Kane's flippant words held more truth than he could ever have known.

Alex dropped her head back into her hands. No, she couldn't have, not again, not now. It wasn't possible, was it? Yes, of course it was possible. Most things were possible. But was it likely? She'd been asleep and woken up to find the shirt torn. She'd been asleep and woken up to find the horse stranded out on The Reach. Both times, she'd been asleep and when she'd woken, something bad had happened. The common denominator in both incidents was the fact that she'd been asleep. Beseechingly, she looked up at Jodie. 'I couldn't have, could I? Not now, not after all this time.'

Jodie sat down, the weight of the possibility knocking the wind out of her.

'What?' Jack said, looking from Jodie to Alex and back again. 'You couldn't have done what?'

Jodie and Alex stared at each other.

'I used to sleepwalk,' Alex said, not taking her eyes off Jodie's face.

The kitchen, except for the heavy ticking of the clock, fell silent.

Alex couldn't afford to believe it was possible. She couldn't have ripped her own shirt and put her own horse out on The Reach, could she? She'd been free of the problem for years now, ever since …

Jodie slid a hand across the table and took hold of Alex's, squeezing it tightly. Alex looked at Jodie through horrified eyes. 'Could I have done it, Jodie? Could I?'

'Bullshit!' Kane said emphatically, before Jodie could answer, not that she wanted to. For one thing, she didn't know the answer, not for certain.

'Are you seriously saying you think you did both of those things in your sleep?' He gave a derisory snort that turned to laughter. Jack joined in.

'Ten years ago, Alex's parents' house burnt down,' Jodie said quietly.

The laughter stopped.

'They found Alex asleep in her father's Range Rover. Scattered in the back, where she'd thrown them, were empty petrol cans. Alex started the fire in her sleep.'

Alex turned her face to Kane. If it were true, then she'd accused him wrongly. He'd merely been in the wrong place at the wrong time regarding the shirt and in the right place at the right time regarding the episode with Holly on the rocks. Her accusations could be little more than wishful thinking. 'I'm sorry,' she said, wide-eyed, zombie-like. 'It could have been me.'

Kane touched her shoulder, a gentle touch that brushed her bare skin. 'I don't believe that for one minute,' he said, scrutinizing her pale, stricken face. 'You wouldn't put a horse at risk, conscious or comatose. You're just not made that way.'

'But, I blamed you. I said some despicable things. You saved my life ... and Holly's and I never even thanked you.'

He smiled, crinkling the tanned skin at the edges of his eyes. 'That's OK. I forgive you. Like I said, I couldn't sleep, so it wasn't like I had anything better to do, was it?'

Alex pushed away from the table and stood up. 'I'm going to check on Holly.'

'Is that a good idea, Alex?' Jodie asked. 'You should be in bed, taking it easy. After what you've been through, I doubt you'll be able to walk in the morning.'

Alex stopped at the door. 'I need to check on Holly, OK?'

Jodie held up a hand in submission. 'OK.'

The shock waiting for Alex when she saw Holly turned her heart over. The mare was flat out, eyes closed, hardly breathing; her bright chestnut coat was caked in dried salt and sand, turning her grey before her years. Jodie had rigged up several drips straight into the horse's bloodstream, and with tubes stretching across her still body, she looked like a broken, discarded puppet that some horrible child no longer had a use for.

Alex stole quietly into the box, closed the door and settled into the corner. If the horse came through this, it would be a miracle. It had taken hours to get it back to the barn. First Kane had walked back to the house to fetch a can of diesel, then he'd walked back to Alex and Holly and filled up the tank on the Land Rover. After that, he'd driven back to the house, picked up the horse trailer and carted it back along the beach to Alex and the horse. It had been hard work trying to get Holly up the ramp and into the box. She wanted desperately to lie down and it took the last of Alex's strength to keep the mare on its feet and inch-by-inch move her in the right direction. Together, she and Kane had shouldered the mare up the ramp until, sweating and breathless, they succeeded in getting her in and closing the door. Alex had to travel back in the trailer, hanging on to Holly, pushing and shoving her slight weight against her to stop her from falling over.

Alex pulled a strand of hay from the rack and put it in her mouth, chewing thoughtfully. Kane had been brilliant – in the end, and she was under no illusion, she couldn't have got Holly back alive without him. She had been horrible to him, accusing him of tearing her shirt, insinuating that he'd stranded the horse out on The Reach. And now the evidence pointed to her as the guilty one.

She closed her eyes, screwing them tight to stop the drumming in her head. She could still hear the deafening boom of the sea. It seemed to fill her head. She rubbed at her temples. Jodie was right, she should be in bed but what if Holly deteriorated further and there was no one with her? She could hardly expect Jodie to stay with her. As far as Jodie was concerned, she'd done her best, now it was up to the horse.

These *so called* professionals - they always did their best. Just like the ones Alex had seen - the therapists.

The ones that said her sleep walking was a *stress thing*, the product of an over active mind; that it was more common in the young and that she'd come through it, grow out of it.

She snatched another strand of hay and chewed on it, deep in thought. Kane hadn't had to save her life; it wasn't in the job description. Jodie hadn't stated, 'You must come to a foreign island, put up with a screwball woman who sleepwalks and tries to kill things and then, if you're not doing anything in particular, just pop along the beach in the dead of night – or early morning – and save her life, an act to which there will be no thanks given or gratitude shown.'

She leant back, resting her head against the partition and closed her eyes. Instantly she opened them. What if it wasn't her? What if her gut reaction had been right? What if it really was Kane?

Around nine the following morning Plug arrived back on the island. He'd phoned to enquire if Alex had made any headway with the book they'd found. When Jodie divulged what had been happening over the past twenty-four hours and suggested that Alex probably hadn't had the opportunity to study it, he'd informed Jodie that he'd be back on the morning tide and no matter what Jodie said, he'd refused to be drawn any further as to why. He arrived just as Jodie was about to serve breakfast and happily took up the offer of sausage, bacon and beans, pulling out a chair and settling at the side of Kane.

He made no attempt to hide his concern when Alex limped into the kitchen and took her place opposite. He waited, watching her intently, until she'd settled, then said bluntly, 'I reckon, in light of what's been happening, that there's something you should know about this place.'

Jodie paused, the frying pan in her hand. 'Will it wait until after breakfast, Plug, or should I serve up?'

Plug shook his head. There wasn't much in life that he considered as grounds for delaying food. 'Nah, I reckon you'd better go ahead and serve up. I'll talk while I eat, if that's OK with you.'

Jodie served the food, while Jack poured coffee. Plug continued to watch Alex, noticing the way she grimaced as she lifted her coffee cup. When Jodie took her place at the table and picked up her fork, Plug said, 'I heard from your friend here -' he nodded at Jodie, '- that you ended up out on The Reach chasing some horse of yours.'

Alex swallowed the strong coffee and nodded.

Plug placed his fork on his plate. 'How much do you know about this place, its history?'

Alex and Jodie exchanged glances. 'What's to know? Jodie asked.

Plug wiped his mouth, his grey eyes flicking to Kane, then Jack, then Jodie before coming to rest on Alex. 'This island has a history and it ain't pretty. It ain't called Mulligan's Reach for nothing and it ain't because of them rocks. It's because of what *happened* on them rocks. I reckon it's time someone told you what happened out there,' Plug said, picking up his fork and shovelling sausage and egg into his mouth, like a little boy gone crazy in the *Pick and Mix*.

Jodie sat frowning, concern puckering her forehead. 'It sounds serious, Plug. It can't be that bad, can it?'

Plug swallowed and took a sip of coffee before saying, 'Depends … it could be.'

'Depends on what?' Jodie said.

'Depends on how that horse got out there,' Plug said, glancing at Kane.

The latter held Plug's gaze and said quietly, 'If you have something to say, I suggest you say it.'

Plug nodded. 'Yeah you're right. OK. Years ago, the island was owned by Sissy and Jacob Mulligan. They had a boy ... Isla. He was a shy, introverted lad. His mother, Sissy, worshipped him and *that* was the problem. Jacob Mulligan was insanely jealous of the mother/son relationship and sent the lad away to the mainland. A week after Isla's departure, Jacob was found drowned, his body washed up, broken and bruised on The Reach. No one knew how it happened; it was a flat, calm night and Jacob was experienced with the ways of the sea. After a year, Sissy eventually managed to track her son down through the authorities and he came back to the island. But he didn't return alone. He'd married a girl on the mainland, Kitty. Sissy saw Kitty as a barrier to her son's affections and set about making her life hell in the hopes that the girl would give up and go back to the mainland. But Kitty fell pregnant and a baby boy, Asak, increased the problem a hundred fold. Now there were two barriers between Sissy and her son. One night, about three weeks after Asak was born, Kitty woke. There was a storm blowing Up ... this place is renowned for its atrocious storms, something to do with the curve of the bay, the way the north wind meets the south head on ...' Plug stopped briefly, considering these geological facts. Then, after scratching at his chin, went on, 'Kitty heard the baby crying and went to its room. It was gone. Standing outside in the approaching storm, Kitty followed the baby's cries into the night. She found herself on the beach heading towards The Reach ...'

'The Reach?' Jodie queried, picking up the coffee pot and refilling everyone's cup.

Plug nodded. 'Kitty followed the cries up onto The Reach, along the top until she got to the point where the rock breaks and the tide floods in. Across the water, lying on the furthermost point was the baby.' Plug looked across at Alex. 'Same place as your horse ended up.'

Alex shivered. Coincidence. That's all.

'Kitty plunged into the water and staggered up onto the rocks ...'

'The same as me,' Alex whispered.

'She grabbed her baby but was too scared to attempt getting back ... '

'*Not* like you,' Kane offered.

'Is this for real?' Jodie asked. 'Only, it sounds like a horror story to me.'

Plug pursed his lips. 'I said it weren't pretty, didn't I? By the time Isla found them, they were completely cut off by the sea. Isla was distraught, shouting and screaming for Kitty to jump, stretching out his hand across the water. But Kitty was terrified of losing the baby. Isla Mulligan called out repeatedly for her to jump, promising to catch her, vowing the baby would be safe. Finally she did. Mulligan reached out for her. Their fingers touched ... briefly. Then she slipped away from him, into the black rush of water, still hanging on to the little 'un. The undercurrent did its worse, sucking them down. You don't stand a chance in them whirlpools between the break in the rocks. There are those who reckon those eddies would drag an elephant down into oblivion. Isla hurled himself into the water after them. They never found the bodies. And there are those who say that on a stormy night, when the wind is in the right direction, you can hear a baby's cries coming from The Reach.'

The kitchen was silent. Kane was the first to speak. 'Good story mate. I'll bet that's snowballed over the years, kept the locals amused over many a pint at closing time.'

'That's horrific,' Alex said, rubbing at her gooseflesh arms, ignoring Kane's blasé attitude, remembering the sound she had *thought* she'd heard the night they found the snake in Mac's box. *That* had sounded like a baby. *And* there had been a storm that night.

'I suppose it was the mother-in-law from hell,' Jodie said.

'It didn't crawl there on its own, did it, mate?' Plug said simply. 'There had to be someone to blame. Always is in these matters. And let's face it, she had to be there or who would have told the story that's been handed down over the years? Who would have known what happened blow for blow? As I say, there's always someone to blame in these matters.'

'Yeah, right,' Alex said. She wanted to direct her comment at Kane. She needed it to be him, because then – it meant it wasn't her.

Plug finished his breakfast and pushed his plate away. The expression on his face looked bothered, unfinished. He sucked at his teeth, his eyes flicking to each of them in turn. 'There's more,' he said quietly.

Chapter 8

'There are those that say the baby, Asak, didn't perish out there in the sea that night ... that the old woman somehow pulled him out, saved him, brought him up. That he survived then, and ... he survives now.'

'Now!' Jodie exclaimed.

Plug nodded. 'Yep. That he lives on the island to this day.'

'Where?' Jodie said, raising her eyebrows in undisguised astonishment. Where would he live?'

'Where do you think he would live?' Plug said. 'Asak Mulligan had Aboriginal blood in him. You only need a drop of that stuff running through your veins and you can live anywhere where there's nature. They're a race born of the land and at one with the land. You've got wildlife on this island, fresh water, cover from the weather, what more would he want?'

Jodie shook her head. 'No, I can't believe that,' she said. 'Why haven't we seen signs of him?'

'Why should you?' Plug challenged. 'Asak Mulligan wouldn't be seen if he didn't want to be.'

Jodie was still shaking her head in disbelief as Kane chipped in.

'The story is widely known. I'd heard it on the mainland before I came here.'

All eyes, except Jack's – who remained staring at the table and looking decidedly shifty - turned to Kane.

'You knew about it before you came to the island?' Jodie said, incredulity sounding in her voice. 'You knew about it and you said nothing?'

Kane shrugged. 'I thought you'd already know the history of the place you called home.'

'We've only been here a few months,' Jodie defended. 'We didn't hear anything. If it was common knowledge, the men working on the house would have told us, surely?'

'Not necessarily,' Plug said. 'Depends if they were local to these parts.'

For a moment, Jodie didn't speak as she digested what Plug was saying. Then she turned to him and with a blank expression said, 'But, if this man exists, he's going to be an old man, a man in his …what?'

Plug pursed his lips and rocked his head gently, from side to side, as if struggling with the maths. Then he offered, 'Late fifties.'

'But that's impossible! An old man, almost sixty years old, living on the island, out in all weathers, killing and living off the land? No, that's just local … '

'Bullshit?' Kane offered.

'Yes, bullshit,' Jodie said, continuing to stare at the side of Plug's head. 'Are you seriously suggesting that this … Asak person, caught, lead, and stranded that manic chestnut horse out on The Reach? That a sixty year old could do that?'

Plug wiped a hand across his mouth and scratched at his chin. 'Yep! That's exactly what I'm suggesting. I've told you. You only need a tiny drop of that Abo' blood and you have *the way* with all things living.'

Alex, so far, had said nothing. Her nanny, Martha, had always said, 'Listen twice,
Alex dear and speak once.' Not something Alex always managed to do. Usually it was the reverse, but this time she'd listened. Kane had known the rumour all along, known in advance of coming to the island, long enough to use it to his own devious advantage, to commit any travesty his sick, bored mind might want to and then

blame it on a rumour. She watched his face, expressionless, innocent - too expressionless, too innocent. He'd done it. As surely as night followed day. He'd ripped her shirt, put Holly out on The Reach, and now, she and Jodie were supposed to fall for this 'cock and bull' story about a part Aboriginal, geriatric weirdo. There was only one weirdo on the island and he was within smelling distance.

'I think you ought to take the story seriously,' Plug continued. 'At least keep a look out for anything abnormal ... '

'As opposed to anything Aboriginal?' Jodie said, with a sly grin. She stacked the plates and carried them to the sink still grinning, then, as Kane and Jack stood up and left the kitchen, she followed them out, leaving Alex sitting alone with Plug.

She tilted her head to look at him. He looked rebuffed. He'd come twenty-five miles to impart this news and no one was taking him seriously. Alex touched his hand and he turned to look at her. 'Thank you,' she said. 'Thanks for coming all the way out here to tell us this. I'm sure there are those that believe rumours and superstition like this but Jodie has her head wrapped in hard, solid facts. That's what schooling does for people like Jodie. Don't be put out because she ridicules what you say.'

Plug sucked at his teeth and said sharply, 'I ain't put out, Missy. I'm concerned that that horse of yours ended up out there on The Reach. That ain't normal by any stretch of the imagination.'

Alex didn't answer. She didn't say what she thought, that no, it wasn't normal for Holly to end up out on The Reach, but neither was what Plug was suggesting. An old man of almost pensionable age catching and leading

Holly? Not possible. She lowered her head to look at Plug who was sitting staring at the table, as if he had all the worries in the world piled on his shoulders. 'Listen,' she said, suddenly grasping an idea. 'How about you stay the night and tomorrow we could take another ride out to that shack and have another poke around? You found the book the first time and if I hadn't been such a wimp, moaning on about the smell and everything, we might have found more. I think we overlooked something.'

Plug raised his head and looked at her. 'Yeah?'

'Yeah.'

His face crept into a grin. The old Plug was back. 'Well, I reckon we could. But I don't think we missed anything the first time.'

Alex probably agreed with him but she wasn't likely to say so. Plug Towers was a lonely man. It showed in his gushing acceptance of hospitality, in the fact that he could find the time to return to the island. Plug was the father figure she'd never had. Someone, to whom, perhaps in time, she could tell her innermost fears and hopes, without the risk of her burden becoming too heavy, causing them to walk away.

It wasn't easy being insular.

Around eleven-thirty that night, Alex gave up trying to sleep. Her brain refused to close down. There were so many things to think about. It was made worse by the music belting out from the room next door. Having your eardrums and your sensibility subjected to such classics as *The Wind Beneath My Wings, For The Good Times* and *I Will Always Love You* (fat chance), wasn't exactly preparatory for a good night's sleep. So many hearts ripped at the seams, broken, bleeding, never to be repaired. She'd decided to listen to one more song before bolting into his room and throwing him and his entire C.D. collection through the window. She wondered if she'd physically have the strength to do so but she'd give it a go, anything to shut up lyrics that were actually starting to get to her. Lord, she'd be on the Internet tomorrow, ordering her own copy of *50 All Time Country Classics*.

As the record, *Honey Come Back*, ended, the room went quiet. She'd figured he'd either become as sick and suicidal as she was with the whole thing or fallen asleep. Either way, she'd been relieved and thrown herself onto her stomach in a final attempt at sleep.

Half an hour later, she'd given in, got up and walked down to the barn to check on Holly. She'd been with her for most of the day, just sitting at the back of the box, waiting for the slightest sign that the horse was improving. Just before teatime, Holly had regained consciousness and staggered precariously to her feet. Alex had been elated.

Standing here now, watching the mare absently plucking a strand of hay at a time from the rack, Alex felt overwhelmed. The horse had stood at the gates of hell – and returned. She was battered and bruised, her skin pulled tightly across a rib cage that looked like it was two sizes too big. Her eyes had sunk into their sockets. She looked like a knacker, something even the meat man back home wouldn't touch. But – she was alive and that was all that mattered. Alex could build on that, make her better.

Alex left her in peace and walked back towards the house. It was a beautiful night. Looking up it seemed like a billion stars shone down on the island. Alex had heard it said somewhere that there are more stars in the sky than grains of sand in the whole world, a fact that tonight, she was prepared to believe. It was as if a Godly hand had drawn back the clouds like a dusty stage curtain, revealing the whole magical universe. Mulligan's Reach might be badly placed geologically and subject to storms and squalls, but when it got it right - it got it right.

Alex spun a full circle, overdosing on the sight, taking in the huge grapefruit coloured moon casting its *Super Trouper* light across the sea: a beaming beacon, lighting a mystical pathway to the stars. In that moment her heart felt light, empty of all misery and bitterness. It wasn't possible to feel a single negative emotion on a night like this. Dizzy, she stopped spinning and stood looking out towards the sea, breathing in the salt and flora-perfumed air. Perfect. Bliss.

Out of the darkness, a voice spoke, 'Beautiful, isn't it?'

She spun so fast she almost tripped over her own feet. Sitting on the porch steps, a metre away, was Kane. Other than jeans, with the belt left unbuckled, he wore nothing. She lowered her eyes to his bare feet. On the air another smell drifted - whisky.

'Can't you sleep, either?' he said, moving along the step and tapping it with his hand. 'Come and join me.'

Without knowing why, she sat next to him. He lifted a bottle of Jack Daniels to his lips and swallowed twice before wiping the back of his hand across his mouth. 'Here,' he said, offering the bottle to Alex.

She stared at it. 'Does it help?'

'To a certain point,' he said, continuing to hold the bottle under her nose. She took it from him and wiped the top on her nightdress.

'Scared you'll catch something?' he said into the night, not bothering to look at her.

She closed her eyes and took a slug. It felt like fire as it hit the back of her throat and dropped into her stomach. She'd never tasted Jack Daniels, always considering it a bit American but here she was, sitting all alone with the original American Cowboy, so it didn't seem like there would ever be a more suitable time. She took another swallow, pulled a face and handed the bottle back. He took it and, without wiping the neck as she had, took several gulps.

Alex turned her eyes to the skies just in time to see a shooting star.

'Make a wish,' Kane said, slightly slurring his words 'You never know, it might come true.'

Alex made a wish. The same one she always made. It hadn't come true yet.

'So, what keeps you up with the creatures of the night?' he said.

'Oh, you know, this and that.' She wasn't going to share her thoughts with him. She wouldn't tell him that suddenly there was this very rational fear tapping away inside her head, suggesting that if she should sleep too deeply, who knows what she might wake up to find.

'I've never known anyone like you,' Kane said bluntly. 'Thought I'd seen it all but you really are something else.'

Alex turned to look at him. 'Something else?'

He shoved the bottle at her and while she drank, he said, 'Yeah, something else. I don't know anyone who would have gone out on to those rocks with the tide coming in and attempt to rescue a horse. And then, as if that wasn't enough, you jump into the sea with it. I've never seen anything like it.'

She handed him back the bottle. It was almost empty. He shook it, drained it and produced another from off the step behind him. Opening it, he transferred half the contents into the empty bottle and handed it back to Alex. 'Drink up,' he said. 'There's something sad about a man who drinks alone and I don't really want to figure out what it is.'

Sad wasn't a word she'd associate with Kane Mitchell. 'I don't drink really,' she said. 'Not since …' She stopped.

'Since what?' Kane said.

'Since the past, I guess. I'm a rotten drunk. It makes me cry. I start wishing for the moon and stars.'

Kane tilted the neck of the bottle towards the sky. 'No need to waste wishes on them little beauties. They're here already. Look at them. Have you ever seen anything prettier?'

Alex followed his gaze. No, she hadn't - ever. It was the perfect night. Even his presence was beginning to grow on her. But that was just the whisky working, seeping into her bloodstream, taking away her basic instincts and fears. For a while neither spoke, both wrapped up in themselves and the beauty of the night. From the paddock, a horse whinnied, the thin, high-pitched sound piercing the still, starry night.

Alex listened. 'That's Flying. She has a soft spot for Holly. It's a girl thing.'

'You sure know your horses,' Kane said. 'I'll bet you know the sound of each and every one of them, don't you?'

Alex nodded. Yes, she knew her horses.

'Weighs you down, doesn't it?' Kane murmured. 'Emotional baggage … the longer you carry it, the more it weighs you down and wears you out.'

Alex looked at him. He was watching her, an expression on his face she hadn't seen before. He looked human – open, touchable. 'Are you speaking from experience?' she said, unable to take her eyes from his.

'Suppose I am.'

Without considering the question, she heard her voice ask, 'What happened?'

'Life,' Kane said with a self-deriding laugh. 'Life happened. It has a habit of doing that, hasn't it? Just when you think you have it all sussed out, just when you reckon you have all the answers, life rears its ugly head and bites you in the balls.'

Yes, Alex could relate to that. She hiccupped and without warning blurted, 'Life happened to me too, you know. I lost the man I truly loved *and,* as if that wasn't enough, I *then* lost the baby I *would* have loved, if I'd been given the chance. How ball-biting is that?'

Kane lowered the bottle from his mouth. 'Ditto.'

'Ditto?'

He nodded, a long upward tilt of the head followed by a long downward lowering of the head. His co-ordination was starting to suffer. 'Yep. Ditto. Lost the love of my life -' He paused and looked over his shoulder before whispering, '- Ellie. Her name was Ellie. She died in an automobile accident. I didn't know she was pregnant. She'd told Jack and asked him not to tell me; said she wanted it to be a surprise, something she was going to tell me on our honeymoon … talk about bad timing. We never made the honeymoon. Jack would probably have never told me but they did an autopsy, ripped her apart and put her back together.' He gave a disgusted snort of a laugh. 'Didn't make her work again though, did it? *They* told me she was pregnant. How sick is that? Do you think that was necessary? Should they have told me that, Alex?'

Like the question that had crept out unaided, her hand, of its own accord slid across to his, took it and squeezed it. It felt warm and rough, the hand of a workingman. How would a hand like that feel gliding across her skin, touching places that only a lover should touch, making her hot, making her forget promises made and broken. And afterwards, would she crave for more?

'I'm sorry,' she said, her voice faltering. 'I didn't realise. You somehow get to thinking that you're the only one this sort of thing happens to. You don't realise that there are others out there that have been through the same kind of misery.'

'The trouble is,' Kane said, turning to look at her, 'you're too damn scared to risk it all again. You need to feel *something* just to be sure you're still alive. So instead of risking new emotions you have to keep playing the old ones over and over, even though they almost kill you.'

'I try not to do that anymore,' Alex whispered. 'It still hurts too much.'

Kane didn't answer. Instead she felt his hand tighten around hers and when she turned to look at him, his body seemed much closer than before. She could feel the heat of his flesh settling on her bare arms, coating her skin. A man like this could become a drug - impossible to quit. Raising you up to dizzy heights and plummeting you down to the darkest, deepest depths. This man would have that power.

He coughed to clear his throat and took another deep pull on the bottle, draining it. 'Shouldn't drink, really,' he said, screwing up his eyes. 'It only makes matters worse.'

'Shouldn't listen to that God damned awful music, either,' Alex said bluntly. 'It's enough to *drive* a person to drink ... or worse. Why don't you get some cheerful stuff?'

Kane tried hard to get her into focus. 'Like what?'

Alex shrugged. She hadn't thought that far. This whole episode had come out of the starry night. There had been no warning that she was going to be sitting here, getting progressively sloshed out of her head, looking up at the stars with a paralytic cowboy, who, only an hour ago, had been the worst thing since The Black Death and was now fast turning into a comrade in arms, another poor wounded soul in the battle of love. 'I don't know, something a bit classical, or better still, something without words at all. That should be all right. It's the words that do it. They get to you and eat your heart out. I mean ... Dolly Parton? *I Will Always Love You*? You do yourself no favours listening to that. It's so... hopeless ... helpless ... heartbreaking.'

With the hint of a smile, he said, 'So, you don't think the drinking's a problem, then? Just the music?'

Alex hiccupped and started to laugh, still clutching his hand in hers.

A grin crept beneath the moonlight shining on his face and he burst out laughing.

Chapter 9

Plug had been up since dawn, brewing coffee and making sandwiches. When Alex shuffled into the kitchen, dressed in shorts and a yellow sleeveless vest, clutching at her throbbing head, he said, 'Jeez, what hit you, Missy?'

She made it to the table and sank into a chair, nodding only slightly at the coffee pot that Plug wobbled in front of her. At least, she hoped Plug was wobbling the coffee pot, because if not, it was her head that was wobbling. It felt like it was about to launch itself from her shoulders, take off into the stratosphere and explode into a billion very unattractive pieces. Had she really sat out on the front porch into the early hours of the morning, star gazing, listening to Kane's dulcet Texan drawl and drinking Jack Daniels? Had she really been that stupid? Because, stupidity it was, sitting beneath the hypnotic moon and stars, exchanging blow for blow, details of her past.

She knew Kane's history now, as well as if she'd read the book, seen the video and got the T-shirt. But the information had come at a cost - because now he knew hers. She'd blabbed out everything about Peter - snivelled and sniffed her way through the baby bit; poured her heart out about the lack of love her parents had shown. Thank goodness, she'd resisted his body. Yes, it had got to the point where his closeness, his smell, his hard muscled, warm, semi-naked body had started to appeal. She had had to fight the growing urge to kiss his mouth, to stop the words escaping that were hurting him so much. She had been unbelievably touched by the man. It had been a long time since she'd felt that way and the feeling bothered her.

She took a deep breath and took the coffee Plug offered. It was better to get all thoughts of flesh and Kane Mitchell back where they belonged; rewind her head; go back to before last night.

'You look right crooked,' Plug said, tilting his head to peer beneath her spiky fringe. 'Do you reckon you're up to that old Land Rover and the bumpy ride?'

She put her hand to her mouth and tore out of the kitchen, down the hall and into the bathroom, where, noisily she threw up into the loo. She was so engrossed with retching up her entire digestive system that it wasn't until she dragged herself upright and was wiping her mouth with the back of her hand that she realised Kane had just stepped out of the shower. He stood before her, his lower torso *almost* wrapped in a white towel, the starkness of it making his tanned flesh appear even darker. Dark hair twisted and curled on his muscled chest. He stepped towards her, offering a wet towel for her to wipe her face.

'Jack Daniels?' he said, wincing.

Alex nodded and wiped her face, burying her eyes in the soft cotton fabric, hoping that when she opened them he'd be gone. No such luck.

'I'm glad I caught you,' he said. 'I thought I might ride out and take a look around. Is it OK if I take Mac? Only Jack and I want to try Nightwalker on that black mare of yours later today, so I can't take him.'

Alex nodded. Another wave of nausea was lapping in. 'No problem, take him. I think you'd better leave me to it.' She indicated the toilet with her throbbing head.

He nodded. 'Sorry. Is there anything I can do?'

She shook her head, panicking. She was going to throw up all over him if he didn't get out of there. Suddenly he seemed to understand and legged it to the door, Alex running behind him so that she could lock it. As she sprang the lock, she threw up all over the floor.

Ten minutes later she went back to the kitchen. Plug was busy scouring the sink. 'Any better?' he said, folding the dishcloth and placing it in a solution of bleach.

She did feel better, now that the sick feeling had gone. Her head still hammered away but a couple of painkillers should do the trick. 'Yes, fine thanks. Are you ready, then? Shall we make waves?'

'Yep, but I reckon you ought to have a bite to eat. I don't think we should go bouncing across the sand without something inside you.'

She held up a hand, stilling him. She was just fine the way she was. Right now, she *had* something inside her - her stomach. Anymore talk of food and bouncing across sand and she'd be parting with it. Plug didn't push it; instead, on his way out of the kitchen he grabbed half a fruitcake, a packet of chocolate digestives and a bottle of water.

'I don't reckon we missed anything the first time!' Plug shouted over the noise of the engine, as they tore along the beach, following the tracks Kane had left half an hour previously.

'Well I think we did!' Alex shouted back, even though the painkillers hadn't had time to kick in yet and the sound of her own voice made her wince and screw up her face. 'I've turned that book inside out and there's nothing except a few random pencil marks. My father wouldn't have come all this way just to sit in a disgusting shack reading a book on Genealogy. It just wasn't his style.' She braked and nosed the Land Rover into the damp undergrowth. A blaze of vibrant colour whirled up before them as a flock of raucous cockatoos startled and disappeared skywards towards the dark canopy of the trees. Alex slammed on the brakes and swore under her breath as the Land Rover skidded, ran off the track and collided with a fallen tree. She thrust it into reverse and rammed her foot hard against the accelerator. It had no effect. With difficulty, she found first gear, then reverse again, but it remained rooted. She turned off the engine and jumped out. Plug followed and together they stood staring at it until Alex, scratching her head, said, 'It's not going to move, Arthur. We're going to have to dig it out.'

Plug nodded in agreement before fetching the spade from the back of the Land Rover and setting to. After five minutes, Alex took the spade from him. 'My turn,' she said.

Plug objected. 'Nah. I can't let a lady dig. It ain't right.'

Alex launched the spade at the tree root. 'I'm not a lady, Arthur. Hasn't anyone told you yet?' She threw the mossy soil over her shoulder and swung the spade again. Plug settled on the fallen tree, glancing round at the wild vegetation. 'You need a ranger,' he said, slapping a fly from the back of his neck. 'You need to get some of this lot felled, open up the place a bit. You'd be surprised what'll grow if you change the light pattern. You should get the boys to give a hand while they're here.'

Alex wiped the sweat from her throbbing forehead with the back of a dirty hand leaving a brown smear. 'No thanks! I want *the boys* gone the minute the horses are covered. I want the island back to normal: just Jodie and me; the way it used to be.'

Plug watched her through narrowed eyes. 'Hard work, ain't it?' he said.

Alex leant against the spade handle, screwing up her eyes against the pain, breathing hard. 'Yes,' she panted. 'It is, but don't get any ideas because you're not doing it.'

For a moment Plug looked confused, then he shook his head and said, 'Nah, I don't mean digging. I mean trying to keep people at bay. I mean trying to hide your feelings all the time.'

Alex almost fell off the spade. 'What do you mean?'

Plug patted the tree trunk. 'Come and sit here a spell. Get your breath back.'

She propped the spade against the bonnet and sat next to him.

'I reckon you and that Kane bloke could be a good thing. I was talking to him last night ... well early hours of the morning really. He was pretty gone.'

Ditto, Alex thought.

'The booze had loosened his tongue, I reckon. He doesn't strike me as the kinda bloke to wear his heart on his sleeve normally. He told me how much he admired you. Said he'd never met a woman, or a man, with as much grit. Told me about you jumping that horse of yours off The Reach. Said how he'd given it up for dead but *you* brought it back from the dead. Said he knew your ex, Paul, Peter, or something. That he was a moron and that he should never have walked out on you and the baby. Said he'd have never done a thing like that.' Plug paused and turned to face Alex. Gently he raised a hand and wiped the dirt from her forehead.

'Why don't you give him a chance, Missy? What harm could it do?'

Alex swallowed hard. She was starting to feel sick again.

'Surely you can trust a man who saved your life. He's had it rough you know. I'll bet you didn't know he was married.'

'Yes! I know he was married and I know he lost his unborn child *and* he knows just about everything about me, too. He wasn't the only one spilling out his riotous past, last night. You obviously got the remnants after the party broke up and I went to bed.'

Plug sucked his teeth a bit before saying. 'I don't know what the problem is. If I was a sheila I'd fancy him myself.'

Alex forced a snort. 'Yeah, you and every sheila for miles around.'

Plug squeezed her hand. 'So you do see it then?'

Alex turned, wide-eyed, to face him. 'Yes I see it. I might be stupid but I'm not blind. He's not exactly hard on the eye, is he?'

Plug persisted 'So what's the problem?'

'I don't trust him.'

'But you trust Jodie and she trusts him.'

Alex snorted again. 'Yes, I trust Jodie but she's easily taken in. She tends to only see the good in people. She's too innocent, too gullible, she proved that in her last practice.'

When Plug raised a questioning eyebrow, Alex knew there was no point in trying to avoid the issue, so she said, 'Jodie fell big time for some locum they got in … Harry something or other. Well, good old Harry made misdiagnoses regarding a bull belonging to the biggest Hereford breeder in the South West. Somehow or other, Harry wormed his creepy little way into Jodie's affections and got her to back up his diagnosis. Then, she found the spineless little creep in the drugs cupboard with his flies undone and his hand down the front of the receptionist's bra.'

Plug tried not to grin.

'That Hereford breeder could have taken the practice to the cleaners and ended up ruining Jodie's career. Lord knows why she backed his diagnosis anyway. That's what you get with men. Deceit, lies, heartache, misery …'

'I reckon I git the point,' Plug said, swatting blowies. 'But why didn't the breeder sue the practice? Everyone wants something for nothing these days and it sounds like he had a valid case.'

Alex ignored him and got to her feet. 'Come on; let's have another go at digging this heap out.'

Plug remained straddled across the log. 'You haven't answered my question yet, Missy. Why didn't the breeder sue?'

Alex shrugged.

'C'mon, out with it. I know you know.'

'Because I wrote him a cheque, that's why.'

'Why?'

'Because Jodie could have been ruined. It doesn't matter how many clients like you, it only takes one who doesn't and your good name has gone. She was an idiot to back up the story in the first place but I didn't think it was fair for her to spend the rest of her life paying for it.'

Plug looked astounded. 'I hope Jodie appreciated what you did.'

'Jodie doesn't know what I did … and don't you go telling her, either, Arthur. The incident was over when I signed my name on the cheque.'

A silence fell between them until Alex picked up the spade. Then Plug said, 'Come and sit a spell, I ain't finished yet. Forget Kane and Jodie, I want to talk to you about the island.'

She sat down again. 'What about the island, Arthur?' Time was getting on and the sun was getting higher. The heat was already rising.

Plug rubbed at his chin. 'I know you all think I'm a tile short of a full roof but I'm not. There's a real chance that Asak Mulligan is still alive and living on this island. All rumours are based on some truth.'

'I'm sorry Arthur,' Alex said gently, 'but I can't believe that. I don't think it's possible.'

Plug watched her with concerned eyes. 'So, you're sticking with your original theory and blaming Kane for everything?'

Alex shrugged. 'What other explanation could there be? And let's face it, he's pretty screwed up. There's not much to choose between the two of us, as to who's the biggest weirdo.'

He shook his head. 'You're making a big mistake, Missy.'

'It wouldn't be the first time, Arthur. Now, come on. Let's get this dug out and be on our way.' She swung the shovel, aware that he was watching her. She didn't want to upset him but what he was saying just wasn't possible. She turned her back to him to avoid his gaze and swung the shovel again.

Ten minutes later, they climbed into the Land Rover. Alex turned the key, reversed it and smiling across at Plug, said, 'Right. Let's make waves then.'

Plug nodded vacantly. His attention was held by something straight ahead of them, moving through the undergrowth.

Chapter 10

At The Reach, Kane reined in the grey horse and stood watching the retreating tide. A slight offshore breeze brought with it the heady perfume of the island's flora and for several minutes, Kane sat quietly, his senses over indulging in the beauty of it all, until Mac became impatient and started to jog beneath him. He ran a hand down the horse's neck and spoke to him. He'd been pleasantly surprised to find that Alex's horse had been a good ride. It wasn't as tall as his horse but its action was better, more fluid. It had taken no time at all to circle the island and the grey was still full of running.

As he turned the horse up along The Reach his thoughts turned to Alex, something they'd been doing ever since he'd pulled her and the chestnut horse out of the sea. He hadn't wanted her to get into his head but there was something about her that wasn't that easy to ignore. There was the obvious, the things that most men went for – blindingly good looks, the perfect figure, the usual sexy stuff, but Alex was deeper than that. If the average woman was likened to a rippling stream then Alex McBride was the Pacific Ocean. Deep. Scary. Fathomless.

As they met the powdery sand, Mac stopped. Kane left his thoughts and spurred the horse forward but it was having none of it, digging in its heels and refusing to budge. Kane spurred it again and this time it reared, its hind legs scrabbling through the sand, almost toppling over. Kane grabbed its mane as it crashed back down and spun until it faced the inner terrain. Kane adjusted his position, shortened the reins and attempted to turn the horse but Mac stood his ground, ears pricked forward, listening to something that was out of Kane's hearing range. Kane stood in the stirrups, aware that the horse could hear or detect something even if he couldn't. And he couldn't. Other than the horse's hard breathing and occasional snort, there was nothing. Off to the left there was a flattened pathway where the Land Rover had entered the vegetation and a little further along Kane could see the excavated area where Alex and Plug had had to dig it out. It looked like an old badger set. He was about to spur the horse again when out of the vegetation came another smell. The horse had caught it first and recognised it, running several paces backwards before half rearing. Kane steadied him, running a hand the length of its shoulder, talking reassuringly in words that came natural. Putting his weight in the stirrups, Kane stood, bending to the side, peering beneath the low hanging branches. He sniffed. Once, twice, then he knew. It was smoke. He turned the horse away back down the beach to give himself distance. When he turned back and cast his eyes above the trees, he saw it - a thick, grey plume corkscrewing skywards through the trees. He estimated it to be a good distance away, probably at the islands heart. For seconds no other fact registered as he sat watching the spiral, then he vaguely remembered Plug telling him in the early hours that he was going out with Alex at dawn, back to where they'd found an old shack. By Plug's brief directions, most of which were too blurred by Jack Daniels, the two things added up. It didn't seem likely that Alex or Plug would have started a fire intentionally – something had to be wrong. The fastest, most direct way was with the horse, but he doubted it had the guts. He urged it forward and this time Mac obeyed, breaking into a lope until he reached the edge of the sand. Kane took hold and applied his spurs. With a mighty leap, Mac took off, crashing into the understorey, landing in the middle of a tall fern, which crumpled like paper under the horse's weight and thrashing legs. Kane grabbed the loose reins and pushed on, finding the track that the Land Rover had taken. The horse broke into a canter, sending Kane low over its neck as branches and fern fronds scraped against them, obliterating Kane's view, leaving him to put his trust in the horse. Several times it missed its footing, sprawling over logs, scrabbling through lichens, almost falling, shaking Kane from the saddle, until the forest gave way and they burst through into a clearing. Kane reined in, spinning in the saddle, frantic to get fresh bearings. Across the clearing, he could just make out tyre tracks where the Land Rover had braked and skidded, and off to the left, an entrance, almost concealed as grasses and fern sprang back protectively, desperate to bar the way. The smoke was stronger now. Long, grey, snaking fingers of it, escaping through the trees, drifting towards them. Kane turned the horse across the clearing and into the smoke.

Ahead of them the track thickened, concealed rock and rotting tree stumps making it almost impossible to make any kind of fast progress. Kane leapt from the horse, grabbed hold of its bridle and led it behind him beating and flattening the way ahead with a narrow switch. Towering fronds enveloped the smoke, trapping it at ground level, blinding the way ahead, making him choke. The horse pranced and crashed behind him, tossing its head, trying to rise above the smell.

An ancient gum tree, its roots loosened by age, crashed down across the path. Kane spun just in time to avoid being flattened but Mac hadn't been as lucky. A jagged branch had speared the horse's shoulder, knocking it to the ground. Blood pumped freely from the wound but the branch was embedded in its flesh. With his hand about to rip the branch out of the horse's muscle, Kane froze. What if it had hit an artery? If he removed it, the horse would surely bleed to death. This, Kane felt was a no win situation: the horse or the woman. He didn't know for sure that Alex was anywhere near the fire - not for sure. And if he wasted time going on, the horse could die. He had to try to get it back while it had enough blood in its body to walk.

Grey, billowing smoke had turned to black as Kane turned away from the horse and back towards the source of the fire. Maybe it wasn't that far now. Perhaps if he could get the horse to its feet, tether it and just go on a little farther? But what were the chances of actually getting it back on its feet? There could be more damage, hidden. It could even have a broken leg and if it did, how could he leave it? Indecision held him glued to the spot for precious seconds while his head battled with his heart. But when it came to it, Mac made the decision for him, as he threw out each foreleg in turn, pushed, staggered to his feet and shook. Kane ran a hand down the horse's blood-soaked neck. The branch was still imbedded and a hurried glance told him that the horse's legs were still intact. He'd been wrong about the animal. It did have guts.

After a second brief look at the horse, Kane left it and went on, tripping and stumbling toward the source.

He called her name. It seemed to hang in the smoke before slowly filtering its way upward and disappearing through the overhanging branches. No answer came. He called again - still nothing. The smoke made him cough. He pulled the neck of his T-shirt up to cover his mouth, pushing slowly forward through dense vegetation.

Without warning, the forest cleared and he stopped dead, his eyes taking in the sight before him, his brain refusing to decipher what he was seeing. The Land Rover stood abandoned, empty. Beyond it was a shack - engulfed on two sides by leaping flames and smoke. He called her name again, once, twice. His voice was lost in the sound of crackling, spitting wood.

Instinct and nothing more told him she was in there. He closed the distance, tearing his T-shirt from his body, stopping for a precious second at the stream to douse it in the water, before sprinting the remaining distance. He lifted his right boot and kicked at the door. It didn't budge. Again, he booted it. It gave slightly, allowing black smoke to squeeze out through the crack. He kicked at it again. This time it opened, flying back and crashing against the side of the shack, the noise muffled by the thick smoke. He called her name again. No one answered. She *had* to be here. He *knew* it.

He took a lungful of air and stepped inside, ramming the wet T-shirt over his mouth and nose. At first, he could make out nothing as the dried-out timber flared and spat. Part of the roof fell in, sparking and bursting into flames. As it touched the ground, it lit the bodies.

Alex was pushed into the corner, head down, her face lying in the squalid dirt. Plug Towers was draped around her, a human fire blanket, protecting her body. Kane moved, bending his body against the scorching heat. Another chunk of roof fell in, hitting him on his left shoulder. He reached Plug Towers and dragged him out on his belly, before turning back into the fire for Alex. Ten seconds and he had her out. Eleven seconds and the walls collapsed, the shack engulfing itself in flames.

He took in the deathlike pallor of their skin, the short, shallow breathing. He had wasted too much time - time spent considering whether to stay with the horse or go on; time spent walking when he should have been running. Should he attempt to revive them? Should he get them back as fast as humanly possible? They both looked like they were too far gone to revive? Why was he wasting more precious time considering alternatives?

Throwing Alex up across his shoulder, he grabbed Plug by his belt and dragged him back to the Land Rover. By the time he got there, he was drenched in sweat.

The horse had followed him and was standing by the side of the Land Rover. There was nothing he could do about it now. It would have to take its chance and wait until someone could come out and get it. He glanced at its blood-streaked skin as he threw Plug into the open back of the Land Rover and then dragged Alex into the front seat.

He turned the key and, as it burst into life, floored the accelerator and prayed. It lurched backwards crashing through the vegetation, sending debris flying into the air. He crashed the gears, got it into first and it lunged forward, sending Alex's body sliding along the seat. He put out a hand to steady her. She was too cold. He dared to take his eyes from the track just long enough to look at her smoked-streaked, pale face. He was going to lose her like he'd lost Ellie. Lose her when he didn't even have her yet. He'd been too slow. He should have told her how he felt. He'd tried last night but the drink had got in the way and he'd ended up spurting on about his past and then listening to hers. For the first time since Ellie's death, it struck Kane that there was nothing you could do about the past, it was the here and now that mattered.

He looked up into the rear view mirror and then back to the track. His eyes flashed back to the mirror - the horse was following.

As the Land Rover burst onto the beach, the horse was still there. And as Kane pushed his boot to the floor, thrashing the engine and ramming it into fourth, the horse settled into a steady gallop at the side of the Land Rover. Blood showered from its wound, flying back in the draft of speed.

It was the farthest half-mile he had ever driven.

He could see the house now as he leant on the horn, shattering the idyllic peace and quiet of the island, sending seabirds, feeding at the water's edge, lifting and wheeling away. He saw the kitchen door open and Jodie come rushing out. Christ, he thought, was she in for a shock? There was no way he could lessen it.

He braked, slithering to a halt centimetres from the kitchen door, sending up a ten-foot wave of sand. He leapt from the Land Rover and shouted, 'Get the Flying Doctor!'

Jodie's mouth opened and closed but no words came out. Jack ran out of the house, stopped, weighed up the situation in a stride, turned and ran back in.

Kane snapped, 'Jodie, move it!'

She stood rooted to the spot, shaking her head, mouthing silent words, unable to take her eyes off Alex, slumped motionless across the front seat. Kane was dragging Plug up the steps, as Jack tore out of the house. 'They're on their way.'

Kane looked at him briefly. 'For Christ's sake, shake her. She's a bloody vet, she's needed. There's a horse dying over there, not to mention this pair.'

Jack looked horrified.

Kane cut across him and grabbed hold of Jodie by her upper arms. 'Move it woman! Do you want her to die? Don't you keep oxygen here?'

Jodie nodded vaguely, pointing.

Jack shot back into the house, shouting, 'I'll find it!' The kitchen door crashed behind him.

Kane wrenched open the Land Rover door and pulled Alex out, cradling her in his arms. Her head hung limply like a broken doll that some spoilt child had tired of. He carried her up the steps and laid her at the side of Plug.

Jack brought the oxygen, strapping one mask on Plug and giving the other to Kane. Jodie settled on the veranda steps, stunned and grey, watching as Jack caught the horse and led it to the stables

Kane straddled Alex, lifting her chin, tilting back her head. Then, pinching her nostrils, he put his mouth over hers, breathing into her body, forcing her lungs to rise and fall. After five minutes he stopped, sitting back on his heels, staring at her chest, willing it to breath. He could see nothing. He moved his body back over her and tried again.

Hands tried to take her from him and he struck out.

Jack caught his fist. 'It's OK, these people will help, Kane. They know what they're doing. Let her go, Kane.'

He laughed, helplessly. 'They knew what they were doing with Ellie,' he said. 'And they still let her die, didn't they?'

'They couldn't do anything for Ellie, Kane. It was hopeless. Let them help Alex.'

'I should have been there,' Kane said, cradling Alex in his arms. 'I should have been there.'

Jack laid a hand on Kane's shoulder and squeezed. 'It wasn't your fault Kane. There was nothing you could do. It was an accident.' Kane's face didn't register so Jack said quietly, 'Let her go, Kane. Let them try to save her.'

This time the words seemed to get through and Kane moved away giving the paramedics access. They worked methodically checking vital signs, thrusting needles into veins, massaging her barely beating heart, rigging her up to a respirator. No one spoke. They didn't need to. Kane knew the system. He knew the signs. They never told you anything, these bloody people. They wouldn't have told him Ellie was dead in her car with her legs half sliced off at the thighs, if he hadn't pushed the police aside and seen it with his own eyes.

The dark haired paramedic spoke to the doctor. 'I'm ready here, Tom. *Now* would be good!' Then he cast a look in Kane's direction. 'We need to get them to hospital, pronto. I won't beat around the bush mate, they're in a bad way.'

Jodie let out a huge sob, tears streaming down her white face. 'Are they going to die?'

The young doctor helped to lift Plug onto the stretcher. 'We'll know more when we can get them to hospital. The man seems to have taken in more smoke but the lady has had a nasty blow to the back of her head. We don't know the extent of that yet. I'll be honest, it's gonna be touch and go.'

Jodie turned her head and threw up.

They loaded the stretchers into the air ambulance. Jack put out a hand catching Kane by the arm, as he was about to climb in. 'She's tough. She'll make it you know.'

Their eyes met. Kane nodded, but his head said, 'Yeah, just like Ellie.'

As they lifted off, Alex's breathing worsened.

The paramedic shouted across the sound of the whirling blades, 'We're losing her Tom! She's crashed!'

'Paddles!'

'Charging ... two hundred ... clear.'

Thud. Thud.

'Nothing!'

'Charging ... three hundred ... clear!'

Thud. Thud.

'Nothing.'

'Charging ... three sixty ... clear!'

Thud. Thud.

'She's back! We've got her. Get another line in there.'

Kane saw the anguish in the paramedic's face as he thrust another line into her arm, increased her oxygen intake and tried to hide the fact that she was barely hanging on. He forced a smile. 'Try talking to her Mr Mitchell. Hearing is the last sense to go.'

Kane winced. Christ, how he hated her right now. How dare she put him through this? He took her cold, motionless hand in his and raising it to his mouth whispered softly against her fingertips, 'Come on Alex, fight. You know how to do that.' He closed his eyes and for the first time since Ellie had died, prayed to an all mighty God that he didn't even know if he believed in anymore. He prayed that the hospital came in time for both of them, for the feisty woman and the funny little man.

Once more, his prayers weren't answered. Somewhere over the South Pacific Ocean, Arthur 'Plug' Towers lost his fight for life. He suffered a massive heart attack and never regained consciousness.

Chapter 11

Kane sat on the shoreline watching the horizon, waiting for the speck of colour that would prove to be the helicopter bringing Alex back to the island. He raised the bottle to his mouth and swallowed several times, glancing again at his watch for the third time in the last five minutes. It said two thirty.

He wondered if there had been a hitch at the hospital and they'd decided not to discharge Alex after all, but Jodie would have called him if that was the case.

He took another swallow of scotch, grimaced and rammed the cork back into the bottleneck. He knew he shouldn't be drinking in the middle of the day. He had to get a grip on it, but this whole thing with Alex had gone deep. He narrowed his eyes, tightening tired eye muscles, and concentrated on the sky. How she'd managed to pull through this had astounded him. He'd given her up for dead but hadn't counted on the expertise of the medical team and the sheer grit of the woman.

Twice she'd stopped breathing, sending the crash teams flying to her bedside, while he'd looked on helplessly and twice they had jump-started her failing body back into life, where it hung in the balance until the next crisis.

In the early hours of the fifth day, with Kane and Jodie by her bedside, she'd
re-gained consciousness. And that had been the worse time for Kane. She'd made Jodie send him away, refusing to see him. The doctors told him it was to be expected – but *he* hadn't expected it, and it gutted him. And when Jodie broke the news about Arthur not

making it, Alex broke down and had to be put under sedation.

He stopped trying to see her after that and stayed on the island, while Jack and Jodie remained on the mainland

He'd occupied his time with the horses and took to circling the island each
daybreak, frantically searching for any sign that someone else was on the island. When that drew a blank he increased the search to morning and night, driving around the perimeter, looking for footprints in the sand - anything. Nothing materialised, so every lunchtime he took Nightwalker out, criss-crossing the inner island terrain. Still he drew a blank. Even the police, with their top forensic team, couldn't find any proof that the fire had been started intentionally. They'd crawled over the island like ants for three days before concluding that any 'weirdo' would be long gone by now.

Daylight hours were manageable but the nights were hell and just lately he'd seen too many of them through the bottom of a whisky bottle. It helped initially, but the result was always the same. His thoughts turned to the woman who had almost died, and worse still, to thoughts of the woman who *had* died.

Ellie had stopped coming to him in his dreams lately and it tore him up to find her returning, sneaking into his shallow sleep, making him relive that awful time, making him feel the loss all over again. The dreams were so real he'd wake up smelling her, turning his head, expecting to see Elle's chestnut mane of hair, softly falling across his pillow. When it wasn't there, he would get up, and go down to the stables and talk to Nightwalker, spilling out his confused, miserable thoughts, while the horse snuffled at his chest telling him that he understood.

He took another half-slug from the bottle and lowered it as the yellow and black helicopter appeared on the horizon. By the time he had crossed the beach, it had circled and landed next to the house.

The door opened and Jack stepped down. In his hand, he carried a small, marble urn. Arthur Towers had no remaining family. He'd scattered his wife's ashes on the sea, years ago, so there was no family grave either. It therefore seemed the most natural thing to bring his ashes home. Jack turned and offered a hand to Jodie who stepped down and turned back to help Alex out.

Kane barely recognised her. She looked so frail, almost waif-like. Dark circles sat beneath her eyes. She had lost weight, so much that he half expected the fragrant afternoon breeze to lift her up and blow her away before his eyes. She stood before him and from somewhere he found a smile.

She didn't return it, merely turning away and walking towards the house with Jodie.

Jack placed a hand on his shoulder and said quietly, 'It's early days, Kane. Give her time to settle back into things. She needs help to come to terms with this.' His eyes lowered to the urn he held in his hand.

Kane watched as Alex and Jodie went into the house and the door closed behind them. Somehow, it felt like there would always be a closed door between them from now on.

A wind blew up from the east around midnight, whipping up the sea into a swirling, witch's cauldron, carrying the salt-spray across the beach to rain down on the house. Kane found it hard to sleep but it had nothing to do with the wind. It was his over-active mind keeping him awake, giving him little solace. He'd only just drifted off to sleep when something dragged him back to consciousness. He listened hard above the howling of the wind and heard it again. It sounded like a screen door banging. He dragged himself out of bed and pulled on his jeans, yawning.

Jack's bedroom door was open. His bed was empty. Passing Alex's door he stopped to look in. Her duvet was piled high in the centre of the bed, pillows scattered on the wooden floor. He tiptoed across and gently pulled the duvet down so as not to disturb her. He needn't have worried; her bed was empty and cold. She was long gone. Cussing under his breath he tore out of the room.

He was right. The screen door had been left open and the wind was now slamming it relentlessly against the doorframe like a fat wrestler trying for a submission. He stepped out on to the veranda. The black night sky was clear with a million twinkling stars looking down on the island, just like the night he and Alex had sat out on the front porch step and shared a bottle of Jack Daniels. At the time, it had seemed like a beginning. How different things were now.

He dragged his eyes from the heavens and let them drift. All looked perfectly normal but he knew it wasn't. She was out there somewhere.

He stepped down from the veranda and set off against the wind towards the stables. Perhaps she'd thought she had heard something and gone off to check. He knew she was well capable of such stupidity.

The stable door was still bolted. He breathed a sigh of relief. There were no horses missing and as he looked across the yard, he could see the Land Rover still on its hard standing. At least she was on foot. He was talking to himself as he said aloud, 'Come on Kane, think like she would think. I know that's almost a bloody impossibility, but try. Where would she go?'

He headed towards the beach. The wind was worse here and a persistent shower of sand bit against his bare chest. Shielding his eyes as best he could, he scanned along the beach in both directions. Away in the distance, he could just about make out a white spectre-like figure struggling into the squall.

He took off after her, running against the buffeting wind. He was making better progress than she was and the distance between them shortened with each stride he took. Suddenly it came to him. He knew where she was going. '*Donna,*' he said against the wind. 'She's going out in a fucking hurricane to a bloody dead man's boat.'

The boat came into view, tilted and docked, as the outgoing tide had left it in its wake. He could see her quite clearly as she started to climb the ladder up to the deck. When he reached the bottom, she'd gone. He followed her up the ladder and as he jumped onto the deck, she turned and saw him. Her eyes were wilder than the wind, her face a mask of pure misery and hate. She backed towards the wheelhouse, carrying Arthur's remains in her shaking hands.

She spat in contempt. 'What are you doing here? Come to finish me off?'

He didn't much like the look of her. He had known some crazy people in his time and she looked like she was up there with the best of them.

Her voice sliced through the night, 'I said what you are doing here on our boat?'

His forced evaluation of the situation told him, in all probability, it was too late trying to humour her but what choice did he have? 'What do you mean, Alex? *Our* boat.'

'Our boat!' she shrieked irrationally into the wind. 'Arthur's and mine you murdering maniac.'

He tried to keep his eyes off her body as the wind snapped and cracked her shirt against her naked outline. He dragged his eyes away from her jutting breasts. 'Arthur's dead. He died in the fire.'

Incensed eyes watched his approach. 'Don't you think I know that?'

'Then what's all this about? Why are you here?'

She fixed him with drugged eyes, brimming with tears. 'I've brought him home. You can't hurt him now. This is his resting-place. This is what he would have wanted.'

He thought he had never seen such a pathetic sight as the woman who stood before him. There was no way of telling if she was on this planet or not. He spoke quietly as the wind lulled momentarily, 'Alex, do you know who I am?'

She stood before him, teeth chattering, body shaking, eyes closed, tears escaping through her lashes. 'Of course I know who you are … you're the man who killed Arthur.'

He stepped slowly towards her, as he might an injured bird, not wanting to alarm it; to gently pick it up in his large, capable hands; to take it home and make it better.

'Stay away from me,' she hissed. 'Stay away or God help me, I'll kill you.' Her hand closed around a rusty fish-hook that was leaning against the side of the boat, her fingers opening and closing frantically to get a firm hold.

'Alex, I'm not going to hurt you. I've followed you here to help. You shouldn't be out here, not so soon after coming out of hospital. Why couldn't this wait until tomorrow?'

'Tomorrow? Tomorrow?' she shrieked. 'Who knows if they are going to wake up to a tomorrow, with you around?'

He took another step, disguised by a slow, backwards look, as he continued to close the distance between them.

'Let's go home, Alex. We can come back in daylight and sort this out.'

She raised her head, her short hair erect in the wind, her eyes huge and pathetic in a ghostly-white face.

'Alex, let's go home.'

Hopelessness bubbled up in her throat and escaped as a sob. In that moment, Kane took the remaining step, dragging her into his arms, crushing her against his bare chest. She struggled, dropped the fish-hook and hit out, raining down blows, one after the other, the sound of her fist hitting flesh filling the night. He took the blows, barely moving. Arthur's urn fell and rolled away across the deck, spinning like a top as it hit the side of the boat. Her arms grew tired and eventually she stopped the onslaught, half collapsing as Kane held her against him.

When he spoke, his voice faltered, 'It wasn't me, Alex. I didn't do those things. There is, or was, someone else on this island. I've searched and searched but I haven't found a single trace of anyone. The police had tracker dogs all over the island. They couldn't come up with anything either. But that doesn't mean there isn't someone here … somewhere. We just haven't found him yet.'

Alex pulled away. 'What, a sixty-year-old geriatric who has a passion for women's clothing, stranding horses and killing a sweet, harmless man?'

When Kane didn't answer, she added, 'Just go away and leave me alone.'

He shook his head. 'I can't do that.'

'I strongly suggest that you do,' she said.

The wind abated as they stood before each other, eyes locked, jaws set, each fighting their own demons.

He pushed his hair back and scratched the back of his head. 'I'm not going anywhere, Alex. One of us has to see sense here and I really think it's going to have to be you. Do what you want with Arthur. -' He waved a hand at the urn lying on the deck, '- because we're going home … together.'

Her chin came up in defiance. 'I'm going nowhere with you.'

He dropped his head in his hands and rubbed his face. Then, looking down into her determined, demented face, shouted, 'Look you stupid woman, I'm standing here freezing my balls off in the middle of a fucking hurricane! Now admit defeat for once in your God-damned, crazy, bloody life, and come with me!'

'I'd rather drop dead and go to Hell!'

'Then you've nothing to lose, have you? Now are we going to do this the adult way or are you going to continue throwing your toys out of your bloody pram?'

'Got it in one!' she screamed and hurled an empty paint can at his head. As it whizzed past his left ear like a newly launched rocket, he moved, yanking her into his arms and over his shoulder. 'You sure are one cussed female. Now we've fucked around long enough out here in this lousy weather, we're going home.' He nodded towards the urn. 'Say goodbye to Arthur, because we're leaving.'

He carried her down the ladder and along the beach. Although at first she struggled, kicked, and screamed, she soon grew tired and gave in.

It took a long time to get back to the house as they battled head on against the wind. Secretly, he was thankful she had lost weight. He frog marched her straight through the house, hurled her into the shower, turned it on and left her there, standing under the warm water raining down on her thin, shaking body.

The pandemonium woke the others and they appeared together from Jodie's room. Kane showed no surprise that they appeared together from the same bed. Little would surprise him, these days. He regaled them with the episode. When he had finished, they didn't speak for several minutes. Then, Jodie, shaking her head - half dazed by what Kane was saying - walked over to the kettle and flicked it on. Jack was the first to speak and with raised brows said, 'Does she *really* believe you're responsible for everything that's happened?'

Kane rubbed at his stubble chin, sighing, 'Yeah. I reckon she does.'

'Christ!'

They all turned as the door opened. Alex walked in wrapped in a bath-towel.

Jodie pulled a chair from under the table. 'Sit down, Alex,' she said, handing her a mug of coffee. 'I think it's time we sorted one or two things out here.'

Jack stood up to leave.

'No Jack, stay, and you too, Kane. This is something we *all* need to sort out. It involves us all.' Jodie sat on the edge of the table and faced Alex. 'What do you think you're doing tearing around in the dark, on your own, two minutes after coming home? Someone out there killed Arthur and almost killed you. Kane can't keep saving you from yourself, you know. You really are becoming your own worst enemy.'

Alex's head came up. 'How can you say that? You're supposed to be my friend. The one person on this crazy planet that actually believes in me.'

'I *am* your friend and I *do* believe in you. That's exactly why I *can* say it.'

'He's responsible for killing Arthur and …'

'No he isn't!' Jodie snapped, making them all jump. 'He isn't and you know he isn't.'

'I know no such thing,' she said, casting her eyes over him briefly. 'Who knows what losing your entire world might do to a person?'

Jodie was saying something but Kane wasn't listening. He was watching, again, the playback in his mind's eye. Ellie's car skidding out of control, crashing through the inadequate barrier up on the high-top road. He watched it, tumbling and turning, gorging into the hillside, leaving the scar on the landscape that remained months afterwards, serving as a constant reminder to him. If only he'd driven the kids back.

'Kane!'

He looked across at Jodie like he'd lost the plot.

Jodie looked at Jack. He shook his head.

'Right that's it!' Jodie said. 'I'm going to ask you this once, Alex, and I mean once and you are going to give me an answer … *once*. And after that, we are *never* coming back to this again.' She paused to take a deep breath. 'Alex, do you believe Kane killed Plug? Because if you do, I'm calling the police now and having Kane arrested.'

No one spoke. Only the steady tick-tock of the kitchen clock fractured the silence.

'Alex!'

'Yes! No. I don't know.' How much time had she given to this question already – hours, days, seemingly, half a lifetime? Her head kept coming up with rational, sensible, Alex-type answers, telling her that she had it wrong; that Kane wasn't the culprit, while her heart protectively informed her that he was. And it was so much easier, far less damaging, to believe her heart, because then she could go on hating him and with hate came distance, and with distance came safety.

'Alex. We need an answer and none of us are going to bed until we have one. Do you believe Kane killed Plug?'

She dropped her head into her hands and closed her eyes. Arthur had liked Kane.

'Alex!'

She shook her head. 'I guess not.'

Jack let out his breath and Kane sank wearily into a chair, dropping his head into his hands and closing his eyes.

'That's the end of it,' Jodie said. '*The absolute end.*'

Chapter 12

The wind blew itself out over night. Morning brought a bright, clear day.

Jodie rapped on Kane's bedroom door and rushed in. He was still asleep. She pulled the duvet back. 'Kane, wake up.'

His eyes shot open and he was out of bed before he realised Jodie was standing there and he didn't have a stitch on. 'Christ, what's wrong now?'

She turned her back as he slid into his shorts. 'It's Alex. She's going out to look for the person that killed Arthur. She said they found something that day of the fire but she hasn't been able to remember what it was.'

'There's no peace is there?' he grumbled, dragging on his jeans. 'At least when she was hospitalised we knew where she was. Now she's going to chase her backside off until she comes up with an answer. And if she doesn't find one, her quirky brain will fit me up again for everything. Christ, I only survived by the skin of my teeth last night.'

'We won't have anymore of that nonsense. It's finished,' Jodie said. 'Alex has to get back into the real world.'

He raised an eyebrow. 'Does she know how?'

Jodie shrugged.

'What makes her think she can find something when I can't and neither can the police? Does she really think we weren't trying?' He tucked his T-shirt into his jeans and buckled up his belt.

'Do *you* think someone is out there … someone who wants to kill her?' Jodie asked quietly, watching his face.

He struggled to pull on his boots. 'I seriously doubt that shack spontaneously combusted and Alex knocked herself unconscious. Someone has to be responsible for this little lot.' He stomped into the second boot. 'Probably some sick bastard who's come ashore and thinks he's a modern day Robinson Crusoe. But I'll hand it to him, whoever he is, he's more elusive than the Scarlet Pimpernel.'

He found her in the stables tacking up the chestnut mare he had pulled out of the sea.

As he reached the loose box she spun round, her eyes wide.

'What are you doing?' he said.

'I'm going to find the *thing* or *person* that killed Arthur.' She paused and turned back to the horse. 'But then I'm sure Jodie's already told you that?'

'Yes, Jodie's told me.' He reached out and touched her shoulder, turning her towards him. He studied her face, determined, sad, a mix of emotions.

'I'm coming with you, Alex. You and Jodie are to go nowhere on this island without either Jack or me present. It isn't safe.'

'And I take it I drew the short straw?' she said with eyes narrowed, watching his face, seeing the sincerity in his eyes and wishing she couldn't.

He didn't comment.

'You don't have to play the white knight in shining armour, you know. If you weren't here, Jodie and I would have to sort this mess out for ourselves.' She pulled her gaze away from his and slipped back the bolt on the door.

He remained rooted in the doorway, blocking her exit. When she looked back at him, silently requesting him to move, he shook his head. 'You're going nowhere without me, lady. There's something out there with an agenda and for some unknown reason you are on it. And don't go thinking I'm some sort of twenty-first century hero because I'm not. Where I come from men protect women.'

Alex raised her eyebrows. 'How quaint.'

He shook his head in reply to her sarcasm before leaning over and bolting the door. 'You stay there until I've tacked up. If you move a muscle or a hair you'll wish you hadn't.'

She watched him saunter off to the tack room, disappear for several moments and walk back to Mac's box. She listened to his boots clicking on the tiled floor and found the sound of it strangely reassuring.

They rode on in silence until they came to the spot where, two and a half weeks ago, the Land Rover had broken into the under storey and forced a pathway through. She turned the horse into the trees without a word and Kane followed a length behind. Five minutes later, they broke through the canopy into the clearing where the shack had stood.

Nothing remained except a carpet of grey ash. She didn't know what she was looking for, but there was something. She had tried for so long to push all memories of that awful day out of her head but little things kept coming back. She could remember going into the shack with Arthur. She had been on her hands and knees, digging in the dirt, when something hit her on the back of her head. After that, she only knew what people had told her.

She jumped down from Holly and tied the reins to a branch. Kane reined in beside her but remained on the horse, crossing his right leg over the front of the saddle, watching as she bridged the stream and walked slowly toward the burnt-out shack.

Nothing remained to tell any one what had happened here - that a good, decent, honest man had lost his life. Without knowing why she dropped to her knees, and started scratching in the ashes, digging with her bare hands until the ash filled her nails and blackened them. Suddenly she stopped. She closed her eyes and it came to her, like a released demon lifting upwards through her subconscious and into that part of her brain that remembered exactly what she'd found that day.

'Kane!' She sprang to her feet. 'Kane, come here, quick.'

He threw his leg over the horse's back and went to her.

'This is it. This is what I'd forgotten.'

'Forgotten what exactly?'

'This.' She dropped to the floor wafting ash and charcoal. 'Here, it's here, look.'

He knelt beside her as her hands uncovered a flat, oblong stone. 'It's a grave. We found it just before … before …'

He moved her gently out of the way and rubbed the remaining ashes from the stone. It had been crudely engraved, the letters fractured and bruised by time. He picked up a stick and pressed it into the digits releasing ash and mud until each letter made sense. The letters spelt out G. R. A. He brushed ash from the last remaining digit, which produced a letter N. 'Does that make any sense?' he asked quietly, watching her face crease into a frown and noting the dark circles beneath her eyes.

'I don't know if it does or not. What does it say?'

Kane blew the ash away. 'It says Gran.'

Alex sat back on her heels. 'Gran? Do you mean Gran as in Grandma?'

Kane shrugged 'I don't know. Why would …'

Alex cut in, 'Gran means Grandma. Don't you see? Arthur was right. Isla Mulligan's baby *did* survive.'

He shook his head. 'Well, I guess if you're the kind that believes in fairy tales it has a certain kind of hook.'

Alex ran her hand over the flat stone. 'No, listen. It has to be true. This is the grave of Isla Mulligan's mother, Asak Mulligan's grandmother. She did save her grandchild and when she died, he buried her here. There's no other explanation. She only had one grandchild, Asak. No one else would call her gran.'

'I guess it makes sense,' Kane said.

Alex stood up. 'Hold on a minute. That means Arthur was right and we have to go back to the ridiculous theory that we have a sixty-year-old man living on our island, who is capable of murder and Lord knows what.'

Kane stood up. 'Actually, it means something else,' he said, watching her face. 'It means that *you* are living on the island of a sixty-year-old man who is capable of murder and Lord knows what.'

'What!'

Kane took her arm. 'Alex, if this man *is* alive, he's living on *his* island. It was never your father's in the first place.'

'Oh Lord.'

'Let's look on the good side. At least we know what we are up against now.'

'It sounds just crazy enough to be true,' Jack said, pouring coffee, while Jodie served breakfast.

Jodie placed the plates on the table. 'So what does this all mean?' she said.

'It means,' Kane said, picking up his fork and pointing it at Jodie and then at Alex. 'That neither of you go *anywhere* on this island alone, until we've found him.'

'So,' Jack said, nodding at Kane. 'I take it the heat's off you, now. The lady no longer believes you stranded the horse, ripped her shirt, knocked her unconscious, set fire to the shack and killed Plug Towers?'

All eyes turned to Alex, who sat staring at the breakfast set out before her. Slowly she raised her head, grimaced and said quietly to Kane, 'Would you like one of my sausages? I can't manage two.'

'I guess as apologies go, that's pretty original,' Jack said, trying to keep a straight face.

Alex rested after breakfast, waking around eleven and finding Jack in the kitchen stitching a pair of broken reins.

'Have you seen Kane?'

Jack nodded. 'The delivery lady dropped some stuff off for Jodie, penicillin, anti-dote, that kind of thing. Kane's showing her around the island.'

'Oh.'

The delivery lady, as Jack called her, was a little more than a delivery lady. Ruth Tarring piloted her own helicopter, making deliveries from the mainland to the surrounding islands. She'd taken over the business after her father, *Bluey* Tarring, had suffered a minor heart attack while landing on Green's Island. Ruth looked like a Barbie Doll: tall, blonde, and beautiful. And that wasn't all; she had a nature to match. Alex had never heard an unkind syllable spill out of her pretty, pouting mouth. In some ways, Alex was jealous. Sometimes she wished she could have the character and easy going nature of Ruth. Sometimes she just wished she could be different. Someone once told her, 'you can't do anything about the cards you are dealt but you can do something about how you play them.' Sometimes she felt like she hadn't quite grasped this theory.

'Anything I can help you with?' Jack said, jolting her mind back.

'I was going to ask him if he would come to Arthur's boat with me. I made a mistake last night. Arthur wouldn't want to be dry-docked. I want to fetch him back. Only Kane said Jodie and I have to be chaperoned and believe it or not Jack, that sounds just fine to me.'

Jack set the leatherwork aside. The merest hint of a smile tugged at his mouth. 'No problem. I can take you there but we'll have to take the horses or walk. Kane's got the Land Rover.'

She shrugged. 'A walk sounds fine.'

'I'll just go and tell Jodie we're locking her in … she's in the bath.'

Alex shuddered. How had it come to this?

Jack walked by her side along the beach. He wasn't quite as tall as Kane but she still had trouble keeping up with his longer stride. They walked in silence until they reached the boat. Alex fetched the urn from the wheelhouse where Kane had left it last night.

They climbed down off the boat and Jack said, 'Let's sit a while here on the shaded side; we can talk.'

She sat by his side and he produced some doughnuts from his pocket, wrapped in a serviette. 'I reckon you had better eat this, you could do with a bit of flesh on your bones.'

'Thanks,' she said, taking the freshly baked doughnut and biting into it. 'I never knew Jodie even knew how to cook. You and your brother have sure brought out the domestic side of her. I rarely see her these days without an apron on or flour smudged on her nose.'

Jack grinned. 'Yeah, she's OK. A real lady.'

She caught the tone of comparison in his voice. 'You don't like me very much do you Jack?' she said, straight to the point.

'I don't reckon you like yourself very much, if you ask me,' he said, matching her bluntness. 'You seem to give yourself just as hard a time as you give everyone else. Always beating yourself up over something.'

'I didn't know you were a psychiatrist, Jack. No wonder it didn't take you long to figure out how to creep your way into Jodie's bed.'

'Leave Jodie out of this,' he said sharply, his face deadly serious. 'Why do you have to do that?'

'What?'

'Try to rip apart everyone you care about?'

She turned to look at him. 'How do you know what I do? You and your brother have only been here for a couple of months and you both think you know me.'

He wiped his mouth on the serviette. 'You're not that hard to figure. Pretty easy really. You've been hurt. You had one disastrous relationship and he left you. Instead of putting it down to experience, picking up the pieces and getting on with your life, you've tarred every man with the same brush and made it your life's work never to trust any one again.'

'I'll kill Jodie when I get back. So this is what you talk about afterwards ... me and my sad little life.'

'I've told you to leave Jodie out of this. She cares about you more than you will ever know. Did you know she cried herself to sleep every night for a fortnight, while you were in hospital? And you think no one cares?'

'I've never doubted Jodie's love, everyone else's maybe, but never Jodie. She has always been there for me and always will be,' she said defensively.

Jack cocked an eyebrow. 'If you trust Jodie why not try to trust others?'

Alex remembered Arthur saying much the same thing. 'Is this leading somewhere, Jack?'

'There's no fooling you is there?' he said sarcastically, finishing his doughnut.

'You'd be surprised; it has been known.'

He offered her another doughnut. She took it. He waited until she bit into it before he said, 'You can trust Kane. He wouldn't leave you pregnant and alone. He'd love you for the rest of your life ... if you can only find the guts to let him.'

She coughed so badly she almost choked and Jack had to thump her hard between her shoulder blades to dislodge the food before she could breath. 'Christ Jack, where did that come from? Has that brother of yours put you up to this?'

Jack almost choked himself. 'Hell no! If he knew we were having this conversation, he'd kill me. He's almost as screwed up as you. Don't tell me you haven't noticed?'

She looked at him through wide, guarded eyes. 'Why are you doing this to me, Jack? What have I done to you? Are you taking Jodie back to Texas with you and leaving me your brother as the booby prize?'

He laughed loudly. 'Women would kill for a bit of my brother. He drives them crazy.'

She didn't doubt it.

'I can't trust your brother anymore than I can trust any man, Jack. Oh, he's very convincing and you could almost make the mistake of believing he means every thing that comes out of his beautiful mouth, but as you said, women love him. He can have his choice and probably does on a frequent basis. I could never trust him.'

Jack swallowed the last piece of doughnut, and then he turned to her. 'Listen to me, Alex. I'm going to tell you something now and I don't want you breathing a word of this to Kane. It would blow his image. Do you know how many women there have been since his wife, Ellie?'

She shrugged her shoulders. Did she really want to know about the endless string of women? How he'd driven them insane with desire, until they'd laid back in total surrender and let him use every inch of their bodies? And afterwards, how he'd walked away on to his next conquest. 'I don't know Jack. You tell me, but keep it in nice round figures. It's much simpler for my addled, drugged-up brain to cope with.'

He dusted sand from his jeans and turned to look at her. 'None.'

She looked right back at him, eyebrows raised. 'None?'

'None. None after Ellie and not that many before. He's a one-woman man.'

'A one-woman man?' she scoffed. 'Well, why is he out right now, showing Miss Barbie Doll around *my* island?'

Jack stood up and offered her a hand. She took it. 'Well?'

'Well, I never said he wasn't devious.'

'Devious? Or just hedging his bets? If his manly charm doesn't work on me, he has the next little filly interested and sniffing at his bucket of oats.'

Jack pulled a face. 'I don't know where all your nonsense comes from. Is it natural or do you have to work at it? I've told you he isn't like that.'

They started for home, Jack carrying Arthur's ashes. 'And besides,' he said, as they walked, 'why would he save your life twice and come out in a hurricane to find you? Why would he sit by your bed every day and night until you regained consciousness? Don't you think that's pushing it a bit far? If he could have anyone, why wouldn't he pull on his boots and run for his life? I would. There are a hell of a lot less complicated women than you out there, you know.'

'Well, like you said Jack, he's as screwed up as I am.'

He was about to answer her back, when the sound of the Land Rover made him stop. They turned as Kane and Ruth slowed to a halt beside them. Alex didn't miss the questioning look Kane cast his younger brother. It passed quickly, as Jack explained. 'We've just fetched Arthur's ashes from the boat.'

Ruth looked a picture sitting at his side. He dark and handsome, she blonde and beautiful. Alex felt her heart lurch.

'Well Ruth, what do you think of my island?' she said, as sweetly as possible. 'I hope Kane has managed to keep his mind on the driving.'

Ruth was a nice person, the sarcasm washed straight over her beautiful head. 'He's been the perfect guide and gentleman, Miss McBride. It was so kind of you to let me look round the island and I do hope that you're feeling better after your horrible accident.'

Alex waved a hand. 'I'm fine now. Thank you.'

Kane touched his hat, slipped the Land Rover into gear and pulled away.

As they walked on, following in the wake of the vehicle, Jack looked down on her, saying, 'Why do you do that?'

'What?'

'Have to deliver innuendos.'

She shrugged. 'I just don't seem able to stop myself.'

'Ever asked yourself why?'

He was watching her expression. 'Oh, I don't know Jack, you tell me. You seem to have all the answers around here. You tell me.'

Without warning, he thrust his hand over her left breast, pressing hard. 'Can you feel it? Can you?'

'What?' she gasped, not knowing if she was imagining it or if it was really happening. She knew her medication wasn't out of her system yet but was she really hallucinating?

'Hurry up, Alex, before Kane sees me in the rear mirror and comes back and drops me where I'm standing.'

'What?' she managed to squeak.

'Can't you feel your heart racing? Christ Alex, it sounds like an out of control train.' He moved his hand, staring down into her flustered face. 'If you want to know why you react the way you do every time you see the man, listen to your heart.'

She took a deep breath. Jack Mitchell was almost as dangerous as his brother. Why couldn't they just explain things like normal human beings? Why did they have to try to analyse her every thought and action. Her face burned. She didn't know what to say. It wasn't every day an almost complete stranger grabbed her breast. She felt quite unsteady.

Jack noticed because he took her hand. 'Come on, Alex, I think you're getting tired. You shouldn't be out riding and walking; it's too soon. Let's get back.' As an after thought he added, 'What are you doing with Plug's ashes?'

She glanced across at the urn, her face still burning, her breast still tingling from his touch, the words still buzzing around her head - *listen to your heart*. 'I'm going to scatter them on the sea … tonight. I'm going to set him free.'

'Are we all invited?'

She nodded, 'Of course. That's if your brother's finished playing tour guide and is available.'

Jack gave her a knowing wink. 'He'll be there.' He squeezed her hand and laughed, pulling the peak of her cap down over her eyes. From beneath the cap she said, 'And another thing, we don't call Arthur, Plug anymore…we *all* call him Arthur.'

Herringbone-pink stained the early evening sky as the sun slipped away for another day. The tide had turned and was now softly breaking on the cooling sand. They stood side by side, the four of them, saying nothing. Kane and Jack wore evening dress and Kane looked as if he was auditioning for the new James Bond part, he looked so dashing. Jodie wore a full-length, dark blue, satin dress, while Alex looked beautiful, but frail, in long black lace. They stood in silence on the loading ramp; the first place Alex had seen Arthur. The warm sea lapped quietly around them.

Kane handed her Arthur's urn. His fingers touched hers briefly as she took it from him and stepped forward.

'Does anyone want to say anything?' she asked quietly.

Jack and Jodie shook their heads but Kane stepped forward to stand next to her, his face dark. He cast a brief glance at the marble urn that held the final remains of the man, who, in all probability, had saved Alex's life by giving his own - a selfless human being. He spoke softly. 'This shouldn't have happened, Arthur. You were right, Asak Mulligan is out there.' Then, in an undertone that no one else heard, he said, 'I know what you did, and I know why. Thank you.'

Alex took a step nearer to the water. She began in a quiet voice she didn't quite trust as she clutched the urn against her chest. 'What do you say in a moment like this, Arthur? I only knew you for a short time but it was as if I'd known you all of my life. I wish we could have met a long time ago and then you would have been in my life for longer. I would have liked that.' She stopped to take a breath and blink back tears, and then in a broken whisper she went on, 'You shouldn't have lost your life for me, Arthur. No one deserves that.'

She removed the lid from the urn and looked into it through welling tears. 'It doesn't look much to show for the life of a good man, just a few ashes in the bottom of an urn, but these ashes are still you Arthur and I pray to God you find your way home.'

She turned the urn upside down and they watched in silence, as Arthur 'Plug' Towers drifted out in a grey, powdery cloud that swirled in the evening breeze before settling on the water to begin his final sea voyage.

Kane pulled a can of lager from his jacket pocket, snapped back the ring pull and tipped it slowly into the sea. 'To see you on your way, Arthur.'

Jack poured Champagne, handing a glass to each of them. 'To Arthur,' he said, raising his glass. 'A good bloke; may he rest in peace.'

'To Arthur,' the others chorused.

Alex added, 'Look out for him Betsy. He was a good man and no one's laughing at him anymore.' Tears slid down her cheeks.

Kane handed her a handkerchief then sat down on the side of the ramp. 'Sit down, Alex,' he said quietly. 'Let's talk.'

Casting off her shoes, she sat down next to him, dangling her legs off the platform above the water. Jack touched Kane briefly on the shoulder then, leaving a bottle of Brut, took the other and walked with Jodie along the ramp to the beach.

'We will find Asak Mulligan you know,' Kane said seriously, turning to look at her sad, wet face. 'He won't get away with killing Arthur. You do know that don't you?'

She took a deep breath, fighting to keep her voice level. 'Let's not talk about that right now. This is Arthur's moment. I don't want to spoil it with thoughts about the man who killed him.' She turned her head to look at Jodie and Jack sitting on the beach at the edge of the ramp. They looked so right together, so easy, so uncomplicated. She supposed it had happened when she was in hospital. Jodie needed a shoulder and Jack had provided it. 'I might go back up to the house. It's been a long day and I'm feeling tired.'

'Don't do that, Alex. I think it's time we talked.' He turned to look out at the raspberry-ripple sunset, blazing across the horizon. 'It's time I told you how I feel. I've tried so many times *not* to tell you this over the past few weeks, because, truth be known, I'm scared shitless. But I have to say it. You've gotten to me, Alex. Somehow you've made me dare to believe that I can actually feel something again, actually love someone … after Ellie. I thought that Ellie was the only one for me, that love, true, *real* love only came once in a lifetime … and that was if you were lucky.' He pushed a hand through his hair and gave a half laugh before continuing. 'You're nothing like Ellie, of course. She was whole. You're fragmented. But I swear to God I can put you back together again. I can make you stronger than before.' He turned towards her and with a look that almost made her cry, kissed her mouth.

And afterwards, later, in the darkness and security of her bedroom, she might think that it had been the most natural thing in the world, to have been kissed by Kane Mitchell, but right now she still couldn't allow the luxury of such a thought. She pulled away.

Kane touched her face, turning her towards him again. 'Why are you so scared Alex? If I can take the risk, can't you? What do you think I'm going to do to you that's so bad?'

Was he serious? Couldn't he *see* what he was capable of doing to her?

He had the power.

She had known it from the very first time she'd heard his voice - the second his laser eyes had met hers. The words struggled out from their burial ground and spilled, 'You have the power to destroy me.'

His eyes narrowed. He looked confused. 'But ... why would I want to do that?' he said. 'What would that achieve?'

She shook her head. 'I can't risk it. I can't have my heart broken again.'

Kane watched her sad face. 'Love doesn't break hearts, Alex. If it broke your heart, it wasn't love.

She turned away, concentrating hard on the sun slipping slowly over the horizon. She could smell him, pheromones and expensive after-shave, mingling with sea salt and bougainvillaea, a heady, dangerous combination. 'Love broke *your* heart,' she said turning to look at him. 'You said so. You said your heart had been broken, that night we sat on the step and you *made* me drink that awful Jack Daniels.'

Kane raised an eyebrow. 'As I remember, I didn't have to *make* you drink it. You seemed pretty willing to me.'

'Well, I guess even I have my moments of weakness and ...'

'What! The great and powerful Alex McBride has moments of weakness? I don't believe it. And when might that be?'

'I was pretty weak letting Peter into my life. Letting the bastard break my heart. He destroyed me when he left me ... alone and pregnant. That was bad enough. And then ... I lost the baby ...'

'Peter leaving wasn't the *end* of your life, don't you see? It was the beginning. You've just been looking at it from the wrong angle. And when I said my heart had been broken, it wasn't through love, it was through loss. Because I lost Ellie. Because I couldn't protect her. Loss breaks hearts … love doesn't. Loss broke your heart too. You lost Peter, whom at the time you thought you loved, but it was the loss of the baby that broke your heart.'

If she listened to his words, or worse still, started to believe them, then she was finished. Dead in the water.

She touched his arm and held his gaze as she whispered, 'I know you think you've got it all worked out, but, really, you haven't.' She placed her unfinished glass of Champagne on the decking, got to her feet and walked away, back to the house.

The house stood in the last pink rays of the disappearing sunset as Alex climbed the steps, her thoughts still with the conversation she'd just had with Kane. He had sounded sincere, as if he'd meant every word he'd said. And if she hadn't walked away, what might have happened then? What else might he have said? Probably enough to make her start believing it? Best to have walked away. Best to stay strong. He'd be leaving soon, men like that never stayed in one place for long. Men like Kane Mitchell always moved on.

She pushed against the fly screen door and walked into the kitchen. It hit her immediately, a stench so foul that she had to clasp her hand to her mouth. Her eyes flitted around the kitchen as she spun a complete circle. Something wasn't right. Something was in the house.

She tiptoed across the kitchen and opened the door out into the hallway. The smell was much stronger here, leaking through her fingers and creeping into her nostrils. She edged along the wall, close, using it to guide her along the hall and towards the bedrooms. At

Jack's door she stopped. The door was open. She crossed the hall and peered inside. His bed was messed up, half of the duvet hanging off the bed, the rest pulled up and over the headboard. Beneath the duvet still covering the bed, something lay humped and still. Alex glanced around the room. The curtains hung motionless at the open window; blood smeared the sill. She took a step backwards.

The kitchen door slammed, and voices sounded before it went quiet. Suddenly the hall door opened and Kane charged towards her, followed by Jack and Jodie.

'Don't go in there, Alex!' he shouted, reaching her, grabbing her by the arm and pulling her away.

'What is it?' she said, as Jack passed her and entered the room with Kane.

Neither answered.

Kane lifted the duvet.

Chapter 13

'What in God's name is that?' Jodie said, edging nearer to the bed.

Kane let the blood-soaked duvet drop to the floor as he surveyed the mass through narrowed eyes. 'I think we could do with Arthur to tell us that.'

The room fell quiet while they stared at the animal skin, packed and stuffed with entrails and excrement. As they peered at it, dumbfounded, the contents moved and a brown and green snake surfaced through the mass.

Alex took a step backwards. 'It's him, isn't it?' she said in a whisper. 'It's Asak Mulligan. He's done this.' She dragged her eyes away and over to the open window. 'He's been here in the house, while we've been scattering the ashes of the man he killed.'

Kane ripped the sheet free of the mattress, folding each corner to the centre before lifting the whole sick, stinking mess and launching it out of the window.

Jack scratched his head. 'Why my bed?' he asked, confused.

'I don't think it was anything personal,' Kane said shepherding Alex and Jodie from the room. 'Put the coffee on, Jodie, we need to get this thing sorted.'

'We have to find this lunatic,' Kane said, looking at each of them in turn, while Jodie poured coffee. 'We have to go out there and take this place apart until we find him.'

'We need to contact the police,' Jodie said, 'You've tried to find him before, Kane, and failed.' She hadn't meant it to sound like a criticism, but it did.

Kane glanced across at Jodie. 'And so have the police. They tore the place apart looking for him while Alex was on the mainland. Even the dogs came up with nothing.'

Alex stirred her coffee, watching the liquid swirling in the mug. Without looking up, she said quietly, 'Arthur said Asak Mulligan wouldn't be found if he didn't want to be. Said he has *Aboriginal* ways.'

'If that stinking mess in my bed was an example of his Aboriginal ways, then the sooner we flush him out the better,' Jack said. He poured a double measure of Jim Beam into his coffee and offered the bottle to Kane who waved a hand dismissively before saying, 'I suggest we take the Land Rover at daybreak.'

'But what will you do with him, if you catch him?' Jodie asked.

'*When* we catch him,' Kane said

'When you catch him,' Jodie corrected.

Kane took a swallow of coffee before saying, 'We'll hand him over to the authorities. He may feel he has a right to rid his home of trespassers but there's a way to go about things, at least, there is in the civilised world.'

'Asak Mulligan doesn't live in the civilised world,' Alex stated truthfully.

'I agree, but it still doesn't give him the right to go around killing people, does it?' Jack said.

Alex couldn't argue with that.

'We go at daybreak, then. Agreed?' Kane said.

Jack nodded. 'What about this pair? They can't be left alone.'

Kane looked from Jodie to Alex. 'Do you both promise to stay in the house? Lock all the doors and stay put?'

Jodie nodded immediately. 'Sure, we can do that. You can take your mobile. If there's any problem either end we can call each other.'

Kane seemed to accept that. 'And what about you, Alex? Do you agree?'

She didn't look up. She didn't want to feel the intensity of his eyes boring into her. She simply nodded.

'Right,' Kane said. 'In that case I think Jack and I will hit the sack.'

'Hang on,' Jack said. 'Aren't you forgetting something? I don't have a sack to hit.'

Kane raised his eyebrows, halting the coffee cup half-way to his mouth. 'Come off it Jack, we all know you've been sharing Jodie's pit for several nights now. It's not exactly the secret of the century.'

Jack looked a bit shifty, scratched his head and blushed, but his high colour was nothing compared to Jodie's. She looked like an over-ripe plum. She hadn't realised anyone knew about her night-time liaisons with Jack. Alex had appeared too wrapped up in her personal vendetta to have noticed and Jodie hadn't wanted to flaunt their growing relationship while things were as they were.

Kane got up from the table, walked over to the sink and put his mug on the drainer. Jack followed and together they left the kitchen. As the door closed behind them, Jodie slid her hand across the table and took hold of Alex's. She squeezed it gently and said, 'I saw what Kane tried to do down on the beach, Alex, and I saw your response. Don't you think if someone like Kane has managed to find you, on an island discreetly tucked away in the Pacific Ocean, then it was meant to be? If this isn't fate then I don't know what is.' She paused to let the words sink in, and then said, 'Why don't you give him a chance, Alex?'

Alex opened her mouth to speak but no words came. What could she say? She had walked away from Kane when he was offering his love. How much effort and faith had that taken on his part? She'd more or less told him by words and actions that she wasn't interested. But was that the truth? Perhaps it was time to move on, away from the disastrous relationship with Peter, away from the sad yesterdays. But mostly, wasn't it time she moved on from her own set-in-stone beliefs? She had spent six years wallowing in self-pity, pushing people away and feeling sorry for herself. What had that achieved other than making her bitter and not a very nice-to-know person? Nanny Martha used to say, *'Pack up your troubles in your old kit bag and smile, smile, smile.'* She remembered Arthur's words, the day he had stood in the kitchen. 'You'd better watch that, Missy, that smiling could become a habit.' She needed to pack up her troubles and walk away from them. She needed to begin another journey, to venture beyond the horizon. But what if she got it wrong again? What if moving on took her in the wrong direction? What if she arrived in a place from which, despite time and healing, she could never return?

Jodie squeezed her hand again and said in a whisper, 'Let go Alex. Kane isn't Peter. I know you can trust him.'

'Can I?' she whispered.

'Yes, Alex, you can.'

She took a deep breath and let it out. Perhaps there was only one way to find out. And although it was going to take the most enormous leap of faith, perhaps the time to launch herself off the cliff and free-fall was right now.

Around midnight, Alex quietly turned the handle on Kane's bedroom door and stepped inside his room. Pale moonlight flooded in through the open curtains, spotlighting his naked body lying stretched out on the bed. Soundlessly, she crossed the room, halting and turning at the open window, standing with her back pressed tightly against the cool sill. For moments she watched his steady, rhythmic breathing, then, softly, like a prayer uttered in reverence, she spoke his name, and before it had dissolved into the stillness of the room, he opened his eyes and turned his head towards her. The perfumed breeze lifted the curtain, billowing it against her bare arms, the slightest, gossamer touch, encouraging her towards him. As she took the first step, he slid his body free of the bed and rose to stand before her, looking down on her flushed, upturned face. No words passed between them as he reached out and caught hold of her nightdress, lifting it over her head and letting it slip to the floor in a pool of silk, before turning her into the moonlight. His eyes moved languidly over her body - the delicate hollow of her throat, the soft swell of her breasts, the gentle curve of her hips. His consuming gaze missed nothing as it returned to her face, flitting from her mouth to her eyes, seeking answers, asking unspoken questions. He raised a hand and tilted her face towards his, peering closer into her eyes, seeing the apprehension and the desire that she had kept under control for such a long time. She closed her eyes and in that moment, he swept her into his arms, carried her across the room and laid her gently on the bed. Then, slowly, as if he had all the time in the world, he climbed astride her naked body.

Alex slipped out of the bedroom window and ran across the yard to the stables, knowing, with each hurried stride, that she was breaking her word. She figured if she stayed a prisoner in her own home, then Asak Mulligan had scored another point and he'd already scored too many.

The horses were stabled having been brought in from the field by Kane and Jack before they'd left, four hours ago. Holly looked up and whinnied a high-pitched greeting. The others looked but continued busily plucking hay from their racks. She gave them each an apple and went into the room at the back of the barn where they kept the tack. She took Holly's saddle down from the saddle horse, switched on the radio and sat down. Glenn Campbell was in the middle of *True Grit*. She turned up the volume, listening as Glenn bleated on. *'The pain of it, will ease a bit, when you find a man with true grit.'* Alex didn't know if she believed in irony. *'Few battles are won alone.'* She turned the volume higher, aware that Kane must have changed radio channels when he'd been in the tack room. It brought him closer. She rubbed saddle soap onto a damp sponge and gently applied it to the saddle flap, her hand slow, up and down, round and round. She closed her eyes, imagining his hard chest beneath her hand, as it had been only a few hours ago, remembering how it had felt.

She took a long, deep breath and let it out slowly. If life should end right now, this very second, she knew she would die happy. Everything else had paled - slipped away into insignificance; nothing else mattered.

Why had she wasted so much time in hating and repelling him? His words from hours ago circled her brain. 'I love you Alex McBride.' Then he'd made love to her, taking her to a place she had never been to before: a special, once in a lifetime place where dreams became reality and reality became dreams. She smiled, remembering vividly every move, every soft and loving touch. Later, he'd repeated the words, gently moving her above him, his eyes roaming over her naked, vulnerable body. And this time she'd made love to him, riding his hard, muscled body, thrust after thrust, stride after stride, driving him on and on … They'd climaxed together, sweat soaking their bodies, clinging, vice like to each other as each spasm deepened. And afterwards, tightly wrapped in the protection of each other's arms, Alex realised that she'd been wrong. It wasn't a once in a lifetime place, it was a niche they would return to time after time after time …

She hadn't said the words - *I love you* - back. She'd keep them in her head a little longer. Work on the evidence, but it looked suspiciously like the jury was about to announce a unanimous verdict. She applied more soap and slid her hand into the saddle's gully, caressing the soap into the leather until it shone like a ripe conker.

Cutting through Garth singing *Friends In Low Places* came Jodie's voice - distant at first, wobbly as if she was running. Then the barn door swung open and she flew down the centre aisle, shouting Alex's name.

Alex stood up, threw the saddle up on to the saddle rack and walked out into the barn. Jodie stopped dead, relief registering on her pink, agitated face. 'Where the hell have you been?' she bawled. 'I've been looking for you everywhere. How irresponsible can you be, disappearing like that? *And* after you promised Kane and Jack that you would stay in the house. What if Asak Mulligan was out here watching and waiting to pounce?'

'In broad daylight?' Alex said. You really think he's going to expose himself in broad daylight? He hasn't yet, why should he now?'

Jodie held out a hand. In it was the book Alex and Plug had found in the shack. 'I think you had better read this,' she said, trying to keep her voice from shaking. 'I was cleaning your room and it fell off the cabinet. When I picked it up the cover had fallen off. The information you were looking for and couldn't find is written on the inside of the cover.'

Alex stared at the book. 'The information I was looking for?'

Jodie nodded.

Slowly, Alex took the book and turned it in her hand before slipping off the cover. Half of it fell away in her hands and floated to the floor.

'I think you'd better sit down, Alex,' Jodie said, upturning a spare water bucket for her.

'Is it that bad?' Alex said as she sat, pushing back hair that had fallen over her eyes.

Jodie waved a hand at the book and said, 'Just read it, Alex. Just read it.'

The handwriting on the cover was her father's, no doubt about it. He had written notes in diary form. She started to read.

Friday 12th – There's no sign of him. The heat drains. The flies are almost unbearable but I'm going to stick it out.

Saturday 13th – Thought I saw something today down by The Reach but it could have been a trick of the light - my mind imagining things.

Sunday14th – It wasn't my imagination. I saw him. He exists!

Monday 15th – Waited for him all day. Nothing.

Tuesday 16th – Nothing.

Wednesday 17th – Am I going mad? Did I see him? There's no sign now.

Thursday 18th – Christ! I saw him. He didn't see me. The strength of the man. He kills with his bare hands. Broke the wallaby's neck like it was a twig.

Friday 19th – He saw me. He knows I'm here. I need to gain his trust. Approach him?

Saturday 2oth – No trace of him.

Sunday 21st - Still no sign.

Monday 22nd – Where is he?

Tuesday 23rd – Called Plug Towers. Can't stay any longer. Come back next month.

Alex looked up at Jodie. 'He found him. My father found him.' Goose flesh ran up her arms. 'It never quite seemed real before ….' Her voice trailed away.

'It's real. It was real the day your shirt was torn and the day Holly was put out on the Reach. And it was real when Arthur died at his hands. It's real Alex, believe it.'

'What if Kane and Jack find him? What if he finds them and …'

'I think you had better read this half,' Jodie said, picking it up from where it had fallen on the cobbles and handing it to her. As Alex took it, Jodie added, 'And check out the top, right-hand corner. Look at that drawing your father's sketched on the cover. It's you.'

Alex stared at the information in her shaking hand. Slowly the truth dawned. She turned huge, bewildered eyes to look at Jodie. 'Oh, shit.'

It was there in black and white. Her family history, right back to Silas McBride who had come out to Australia all those years ago, married his Aborigine princess and had his brood. Their last-born child, Kitty, had married Isla Mulligan when he was banished to the mainland by his jealous father. Isla and Kitty's child was Asak Mulligan – the baby boy who should have died that fateful night out on The Reach but, as it was now obviously apparent, hadn't.

Arthur had got it right and got it wrong. He was right about the baby; it had survived. But he was wrong about her father buying the island. He hadn't bought it – he had inherited it. It had come to him, down through the McBride line.

Alex looked up at Jodie.

Jodie looked down at Alex.

Together, right on cue, they said, 'Oh, shit!'

They came in hot and dusty, wearing the island on their clothes. Jack made a beeline for the fridge and pulled out two cold cans of beer. Throwing one across the table at Kane, he pulled the ring pull and drained the can in one long backward tilt of his head.

Kane dragged out a chair and lowered himself onto it, struggling to pull off his boots. 'There's no sign of him anywhere. If I didn't know better, I'd think we were imagining the whole bloody thing,' he said, his voice a mixture of despondency and annoyance. He snapped open the beer and half drained it.

Alex glanced at Jodie who nodded towards Kane. Taking out the two halves of the jacket from the book's pages, she held them out before Kane, in a hand that was anything but steady.

'What makes me think this isn't your Christmas list come early?' he asked, trying to get the humour back into his voice. 'What is it, Alex?'

'Read it. I think it's pretty self-explanatory,' she said, unable to take her eyes off his face, grizzled with beard shadow, eyes tired from being awake all night making love to her. She was responsible for the way he looked and it pleased her, made her realise that last night had really happened. Before her was the living, breathing proof.

He took them from her hand and read them. A frown appeared and grew in perplexity. He handed them to Jack who read them, said, 'Ouch,' and handed them back.

There was silence, until Kane, looking up at Alex, said in a voice that was strangely tight. 'This madman, this murderer, Asak Mulligan, he's a *relation* of yours?'

'So it appears.'

'And you had no idea?'

'No, of course not. This has come as much of a surprise ... well, shock ...to me as to anyone else.'

Kane rubbed at his stubble and shook his head. 'Well it conclusively proves a number of things, doesn't it? He exists, he's a relation ... however distant ... and your father inherited this place by default because the heir to the throne was still alive and well and living in 'cloud cuckoo' land.' He made no attempt to keep the bitterness out of his voice as he added, 'And it also explains why Mulligan is set on destroying you. Your Father unwittingly left him a picture in the image of his daughter ... a daughter who arrived here on the island and threatened his very existence.'

Alex shook her head. 'But how do we know that Mulligan found this book and this picture?'

Kane raised his eyebrows in disbelief at her innocence. 'He found it. It may not have meant anything to him until you arrived here, but from the day you set foot on the island, that man has had his sights set on your destruction.'

Alex bit her lower lip, her eyes flickering to Jodie and said, 'But what about Jodie? Why hasn't he attempted to hurt her?'

Kane took a deep breath before bluntly stating, 'Just a matter of preference I'd say. Jodie's next on the list. The man won't stop until he has his island back.'

Jack snapped open another beer and drained it.

Alex gazed out to sea. She had grown to love this place in the short time she had lived here and to discover that Asak Mulligan was still alive and living here, on what appeared to be *his* island, filled her with a deep sense of misery – not to mention apprehension.

She turned as a flock of squawking Rosellas startled and burst out of the under storey in a noisy whirring of frantic wings. Her instinct told her that Asak Mulligan had scared them and that at any moment he would step from the vegetation and she would be confronted with Arthur's killer. And then what? He would probably kill her as well. After all, that was what this was all about, wasn't it? A madman fiercely protecting his home. Who wouldn't want to protect something as beautiful and perfect as Mulligan's Reach, to make this their home for the rest of their days? To watch their children playing on the beach, splashing through the outgoing tides, swimming in the warm sea? It was all about to end. They would have to leave, go back to England.

Would Kane want to go to England with her? Would he want to go back to Texas, to Amarillo? Would he want to take her with him? Would he leave her? Could she bear that? No, not now. Not *now*.

Her heart leapt, as a dark figure appeared across the sand, briefly confirming her fears, until her crazy head told her it wasn't Asak Mulligan, it was Kane.

He didn't speak immediately when he reached her but folded his long legs and sat down in the sand next to her. He took her hand and, as if he could read her mind said. 'It'll all work out, Alex. Jack and I will go out and stay out until we find him. You won't need to be afraid of anything, anymore.'

'It's *his* island though, isn't it? I can't inherit something that was never my father's in the first place, can I? She couldn't keep the hopeless tone from her voice.

He draped his arm around her shoulder, pulling her against him and the warmth of him seared into her. 'The place doesn't matter, Alex. As long as you're there and I'm there, we could live on the Moon.'

She turned to him, seeking reassurance in his eyes. 'Do you mean that? *Really* mean it?'

'I *really* mean it. I'll never leave you Alex and I'll love you for the rest of my life if you let me.'

Alex had waited all her life to hear those words. Peter had said he loved her but he'd never said he'd never leave her. She'd just assumed he wouldn't.

'I'm sorry I treated you so badly,' she said, so quietly the sea almost took the words away. 'I've been so wrapped up in my own tiny, cotton-wool padded world for so long that I'd stopped considering everyone else's feelings. I've been an utter, ungrateful bitch.'

He watched her face as her sad eyes flickered up to his. 'We've moved on from there, Alex. Besides, forget it, it's all part of your natural charm and charisma.'

'Really?'

He mock punched her on the arm. 'Really.'

They fell silent for a few moments, each going over stuff in their heads. Kane spoke first. 'What are you thinking about?'

Alex shrugged. 'I was thinking how beautiful this place is and how difficult it's going to be to leave it. I was imagining children playing on the beach.'

Kane nodded. 'Yeah, it's easy to imagine, isn't it? What do you see Alex? I see a little girl bouncing along on a fat pony and her younger brother following on foot, waiting for his turn. But the girl refuses to let him have a turn. She's feisty and takes after her mother.'

Alex mock punched him back. 'That's not a very nice thing to say, is it? And anyway, why haven't they each got a pony? And why is the girl's pony fat?'

Kane started to laugh.

'Come on, why.'

'Because their mother spoils everything on four legs. But that's just another part of her charm.'

Alex gave an unintentional snort and said, 'Blimey, I never knew I had so much going for me, if I had, I might have cast my net a bit wider and hauled in something really dishy.'

Kane pushed her over on to her back and climbed above her, laughing. 'Lady, you couldn't have found anything dishier than me. So we'll have no more talk about casting nets and hauling in anyone else. Got it?'

When she didn't answer he bent and gently kissed her. 'Got it?'

When she still didn't answer he kissed her again and when she reached the point where she could barely breathe, she conceded and said, 'Got it.'

The sound of a helicopter approaching brought them back to the real world. They watched as it approached from the mainland, flew overhead and landed near the house.

'That's going to be the police, isn't it?' Alex said irritably. 'I'll bet Jodie has taken it into her own hands to call them. Why can't she just leave well alone? Now *they're* going to be creeping all over the island until they find him.'

'The police won't find him, Alex,' Kane said, getting to his feet and dusting sand from his jeans. 'He's been living here for almost sixty years virtually undetected. The inner terrain of this island is like unchartered jungle. Your father found him but they won't.'

Alex looked up at him as he stood against the sun. He was her hero: corny, old-fashioned, but she didn't care. It was going to be all right. Kane was in her life and it was going to be all right. 'I suppose we'd better get back and face the music then,' she said, accepting Kane's hand. 'Go back and see what our little Jodie has buggered up this time.

They were half way across the beach, hand in hand, when the helicopter passed overhead and headed back out over the sea.

'Looks like they've gone already,' Alex said, grinning.

They mounted the veranda steps and Kane held open the kitchen door. She dodged under his arm, half-aware of the voices coming from the kitchen. Abruptly she stopped. Even Kane walking into her didn't move her. She knew the voice floating towards her. Her eyes flew from Jack to Jodie, and settled on the third person seated at the table.

The tall, blonde-haired man stood up, exchanging a non-committal look with Kane, then walked towards her smiling, his hand outstretched. The word fell out of her mouth leaving her jaw gaping, 'Peter!'

She felt Kane's hand tighten on her waist.

'How are you, Alexandra?' he said, breaking Kane's hold, engulfing her stiff body in his. He lowered his mouth to hers and kissed her hard. She pushed against his chest, breaking away, backing across the kitchen towards the sink, hands clutching at the work surface for support. He dragged a hand through salon-streaked hair, laughing nervously as he followed her across the kitchen. 'I've been a bloody fool, an utter idiot, Alexandra. I know it's a little late in the day but I've finally come to my senses. She was staring at him, unable to accept that here, after all this time, stood the man she had loved and lost. Her lower lip quivered involuntarily as she said, 'How did you find me?'

'Anthony told me where …'

'Bowbridge? Anthony Bowbridge told you? I'll sue him. He had no right to divulge such information. What happened to client confidentiality?'

'Well, it did take a couple of bottles of decent plonk and two tickets for *Whistle Down the Wind*,' he said, trying a splash of his usual humour; humour that had once appealed but now fell flat.

Alex turned towards him and raised her chin. 'I'm surprised you considered me worth it. I would have thought a bottle of coke and two tickets to the local flea-pit would have done it.'

Peter closed the distance and Alex thrust out a hand, halting his approach. 'No, don't come any nearer. I don't think I can hold myself responsible for what I might do to you.'

Peter stopped and pushed his hands deep into his pockets, taking up the stance of a naughty boy, kicking his shoe toe against the floor tiles. Sulkily he looked up and then grinned, the action of it crinkling his eyes. 'I know I've left it rather late but I thought our child might want to meet its father.'

If, in that moment, Alex could have been anywhere else in the world simply by wishing, then she would have been – Timbuktu, the Moon, hell, anywhere except standing in her own kitchen confronted by the father of her dead child. If he hadn't grinned, if he could've just looked a little more sincere, she probably wouldn't have picked up the coffee pot and hurled it at his head. Before it missed him by a whisker and crashed against the wall, she'd flung open the hall door and stormed out.

Chapter 14

It was no way to handle the situation, Alex knew that. She couldn't remain pacing up and down her room like a caged tiger with a bad attitude forever. She had to take control, get the whole thing into perspective. Peter had come back. So what? She could handle it. But why had he come back? To see his child? But there wasn't a child. But he didn't know that. Why did he want to see his child after six years? Perhaps he wanted to salve his conscience. No, that couldn't be right. Peter didn't have a conscience. Perhaps he was dying. Yes, that was it. He'd discovered he only had a few months to live and he wanted to make things right. 'One thing's for sure, Peter,' she said aloud as she stopped pacing and started to rip off her grimy clothes. 'You had *better* be dying because if not, I'm going to kill you! And don't expect it to be quick and painless.'

She jumped, as Jodie walked in carrying two mugs of coffee. 'It's only instant I'm afraid; the coffee pot has just met its demise. Jack's clearing up coffee grindings as we speak.'

Alex wrapped a towel around her naked body and snapped. 'Well don't be expecting me to apologise, Jodie. The only thing I'm sorry about is that it didn't hit him on the head, knock some sense into it. How dare he just breeze in like that?'

Jodie handed Alex the coffee and slumped down onto the bed. 'He's waiting for you in the lounge. I think you'd better hear him out, don't you?'

Alex didn't want to hear him out. She'd heard enough of his bare-faced lies to last her a lifetime.

'Kane's gone to his room,' Jodie continued, swilling her coffee, watching it spinning. 'He said to say you know where he is if you want him.'

Alex wanted him. She wanted him to take her in his arms and tell her again that all this madness would soon be ended; that Asak Mulligan would be caught and Peter would be on a plane home before the end of the day. She sat next to Jodie. 'I don't know what to say to him, Jodie. I hardly trust myself in his presence.'

They sat in silence, each going over things in their heads, and then Jodie said, 'Have your shower, get dressed, then take a deep breath and go and speak to him. It only has to be done once. See what he has to say. By the way, I've put a triple vodka in the coffee. Thought we might need it.'

'We?'

Jodie nodded and took a slurp.

'Why we?' Alex said, staring at Jodie as the alcohol caught the back of her throat and she started coughing. '*You* aren't in shock.'

Jodie spluttered a bit and said, 'Not in shock … not in frigging shock? You have to be joking? In the space of less than twenty-four hours Peter Pan has materialised from thin air … flown in from frigging *Never Never Land,* and we've discovered that we have a psychopath living on the island. And you say I'm not in shock? Trust me, Alex, we are all sharing this with you.'

Alex had to smile. Jodie could be quite funny when she tried.

'You know what?' Jodie said giggling, swigging coffee and pulling a face. 'Living with you might be hell but it's never boring.'

By the time Alex had showered and changed, Jodie had dinner underway. She and Jack were in the kitchen, keeping a low profile, while Peter sat waiting in the lounge. Kane was in his room listening to something classical that Alex couldn't recognise. She smiled to herself as she walked down the hall. At least he'd stopped the country songs with the wrist-slitting lyrics. She just hoped he wasn't hitting the Jack Daniels.

As she walked into the lounge, Peter stood up and walked towards her. He attempted to kiss her cheek but she was ready for him this time and turned her head, leaving his kisses to land in mid-air. She sat down and indicated to Peter that he should do the same. He chose to sit opposite, rearranging the already immaculate creases in his trousers and said cheerfully, 'I took it upon myself to put some music on while I was waiting, I hope you don't mind.'

Alex shrugged. She hadn't even realised there was music playing. Her mind was set on trying to remain calm and not hurling the next available object at Peter's head.

Noises were coming from the kitchen - saucepan lids and crockery, interspersed by the odd giggle and scream. It sounded very much to Alex like Jodie was still on the vodka!

'I've been searching through your collection of C.D.'s for our song, but I couldn't find it,' Peter said.

Alex frowned. 'Our song? Which one was that? Oh yes, I remember, '*Leaving On A Jet Plane*,' wasn't it?

Peter slid off the sofa and closed the gap between them on his knees. He took Alex's hands and peering into her face, said, 'I can't justify what I did, Alex, and I realise you have good reason to be bitter.'

'Bully for you,' she said, meeting the pure blue of his eyes.

He placed a finger under her chin and raised her face. 'I was a fool, an idiot.' His face collapsed into a fair impersonation of sincerity. 'When you told me about the baby, I panicked. I only saw chains and dirty nappies and staying home at night, and …'

'And you didn't have the decency to discuss it with me? You think I deserved to be dumped like that?'

Peter shook his head. 'No. Of course not. I just panicked. Surely, you can find it in your heart to forgive me. I really do want to get to know my child.'

Alex snatched her hands away and stood up. 'There is no child. I lost it. And even if I hadn't, I doubt I would want to introduce it to you. A child needs a full time father, Peter, not someone who sees fit to only visit once every six years.'

Peter got to his feet and faced her. 'I'm sorry. I didn't know - about the baby I mean.'

'Of course you didn't know. How could you? You didn't stick around long enough, did you?'

'No, I didn't but I've seen the error of my ways and I've come back. We can still carry on where we left off. It doesn't matter about the baby …'

'What!' Alex snapped. 'It matters to *me* about the baby. It mattered then and it matters now. It was a lost life, Peter. A little lost, harmless, innocent life.'

Peter ran a hand through his hair. He was starting to sweat. The reunion wasn't going as he'd planned. He was making stupid statements. 'When I say it doesn't matter about the baby, what I mean is, I know I said I came back to see my child but it doesn't matter if there isn't one. I still want you, Alex.'

Alex crossed her arms tightly across her chest before she lost control and struck out at him.

'Just give me another chance,' he pleaded. 'I know you still love me, just as much as I love you. Give me one more chance and we'll have more babies if that's what you want and I won't run out on you next time, I promise.'

Alex felt her fingers biting into her ribs; she was trying so hard not to strike him. He put a hand on her shoulder and turned her towards him. 'Look into my eyes, Alex, and tell me you don't still love me, and I'll go.'

Alex could no more trust her voice than she could her fists.

Peter grinned. 'There! You see. I was right. You do still love me. I knew it!'

Just then, the kitchen door creaked slowly open and Jodie's head appeared around it grinning. 'Dinner is served,' she said nervously, her gaze flicking from Alex to Peter and back again. 'Are you coming?'

Alex shook her head. She needed space, not to be sitting at the same table as Peter, making polite conversation as if the last six years were so unimportant that they could be swept away in a few brief, apologetic sentences. Jodie closed the kitchen door as Alex stood up, walked to the outside door and stepped out into the early evening dusk.

Peter followed at a snail's pace. He'd come too far to give up now. He joined her on the front porch and sat beside her on the step. She turned her head briefly, looking into eyes that she had once thought of as beautiful but now those very same eyes lacked something. She remembered his mouth stronger than this. She'd never noticed before the way it flickered slightly at the corners as if he was having trouble maintaining the sincerity of his smile.

'I am so sorry, Alex. Please say you'll forgive me. I've been an utter fool. There's never been anyone else, you know. It's always been you. Just please say that you'll forgive me.'

Without a moment's hesitation the words tumbled out, surprising her as much as Peter. 'I forgive you.' She held her breath, blinked and listened, waiting for the sky to fall in or for the world to stop turning but nothing happened, just silence. She started to giggle and he silenced her with a passionless kiss.

'God, I really thought I'd cooked my goose this time. Thank you,' he said, pulling away and starting to babble. 'Thank you. Thank you. I only need this one chance. I swear you'll never regret it, not this time, darling. I love you … '

'Peter,' she said gently, taking his beaming, boyish face in her hands and looking deep into his cerulean eyes. 'Peter, I forgive you, because it doesn't matter anymore …'

'Darling,' he cut in. 'Of course it doesn't matter anymore. That's what I've been trying to tell you. We were made for each other … '

'Peter, it doesn't matter anymore because I've moved on.'

His face collapsed. He looked as if someone had taken away his favourite little blue car. 'But … '

'You're welcome to stay for a few days, until you get your travel plans sorted, but after that you're not welcome here.'

Alex looked up at the stars starting to appear in the night sky and then across to the beach and out to sea. It was beautiful. But it wasn't special. Not with Peter sitting next to her. Not like it had been the night she'd sat on the step with Kane and they'd drunk Jack Daniels and poured out their hearts to each other. She turned to Peter and the words came without thinking or preparation. 'I don't love you Peter. I don't think I ever did but I'll always be eternally grateful to you because you see, you taught me what love *wasn't*. You gave me an example that I could test all others against and I've found someone that I truly love.'

Peter's smile disappeared and his face blanked over. 'Who?' he said, staring at her. 'Who could you possibly find to love on an island?'

'Kane.'

'Kane!' he spat. 'That bloody Lone Ranger. Christ, Alexandra.' His eyes searched hers. He didn't like what he saw. 'Kane?' he repeated.

She nodded.

'But you can't love *him*. He's just a cowboy, no breeding, no class, a permanent no-hoper. You can't be serious? He's not the settling down sort.'

'And you are, I suppose? You, who disappeared out of my life faster than horse-shit off a shovel!'

'Yes. I am now,' he said urgently, choosing to ignore her crudity. 'Just give me the chance to prove it to you.'

'You ask too much, Peter.'

'But Mitchell will use you up and throw you aside. He's a saddle bum. Why, he covers more flesh than that cranky horse of his. He has a woman in every state, every harbour, every town. You don't know him.'

'I know enough,' she said quietly, seeing again Kane's nude body lying on the bed, watching him rise and walk towards her, feeling his touch as he'd carried her to his bed. Hardly daring to breathe as he'd settled gently above her before slowly exploring every centimetre of her flesh.

'But, Alexandra, you don't know what you're saying,' he bleated. 'Let's wait until the morning and we can talk about it then. Things always look better in the morning.'

She smiled. 'Peter, you can wait until hell freezes over, the answer will still be the same. My old nanny Martha used to say, '*It takes a fresh fall of snow to clear away an old one.*'

'She sounds as confused as you,' Peter bitched, not attempting to understand the simile.

'Yes, you're right, I have been confused. But things are clearer now. I can see that it wasn't meant to be. I can see that if you'd stayed, Lord only knows what kind of a miserable, pointless life I'd be living now.' She stopped to look into his nervous, flitting eyes. 'Leaving me was the best thing you ever did for me. I don't want you back, Peter. It was over the day you walked away.'

'Mitchell will break your heart,' he stated bluntly.

She shook her head. 'No he won't ... you see, love doesn't break hearts, that's something else I've been confused about.'

'But what about me?' he moaned, dropping his head into his hands. 'What am I going to do now? The deal in Brazil went pear-shaped. It blew up in my face. I've lost everything I had, Alexandra, everything. The bank's on to me. There's nothing left.'

A part of Alex cheered. A part of her executed a one-man Mexican wave, a triumphant rolled-fist salute, a thumbs-up, a chorus of Hallelujah. After all this time Peter was about to count the cost of his irresponsible, childish ways. 'What goes around comes around. It's Karma time Peter. Pay up.'

'I suppose that's another one of Mitchell's bloody ridiculous beliefs.'

'No, that's one of mine.'

'He's poisoned your mind, he's ... '

She cut in, grabbing his chin, turning his face to hers. 'Peter, you idiot, you still don't get it, do you? There was a time when you could have had every single penny I owned. You didn't have to take a detour through my pants to get to my cheque book. All you had to do was to love the baby and me as much as I loved you. But you couldn't could you? You could have fed off me like the blood-sucking leech you really are, but you blew it big time. You came back too late – thank The Lord.'

'But ...'

'Forget it, Peter, it's over. There's no more to be said.'

'But I didn't want to be a father,' he whined. 'I wanted a career. '

'Well, as far as I can see there's nothing to stop you now, is there?'

His whole face fell into a pout as he went for broke. 'But the lights are still on for you, Alexandra.'

She raised her head defiantly, peering deep into eyes that were shallow and manipulative. 'Then do yourself a favour, Peter ... turn them off, save power.'

'I don't remember you being this cold,' he said, refusing to accept defeat graciously. 'That cowboy has done this to you.'

'No Peter, *you* did this to me. Six years of grieving for a man that didn't want me, and a baby that disappeared down the toilet will do that to a person.'

'Christ, what have I done?'

'I've told you. You've shown me what love isn't.'

She wanted to laugh and cry both at the same time. Peter had done something marvellous, and he didn't even know it. Flinging her arms around his neck, eyes shining with joyous tears, she said, 'Thank you, Peter. From the bottom of my stupid heart, thank you.' Then she kissed him.

They didn't hear the lounge door as Kane let it click shut and with a relieved smile on his face, went back to his room, knowing that he was guilty of eavesdropping, but not really giving a damn.

Chapter 15

The irritating ring-tone of Jodie's mobile pierced the stillness. It was answered on the seventh ring. Alex smiled into the pillow and turned over, imagining what Jodie must be up to not to answer it before. It didn't register that it was too early to be receiving normal phone calls. She snuggled deeper down the bed and returned to the dream she'd been woken from – it was too nice to leave prematurely. Thirty minutes later her bedroom door opened, light from the hallway flooded in and Jack appeared at her bedside. A voice hissed, 'Alex, are you awake? It's me, Jack.'

She turned over, screwing up her eyes against the light. 'What time is it? What's wrong?'

He flicked on the bedside light. 'It's three-fifteen; Jodie's father's just phoned. Her mum's had a heart attack; she's in intensive care. We have to go to England.'

She leapt out of bed, exposing herself to Jack, who politely looked away as she shoved her arms into a night shirt and buttoned it, mumbling, 'Sorry, Jack.'

He waved a hand dismissively. He'd been surprised to find her in her own bed and had, in fact, gone to Kane's room first, only to find his bed cold and empty.

'Does Jodie want me to go with her or are you going?' she said, taking in the fact he was fully dressed and definitely looked like he was going *somewhere*.

'I said I'd go with her, if it's OK with you,' he said carefully, watching her reaction. 'But I don't want to step on anyone's toes.'

Alex had come to like Jack. Even though he did have a very 'hands on' approach to certain subjects! He was a sound-kind-of-guy and very obviously perfect for Jodie. 'That's not a problem, Jack. 'Where is she?'

They found Jodie in the kitchen shoving her passport, plastic cards and wallet into her bag. She looked up as they came in. Alex put her arms around her and hugged her hard. Neither spoke for a few minutes, then Alex said, 'Jack says he's going with you. Will you be all right?'

'Yes,' she said, a slight tremor in her voice. 'Will you?'

'I'll be fine. Don't give me a second thought, Jodie. You and Jack, just get yourselves to England and your mum. Nothing else is important. Tell your dad to bring her over here to convalesce when she comes out of hospital.'

'*If* she comes out of hospital,' Jodie said, tears welling up.

'No, *when* she comes out, Jodie. Your mum's strong, she'll make it.' Alex had temporarily forgotten that by that time she probably wouldn't even be on the island herself.

Jodie bit her lip, tears closer to falling. 'Sometimes I see why I love you so much.'

'Only sometimes?' Alex said, brushing it off before the lump in her throat stopped all speech. Then she added quietly so that only Jodie could hear, 'You hang on to Jack, he's all right. A big improvement on that lecherous locum who couldn't keep his trousers zipped.'

Tears slipped down Jodie's face and Alex wiped them quickly away with the cuff of her nightshirt. Above the house the sound of a helicopter whirred. 'Get going, there's the helicopter.' She turned to Jack who had been quietly watching the two of them. 'Look after her, Jack. Make sure she eats something. Don't let her worry herself sick and bring her home safely.' Again, Alex wasn't thinking that this soon wouldn't be home.

Jack nodded, then bent and kissed her on the cheek shyly, whispering in her ear on the way up, 'You take care. Don't go *anywhere* without Kane and don't go worrying about that other Pratt. He's not worth it.'

'Go on, go, both of you,' she said, blinking back tears and pushing them out of the door. She watched as Jack took Jodie's hand and, heads bent against the turbulence, ran towards the 'copter. She remained at the door while Jack helped Jodie in, slammed the door and the big machine rose, turned and flew off across the sea. Poor Jodie. She didn't deserve this. She rubbed her eyes before turning and going back into the kitchen. There didn't seem to be much point in going back to bed. She hadn't managed to sleep much before they left and now it would be impossible. She could only imagine what Jodie must be going through. The Lowers had a strong family bond, not like her relationship had been with her parents.

Absently, with her thoughts with Jodie somewhere over the Pacific Ocean, she flicked on the kettle and spooned coffee into a mug. Peter walked in rubbing sleep from his eyes. His hair was a mess and he wore nothing, except a pair of silk boxer shorts loosely slung around his slim waist. She pushed her coffee towards him across the table as he slumped down, and made herself another.

'What the hell is all the noise around here?' he said, over the top of the coffee mug. 'I thought I heard a chopper.'

She told him what had happened.

'Oh, right,' he said grinning. 'So there's just you and me here.'

'And Kane.'

'And Kane,' he repeated, like he was of little or no consequence. He looked round the kitchen, taking in the general tidiness. 'What do you do here all day anyway?'

'Tend to the horses mainly. You can help if you like,' Alex said, knowing what Peter's reaction would be. He'd never liked getting his hands dirty, at least, not literally.

He smoothed back his hair into a semblance of tidy and pulled a face. 'Er, no thanks, I still feel a bit jet lagged. I think I might just go back to bed for a while, give the day a chance to warm up.'

'You do that,' she said.

He grinned and put his half empty coffee cup on the table. 'Where is Kane, anyway? I thought he'd be up and out there by now, roping, rolling and branding.'

Alex refused to take the bait.

Peter watched her, his eyes burrowing through the thin nightshirt, taking in every line and curve as she rinsed out her coffee mug, dried it and placed it in the cupboard. 'You can always change your mind, Alex. Remember what I said last night? I won't make the same mistake twice and it's only going to be a matter of time before Mitchell leaves the island and gallops on to his next conquest.'

Alex threw the tea towel into the sink and turned towards him. 'What makes you think he's going to walk, Peter? What suddenly makes you an all knowing, all wise, agony aunt? As I remember you couldn't even work out your own relationship.'

'And I've said I'm sorry, haven't I? I've apologised. I've said we can try again, have more babies, anything you want.'

'As long as I'm prepared to keep you for the rest of your life?' she said with a laugh.

He pulled a face and scratched his head. 'Not exactly. I could always find a job.'

Alex bit her lip.

'I could.'

'Come off it, Peter. I don't know if you've noticed but we're a bit short on corner shops around here.'

Peter's face turned serious. 'I could get a job on the mainland. I'd do that for you, Alex. If it meant we could give it another go.' He drained his cup and placed it before him. 'What do you say? Can we try again? Say you'll tell the cowboy to walk. It's only bringing forward the inevitable. He's not the staying kind, Alex. Just because he's good in bed doesn't mean he's husband material.'

Alex wondered briefly how Peter knew Kane was good in bed. And as a warm, embarrassed glow seeped into her cheeks at the memory of Kane's ability, she realised that, like everything else, Peter was *way* out of touch. Kane wasn't good in bed, he was unbelievably *bad* – in the nicest, most fantastic way!

'And another thing,' Peter went on, not noticing Alex's flushed face. 'Did you know he was married?'

'Ellie,' Alex said.

Peter looked surprised. 'Oh, so he told you.'

Alex nodded.

'I'll bet he didn't tell you about the three-in-a-bed, drunken orgies at Bristol, did he?'

'No I didn't,' a voice from the door said.

Peter almost fell off his chair as they turned to see Kane push himself off the doorframe, where he'd been standing unnoticed, and walk towards Alex.

He slipped an arm around her shoulder and kissed the top of her head before turning towards Peter. 'I didn't tell her that one, Gregson, because I haven't heard it but obviously you have so perhaps you'd like to tell us both.'

Peter coloured up, holding up his hands. 'I could have been wrong. You know what these campuses are like. It could have just been one-in-a-bed.'

Kane glowered at him and looked like he was about to stroll over and punch Peter's lights out.

Alex slipped her arm around Kane's waist. 'We all have history, Peter. Look at mine. You won't find worse than that. I was taken in by a penny-pinching coward. Perhaps you know him. Oh yes, of course you do. It was you!'

Peter stood up.

'Going to run away again?' Alex said snidely.

Peter sat.

Kane ignored him and turned to Alex. 'I'm sorry to hear about Jodie's mum.'

Alex smiled but said nothing as the mention of Jodie's name brought everything into perspective. What did it matter if Peter had returned? He'd be gone again soon – and sooner than that, if he didn't change his attitude towards Kane.

'I think I'll go and get dressed,' Peter said, finding a way out of the situation.

'I'll go and sort out the horses,' Kane said, his eyes lingering on her. 'Lock the door when I've gone and I guess you'd better bring Peter up to date on our friendly neighbourhood lunatic, just in case he goes walkabout and doesn't come back. We can't have that now, can we?'

Alex kept a straight face as Peter shuffled off. Perhaps she wouldn't tell him about Asak Mulligan. Peter was a rat. He deserved a rat's comeuppance.

With Jodie gone, Alex cooked breakfast. It was still sitting on the hot plate waiting for Kane to return from bringing in the horses when Alex decided to go and see what was keeping him. She stood for moments on the veranda looking towards the barn. Kane had said she wasn't to go anywhere without him, and Jack had said the same only hours before, but surely crossing the yard to meet Kane in the barn wasn't considered as going somewhere without him? She looked left and then right and then jumped down the steps and jogged to the barn. The door was open and she ran in. At first, she couldn't see him and then she noticed that Nightwalker's door was open. She hurried down the aisle and called Kane's name. At the sound of it, he stood up, waving his hand, indicating that she should keep her voice down and then he sank back to his knees. As she neared the box, her eyes fell on the subject of Kane's concentration. His horse was down, flat out, virtually collapsed.

'What's wrong with him?' Alex whispered, entering the box and crouching by Kane's side, looking incomprehensibly from the horse to Kane and back again.

He didn't return her look, just kept his eyes fixed fast on the thoroughbred, but he did answer, 'I don't know yet. I thought it was just a bout of colic but now I'm not so sure.'

Alex pushed up the horse's muzzle exposing bloodless gums. 'He's so pale. Has he eaten?'

'Last night, he took a bit of mix, but nothing since.'

Nightwalker rolled onto his belly, scrabbled to get his rear legs under his torso and giving an almighty heave, hauled himself up to stand swaying unsteadily.

'Does he keep going down?'

Kane nodded.

'It looks like colic.'

'It's more than that. I drenched him at two this morning. I was going to ask Jodie to look at him but …' He shrugged his shoulders.

'Why didn't you, she …'

He cut in. 'She had enough on her plate. Her mother was the first necessity. I'd have put my mother first … if I still had one.'

She touched his arm.

The horse fidgeted, shifting its weight from side to side.

'I think it's poisoning,' Kane said. 'It can't be anything else. But where in God's name is he going to pick up enough poison to do this? There's nothing in the field, nothing in the food chain. He's having nothing that the others aren't getting. I just can't figure it.'

'Could be a bug. Have you jabbed him?'

'Yeah, I pumped him full of anti-biotic as a precaution.'

Walker shuffled to the rear of his box, hanging his head, mucous appearing on the soft pink lining of his nostrils.

Alex dusted hayseeds from her vest. 'I'm going to make a call. We need a vet out here, Kane. This is something more than we can handle. I'll call John Roberts, he's the best vet around these parts … except for Jodie ... but we haven't got Jodie, so second best is going to have to do, OK?' She didn't wait for him to respond, running back to the house and barging through the kitchen door. Peter was sitting at the table, an empty plate before him, shouting at someone on the other end of the phone.

'Hello … I'm sorry you're breaking up … hello … hello ...' He held the phone away from his ear staring at it before dropping it on the table. 'The mobile's dead, flat battery. Have you got another phone?'

She snatched it up staring at it, then at him. 'What? This *is* my phone Peter. Where's yours?'

He grimaced. 'Flat and I seem to have misplaced the charger, think I must have left it back in the hotel on the mainland, that's why I borrowed yours but … '

'You've flattened this as well, haven't you?'

'Sorry.'

She threw the phone onto the table. 'You idiot! We need to call a vet. How are we going to do that without a phone?'

'Jodie's?'

'Jodie's taken hers with her.'

He looked startled. 'Sorry, I didn't realise,' he mumbled, apologetically.

'That's the trouble with you, Peter, you never realise anything. Nice is it, living on the Planet Peter?'

'What about *your* phone charger?' he suggested.

'Mine won't work. I use Jodie's but …'

'She's taken it with her?'

'Well a phone isn't much good without a charger, is it?' Alex said, pacing the kitchen, running her hands through her hair.

'What about the Internet? Couldn't you e-mail?' he suggested lamely.

Alex stopped pacing and pointing a finger at him, nodded. 'Yes. Yes. The Internet. I can e-mail John. It won't be as quick and I'll have to wait for his response but I can try.'

Peter beamed but his face soon fell back into a frown as Alex snapped, 'I don't know why you're grinning, Peter. This is another thoughtless action of yours. You just plough on never thinking of the consequences. You'd just better pray that this works.' She left him sitting at the table and tore off down the hall to the study at the back of the house.

The desk was in its normal state of confusion, with papers, bills and opened letters everywhere but as Alex's eyes settled on the empty space in the centre of the desk she realised that Jodie had taken the notebook with her. She dropped her head into her hands covering out the light and what was happening all around her. What now? They couldn't phone and the computer had gone. She lowered her hands and stood staring out of the window, seeing nothing. The boat! Kane would have to take the motorboat. She dashed back to the kitchen just as Kane came in.

'Is he coming?' he said, hurriedly pouring a glass of water and draining it.

'The phones are dead. I can't make the call,' Alex said, watching his face.

'Christ!'

'You have to take the speedboat. You can be there and back in a couple of hours. It's not ideal but it's all we've got. There's no other way. '

Kane shook his head. 'No, I can't leave you here alone … it's not safe, you know that.'

Peter cut in, 'Er, excuse me, but aren't you forgetting I'm here?'

'I'm trying to,' Kane said through gritted teeth, looking like he might go off at any second.

'Oh great, that makes me feel a lot better.'

'Believe it or not Gregson, your feelings are not top of the agenda,' Kane said.

For seconds they glared at each other, silently waiting for the other to back off.

The sudden sound of splintering wood broke the tension. They were through the door together and racing towards the stables, leaving Peter still sitting at the table, fingering the dead mobile.

They could see as they tore down the aisle that Walker was down again, hooves dancing deliriously above the door as he rolled, trying to dislodge the pain in his belly. Kane stopped dead, turned and ran back in the direction from which he had just come.

Alex flung open the loosebox door and dropped beside the horse, grabbing the head collar, trying to hold him down. Bloody mucous flew through the air as he fought her, splattering her vest and landing in her hair. She pushed her light weight against his shoulder, stretching out her legs, bracing herself against the wall of the stable as another spasm engulfed the horse. It seemed like ages as she struggled to steady it before finally it ceased thrashing and lay still.

She didn't hear Kane come back but she sensed he was there. She turned her head towards him and as her eyes fell across him, she caught her breath.

'Get out of the way, Alex.'

She clung to the horse's neck, unable to believe her eyes.

Kane's arms hung motionless by his sides. In his right hand, he held a gun. 'Get out of the way, Alex. He's not going to make it. He's dying.'

She shook her head, plastering herself closer to the horse as it started to shake again, preparatory to the next spasm. 'No, I won't let you. He's still alive. There's still a chance.'

'He has no chance.' Even from a distance, he saw her eyes narrow defiantly.

'No, you'll have to shoot me first.'

'Get out of the way.'

'No.'

He raised the gun. 'Alex!'

It sounded like the final warning.

She closed her eyes and waited for the explosion. When it didn't come, she opened one eye.

Kane had lowered the gun and was standing at the door. When he spoke his voice faltered. 'Alex, please … come away from the horse.'

She shook her head. 'I can't let you shoot him, Kane. Fetch another drench. We'll pump more antibiotic into him and give him another shot of snake antiserum. What have we got to lose if he's dying anyway? You said Holly wouldn't make it. You were going to put her out of her misery. There's got to be a chance for him, Kane. Please, just give him a chance.'

He looked from her to the horse, then turned and walked away.

By late afternoon, they thought they saw an improvement, but by sundown, Walker had deteriorated. He looked barely conscious. Alex had never willingly given up on anything in her life and the anger and frustration she felt watching the horse slip deeper into the inescapable abyss made her sick. Around eight that night, he fell into a coma. His eyes were mere slits, slowly closing down on the world.

Kane sat cradling Walkers motionless head, while Alex sat in the corner of the box, tears trickling down her cheeks, her nose half-buried in a sodden tissue. Kane looked across at her. 'It's funny isn't it?' he said. 'But I never thought for one minute it would end like this. I thought he'd just wear himself out and die of old age.'

Fresh tears slid down Alex's face. She wanted to speak. She wanted to say something that would make it easier. Things like: 'At least he's had a good life.' Or, 'He knew he was loved.' Or, 'I'm so sorry, Kane, please don't sit there looking like your whole world is about to end because I just can't bear it.' All the things she wanted to say but couldn't. The words were stuck, held back by a massive lump of misery sitting smack in the middle of her chest.

'Reckon we've ridden our last rodeo, old lad,' Kane said softly into the horse's ear. He wiped a splattering of mucus from Walker's nostrils, patted his neck, filthy with dried sweat, and said in a voice hardly audible, 'Be seeing you lad.' He laid the horse's head on the straw and stood up, offering a hand to Alex and pulled her to her feet. 'Its time,' he said thickly. 'Go on up to the house.'

She could only shake her head. She watched, zombie like, as Kane raised the gun-barrel, pointing it at the horse's skull and holding it there for what seemed like an eternity. His hand was steady as he cocked the trigger - and squeezed.

The sound was deafening as it ricocheted from the walls, going on, seemingly forever, like a multi-pile up on an icy motorway - like the one that had claimed Alex's parents' months before. Walker quivered and twitched, his feet paddling through the air, before his muscles relaxed and his body sank into the shavings. A small hole in his forehead trickled blood.

Kane didn't move immediately. It was as if his feet were glued to the spot - the spot from which he had just raised a gun, pointed it at the head of the last thing on earth that linked him with his mother and wife and destroyed it, breaking the link forever. She watched as he lowered the gun, letting it hang limply in his steady hand before he walked across to the horse and knelt by its head. For seconds he said nothing, letting his eyes roam over the chestnut body, taking in the perfection, even in death, of the great animal. Then, in a low voice he said, 'It's the only way I could stop the pain.'

Alex knew that if she lived to be a hundred years old, she would still carry to her grave the vision of Kane Mitchell kneeling over his horse. She was walking away as he spoke.

'Is it OK to bury him on the island, only I reckon he'd like to see his foals born.'

Biting her lip so hard that it bled, she nodded, tears coursing down her cheeks.

Suddenly, he pulled her into the shelter of his arms, crushing her against his chest, rocking her back and forth.

'I heard a shot, is everything all right?'

Kane unwound his arms from Alex and turned to look at Peter. 'It will be,' he said. 'But for now, take Alex back to the house, Peter. I'm going to bury my horse.'

She placed a hand on his arm. 'I'll help you … '

'I'd rather it was just him and me, like the old days. He'd like that.'

Tears threatened again. Bending, she stroked Walker's neck, then turned and left the man and the horse together for the last time.

As she walked back to the house with Peter, she remembered the first time that she had seen the chestnut horse. He had rampaged up the landing ramp then, scattering mere mortals before him. And she had known way back then that Kane Mitchell would make his mark on her life, just as surely as if he had taken a red-hot iron from the camp fire and stamped his brand on her soul. She had just never been that honest with herself to admit it.

They climbed the veranda steps before Peter placed a hand on her shoulder. 'You go in Alex, and I'll go and give Kane a hand.'

She turned to face him. 'He wants to be alone, Peter.'

'I'll help him dig a grave, and then I'll leave him to it. You need a pretty big hole to bury a horse that size.'

'OK. Tell Kane I've locked the doors.'

'You've locked the doors?'

She didn't have the energy or the inclination to explain right now. 'Just tell him, Peter, he will understand.'

He waited for her to close the door and heard the key turn, and then he tracked back to the stables.

Five minutes later, as Alex watched from the window she saw the two of them come out into the night together and walk up to the top pasture carrying shovels.

Peter banged on the door two hours later and she let him in.

'How is he?' she asked, before he was even through the door.

'He's like someone who has just lost his best friend. I think gutted just about covers it,' he said, avoiding her eyes.

'Will he be all right? Shall I go to him?'

He looked at her, his mouth slightly open.

'What?'

He shook his head.

'Peter, what is it?'

He ran mud-dried hands through his hair. 'Shit! I need to say I lied to you about Kane. All those things I said about him … they're not true. He isn't a womaniser, Alex.' He nodded at the white leather sofa. 'Am I too filthy to sit down?'

She shook her head and he sat. He looked all in. For a moment she felt sorry for him.

'When I said all those things I was clutching at straws, trying to score points, trying to get you back into my messed up life. Kane is probably the straightest, most decent person I've ever met. He won't let you down like I did. He won't run out on you when the going gets tough. It wouldn't cross his mind. It just isn't in his genetic make up. The guy is sound and what's more, as far as I know, there's never been anyone since his wife.'

'Thank you.'

'Don't thank me Alex. I've been a selfish bastard, always thinking what was best for me. Even when I came here I had to cause trouble.' He took hold of her hand. 'It's just that when I saw the pair of you come in together, I could see that the two of you were an item. It was written all over your faces. I guess I was just plain jealous. Sorry.' He stood up. 'Mind if I take a shower?'

'Help yourself,' she said, 'It's down the hall on the right.'

As Peter closed the bathroom door she heard the Land Rover start up and walked out onto the veranda in time to see Kane backing it down the centre aisle between the boxes. She looked up into the dark, star speckled sky and said a silent prayer for the man she now knew she loved. A shooting star spun across the jewelled darkness lending hope to her thoughts.

The Land Rover re-appeared, chains rattling across the yard, attached to the horse's legs, dragging its rigor-mortised body across the hard cobbles. Its head hung grotesquely, leaving a trail of burnished chestnut hairs on the dry stones. The pale moonlight caught Kane's features. They looked as if they had been chiselled in granite. She went inside. It would take the best part of the night to fill in the grave.

Kane walked in around five in the morning. Alex had fallen asleep leaning on Peter's chest. As Kane stood before them, she opened her eyes. 'Come on,' he said flatly, holding out his hand to her. I'll make us both a drink.'

They sat at the kitchen table sipping coffee with a good measure of brandy added. He was watching her face as he fished into his breast pocket and dropped something onto the table. 'That's what killed my horse.'

She followed his gaze and frowned. Lying on the table were what appeared to be five small, spear-shaped objects, three inches in length, with feathered tails.

'I don't understand,' she said simply.

He picked one up turning it in his mud stained fingers. 'This, honey, is your old- fashioned, back to basics, blow dart.'

She didn't like the way he said 'honey'. The tone of it distanced him, like they had never been more than casual acquaintances. Never shared the same moment. It held no warmth.

'Are you telling me Nightwalker was darted with these things?'

'That's exactly what I'm telling you. Look, here on the point of this one, it still has hair attached. I found them in his paddock, there are probably more.'

Taking the dart from his hand, she turned it over carefully in her palm. He was right; she could see chestnut hairs still stuck to the point. 'He did this didn't he? Asak Mulligan did this?'

'Well, it wasn't Robin Hood, that's for sure,' he said sourly. 'It was bad enough thinking the poor sod died of poisoning, these things happen. But to think that some sick bastard has taken pleasure in blow darting him with poisoned arrows, it makes me sick to the gut.'

She stretched out her hand across the table touching his fingertips. 'There's nothing I can say is there?'

He moved his hand away, leaving her fingers empty. 'No.'

His one word reply left no doubt in her mind. She swallowed hard. He was blaming her – and rightly so. This whole situation was all her fault. If it wasn't for her insisting that Arthur should take her back to the shack, he would still be alive. And if it wasn't for her insisting that Jodie do something to rectify her mistake with the stallion, Kane would never have come to the island and if he'd never come Walker would still be alive. 'It's all my fault,' she said staring up into his narrowed eyes. 'It's all my fault. Everything that's happened. It's all my fault.'

The nerve in his left cheek pushed into overdrive, twitching away. 'You think so?'

'Yes.'

'And when you say it's all your fault … in triplicate … what do you mean exactly?'

Alex shook her head. She didn't know what to say. He suddenly had another edge to his voice, a hint of sarcasm or anger.

'Where do you get off thinking that everything that happens around this place is down to you?' he said deceptively calmly. 'You're not a nucleus. You don't actually control the whole planet you know. Arthur was here because he chose to be. Walker was here because I chose to bring him here and I'm here because I found something in this God forsaken place that made me remember what it was like to love someone and actually feel alive again. It was my choice. Do you get it yet, Alex?' He half-filled his empty coffee mug with brandy and swallowed it down, grimacing. 'Maybe I was wrong,' he added, screwing up his eyes as the alcohol made them water.

Her head shot up. 'Wrong?' she mumbled. 'Wrong?'

He took another shot of brandy. 'Yeah, *wrong* lady. *Maybe* I'm not ready to settle down yet. *Maybe* it's still too soon after Ellie. *Maybe* this whole situation stinks and I've only just realised it?' He tilted the brandy bottleneck towards her and added, '*Maybe* I'm not the man for you after all and just *maybe* the man for you is in there sleeping on your sofa.'

She thought she was having a heart attack as his words struck one after the other, every emphasised '*maybe,*' ripping and tearing. 'But you said you loved …'

'Loved you?' he cut in. 'Yeah, well, *maybe* you come with too much baggage lady and I've only just realised it. Or, perhaps *I* come with too much baggage and I've only just realised *that*?'

She could only sit and stare at him, her head slowly shaking. It wasn't possible. How could he mean that? It just wasn't possible. He hadn't slept or eaten for days and the brandy, which he was pouring into his mug again, had hit his head like a baseball bat. He snatched up the brandy bottle from the table, half threw his coffee mug into the sink, smashing a glass, and ploughed through the kitchen door into the hall. His bedroom door slammed shut.

Chapter 16

The radio alarm said four-thirty as Alex opened her eyes, red and swollen from crying. She'd wanted to follow Kane to his room after he'd stormed out but she'd finally managed to convince herself that he needed space. Of course he was upset. Of course he was going to doubt everything. He'd just had to shoot and bury his horse -the only thing, other than Jack, that he really had left. And not only that, he'd drunk enough brandy to pickle his brain and he wasn't capable of thinking straight. Alex knew all this, but the words *had* come out of his mouth and once out they could never be taken back. How could this have all gone so wrong so quickly?

She dragged herself out of bed and dressed, pulling on a pair of shorts and a vest, running her hand through her hair and slipping her feet into flip-flops. She had to get out to the field and get the mares in; nothing was going to be safe anymore. If Asak Mulligan could kill one horse, he could kill them all.

Peter was still asleep on the sofa where she had left him and she marvelled at the man's ability to take everything in his stride like it didn't matter – but then it didn't matter to him, did it?

The mares were crowding at the gate jostling for position. Do As I Say stood first in line, cow-kicking and snapping at the others. She cast a look of total disgust when she saw the woman, spun on her heels, barging her way through the others and took off, fly-bucking across the field. Alex cursed. The black demon had been even worse since Kane arrived. She really didn't need this today. Quickly slipping head collars on the other four, she wound them through the gate and ran them down to the stables. After seeing each one installed, she took off back to the field for Do As I Say.

The mare was now on the farthest side of the field, pawing at the loose earth where Kane had buried the stallion. She walked over to it shaking a bucket of oats, speaking in a low, calm voice. It was having none of it, tossing its head snorting, always keeping just out of catching distance. She almost touched its nose, before it reared menacingly above her and took off back towards the gate. She stood watching it go then turned her eyes towards the grave. Nothing remained of the horse except an unmarked mound of orange dirt, piled in the middle of a field in the middle of nowhere. 'It's not even home, is it lad?' she whispered to the grave. 'This wouldn't have happened in Texas, would it?' She sat on the grass and picked up a handful of dry, orange dirt, watching it trickle through her fingers, making a small heap of powdered dust. Looking up she gazed out to sea and again, despite everything that had happened, she had to accept the fact that this was the most beautiful place on earth. But the island caused so much pain and not just for her. It had always had crazy people living on it. Two people had died out there on The Reach. Isla and Kitty Mulligan hadn't stood a chance against the storm that night, just like Arthur hadn't stood a chance. She had thought about that day so much but she still hadn't managed to figure out why Arthur had died and she hadn't.

Crazy people, she thought, crazy, crazy people. And now this madman was out there somewhere, hell bent on destroying her and everything she cared for. She wished Jodie were here. Jodie would know what to do – she missed her so much. Jodie was her rock, always had been, always would be. She jumped at a movement behind her and turned to see the black mare standing there.

'If the mountain won't come to Mohammed, Mohammed must go to the mountain,' she whispered, standing up, slipping the head collar over the horse's ears and starting back across the field.

She was pushing the horse's hindquarters through the gate when her eyes caught a movement across the field near to the newly dug grave. Screwing up her eyes against the sun she climbed up onto the fence to get a better look. She knew, even before her brain could interpret what her eyes were seeing, that the figure standing on the grave was the man who had turned her life into a living night-mare.

He stood looking down towards the house, tall, cloaked head to foot, turning slightly in her direction as she almost fell backwards off the fence. The horse started sidestepping, half dragging her across the ground in a cloud of orange, swirling dust. By the time she had it under control he had gone.

She stormed into the house breathless, letting the screen door slam behind her.

Peter was just surfacing. 'What is it with people around here? Don't they know how to close doors quietly?'

He had one eye open as she panted breathlessly, 'Have you seen Kane? I need Kane. Is he up yet?'

'Haven't seen him,' he said yawning, having the good grace to cover his mouth with his hand.

'Pathetic!' she hissed under her breath as she flew down the hall. There was no answer as she banged on Kane's door, so she barged in. She was still breathing hard as she saw the un-slept-in bed. She spun, her eyes taking in the complete tidiness of the room and this time her brain had no problem taking in what she saw. The room was totally empty of Kane's possessions. Throwing open the wardrobe door so fiercely it broke the hinge, she gasped aloud. Not one single item of his clothing remained. It was as if he had never existed.

She ran down the hall, through the empty kitchen, across the veranda and down to the beach. Screwing up her eyes, she spun, trying to catch a fleeting glimpse of him high tailing it out of her life. The speedboat had gone from its mooring. She shielded her eyes from the blinding sun, frantically scanning the sea for the last physical sign of him, the last dot on the horizon. There was nothing. Nothing!

'Mitchell!' she screamed, causing waders feeding at the water's edge to take off in blind panic, settling way out on the water, where they were safe from the demented woman shrieking at them. She slowly turned a full circle, shaking her head in total disbelief. He couldn't have gone. He wouldn't. He'd said he loved her. Yes, but that was before Peter returned. It was before his horse was murdered. It was before he must have realised, in retrospect, that the woman he thought he loved was more trouble than she was worth. Too high a price to pay. It would have had to be a strong, unbreakable love to survive that. The cold hard truth of it all was – he was gone. The man who had walked into her life, broken down her barriers and made her believe the unbelievable, was gone. She collapsed on to the white, hot sand, rolling over onto her back, as tears slid from her eyes and dried on her flushed cheeks. Her whole world was falling apart at the seams and Kane Mitchell, the man who had promised her the world, had walked out on her, leaving her with an ex-lover and something from the depths of hell.

When the tears ran dry, she dragged herself to her feet, dusted off the sand and with a final glance at the empty boat mooring, and with all thoughts of children riding fat little ponies evicted from her head, walked back to the house.

Peter looked up from the table, fork raised halfway to his mouth. 'God, you look awful. What the hell has happened?'

She waved a hand ineffectually, not wanting to give Peter the pleasure of having been right. He'd said Kane would walk. At least, that's what he'd said before he'd had a touch of humanity and changed into Kane's best mate, helping him dig a grave and singing the cowboy's praises. When she didn't answer, Peter repeated the words.

She shrugged her shoulders and turned her back on him before flicking on the kettle. She focused on the kitchen wall, letting her eyes run along the perfectly straight line of grouting, determined not to let Peter see the state she was in.

'Alex?'

She clutched at the work surface, closed her eyes to stop her tears returning and said in a whisper, 'What?'

'I said what the hell has happened? You look dreadful.'

She turned to face him.

Peter put down his knife and fork and pushed his plate away. 'Oh Lord. What is it? Can it be that bad?'

Alex placed a hand to her mouth to stop her lips from trembling and nodded.

'It's not another horse is it? The thing that killed Kane's stallion wasn't contagious, was it?'

Alex shook her head and sniffed before reaching for the roll of kitchen paper, ripping off half a dozen sheets and blowing her nose. 'No, it's not another horse,' she mumbled through the paper. 'It's Kane.'

'Kane? Kane's dying?'

Alex threw the tissue into the bin and snapped, 'No, stupid. Kane isn't dying, not unless he's hit a reef in the boat he's stolen.'

Peter pulled a face, clearly showing he had no idea what she was talking about.

'You were right, Peter, he's gone ... stolen my boat and taken a leaf out of your book.'

The expression on Peter's face said he was going to need more information than that. 'What do you mean, gone? Why has he stolen your boat?'

'To get off the bloody island and away from me, that's why.'

'Why would he want to do that?'

'I don't know. You tell me. Why did you bugger off?'

'Do we have to go there again? There's only so many times I can say I'm sorry. I told you, I got scared, everybody gets scared now and then ... well, everybody except gutsy, old indomitable you! You're the exception to the rule, obviously.'

Alex took some heart in the fact that Peter didn't really know her, if that's what he thought.

'Maybe Kane's gone over to the mainland and he'll be back later. Perhaps he just needed a bit of space, you know, after what's-it's-name, died ... his horse.'

'He wouldn't leave me with you and besides, he wouldn't take every possession, would he? There's nothing left to even suggest that he was ever here. You could let C.S.I loose in his room and even they wouldn't find anything. No, he's gone all right. It's all become too much, and I can't say I blame him.'

'What's become too much, Alex, and why do I get this niggling feeling that you're not telling me everything? There's more going on here, isn't there? Why did you lock yourself in last night?'

Alex snapped off more kitchen roll and scrubbed at her eyes. Where should she begin? Start at the very beginning? If she started at the beginning, Peter might also leave and then what? But if she didn't start at the beginning he might think she was crazier than she really was. 'It's a long story, Peter,' she said.

'So the sooner you begin, the sooner I'll know what the problem is and perhaps if I know what the problem is I can sort it.'

She didn't have him down as a great sorter of problems, more the instigator but what did she have to lose? She crossed the kitchen and Peter pulled out a chair for her. When she was seated he took her hand and said, 'Go for it and don't leave anything out, except the bit about Kane leaving because he wouldn't do that.'

Alex felt like picking up Peter's plate with the cold congealed egg, half a sausage and two slices of fried bread and hitting him over the head with it, anything to knock some sense and realisation into him. 'OK,' she said, 'I'll try not to dwell on the fact that he's a lying, womanising pig, who, when the going gets tough just packs up his cowboy boots and walks. But I warn you, Peter, after I've told you, you'll probably think me mad.'

The expression on his face, as he tried not to grin, told her that he already thought that. She took several deep breaths and began.

'You need to get the police back here,' he said seriously, when she had finished and the coffee pot was empty.

'There's no point. They found nothing when I was in hospital and Kane and Jack have scoured the island too many times to remember. It's as if Asak Mulligan is made of air and not flesh and blood. He leaves no trace, no footsteps, nothing.'

Peter's face was perfectly serious as he said quietly, 'Perhaps the Police and Kane were looking in all the wrong places.'

She frowned. 'Well, where are the right places, Poirot?'

'The right *place* -' he corrected, '- Singular not plural. The right *place* is close to *you*.'

A shiver ran the length of her spine, making the hair stand up on her neck.

'Sorry,' he said, squeezing her hand, which he still held. 'But to me it's pretty obvious. Asak Mulligan seems out to destroy you, so it makes sense to look near you. If you want to catch a mouse, you bait the trap with what the mouse wants … cheese … or Mars Bar. If you want to catch Asak Mulligan you bait the trap with what he wants … you!'

Alex considered briefly how Peter knew so much about mouse bait before saying, 'But it doesn't make sense. Why kill Nightwalker? Everything else has been directed at me: the ripped blouse, Holly out on the Reach, the fire at the shack that killed Arthur. It wasn't intended to kill Arthur, he just happened to be with me at the time ... wrong place, wrong time ... but the stallion? It doesn't add up.'

Peter looked deep in thought before saying, 'Try this for size. You said he moved with the speed of a much younger man, yes?'

She nodded. She'd only seen him once but one minute he was there, standing on Walker's grave and the next he'd gone, as if a breeze had lifted him away.

'Well, regardless of his speed and athletic ability, in reality he's still a sixty-year old man. At that age, I'd expect certain faculties to be wearing out. Like ... *eyesight.*'

'Yes, so, do you actually have a thread here? Is this leading somewhere because I don't get it if it is?'

He looked her straight in the eyes and speaking very slowly said, 'Eyesight, Alex. He's had Polly once ...'

'Holly!'

'Holly ... he's had Holly once ... what colour is she?'

'She's chestnut.'

'What colour is ... was Kane's horse?'

'Chestnut.'

They stared at each other while his words sunk slowly in. 'Shit!' Alex exploded. 'You mean he got the wrong horse.'

Peter nodded. 'That's exactly what I mean. He made a mistake ... same colour, wrong horse.'

'That's it, Peter! He wouldn't have seen a horse until they arrived on the island. *I* could never make that mistake, but *he* could. Christ, Peter, I never knew you were so clever.'

He grinned, his boyish charm evident.

'I'm going to scour this place until a find a phone charger that works, get these phones working and then I'm going to call the police.'

'I thought you said that was pointless, that they'd never find him.'

'*Kane* said they wouldn't find him. That was *his* opinion. Kane's gone, and as far as I'm concerned, his opinions and barefaced lies have gone with him. Besides, there's no longer a choice. This thing has gone too far; it's out of our hands, beyond our capabilities. They can burn the entire island down to its grass roots if that's what it's going to take to catch Mulligan.'

Peter simply nodded.

'I can't find a charger anywhere,' she said, fifteen minutes later, equally amazed and annoyed. 'I've looked everywhere. They're gone. She dodged under Peter's arm and sat down at the table.

He joined her. 'I looked briefly but I couldn't find mine either, I must have been right the first time when I said I'd left it on the mainland.'

'Oh God! You don't think he's been in the house and taken them do you?'

'No, Alex. If he can't tell the difference between two horses, he's hardly likely to be up to speed with today's technology, is he? He's not out there linked to the Internet or looking up his Abo' cronies on Facebook, is he now?'

She wasn't sure; he seemed quite adept at other things. 'So you don't think he's been in the house then?'

'Don't be silly.'

'Don't tell me not to be silly, Peter, he's been in before,' she wailed, looking nervously at the door, half expecting him to walk through it. 'I've been living this nightmare a lot longer than you.'

'We'll think of something. What time do you usually turn out the horses?'

'Five. Six. Why?'

'I'm going to have to help you. Kane was right, you can't be left alone. Until we discover what's happened to Kane you'll just have to accept my help, like it or not.'

She ignored the mention of his name. 'You'll help?'

'OK, rub it in. I'm a useless, selfish shit, who wouldn't know one end of a horse from the other. Go on, say it.'

When she merely looked at him with raised eyebrows, he added cheekily, 'Yeah, I know. I think I'm going to have to go some to get back into your good books, aren't I?'

She didn't answer him. It wasn't necessary. Peter knew the score.

'Do you think it's safe to put them out?' he said.

Alex shook her head. 'I don't know. I'd decided earlier that it wasn't. That's why I was out at the crack of dawn bringing them in. That's when I saw him. But now, after what you've said, he probably thinks that he's already killed my horse, so if I keep her hidden, she should be safe. And besides, they're fit thoroughbred horses, if I don't turn them out for a while they'll go off their heads …and…if we sit up there with them …just sit and watch them for an hour? Could we do that?'

Peter smiled and squeezed her hand reassuringly. 'Of course, honey. Whatever makes you happy.'

Alex yanked her hand free. 'I hardly think it will make me happy, Peter ... and don't call me honey! I never want to hear that word again.'

Holly stood expectantly at the loosebox door, scraping the ground. She looked confused as the others were led out and she remained. Do As I Say lunged at her in passing, snapping white teeth, missing her ear by a fraction.

Alex cussed loudly, 'Damn black demon! Why didn't he take her with him?'

Peter shouted over the back of Fly, narrowly avoiding the black mare as she careered backwards. 'Don't they still hang horse thieves in Texas?'

'Exactly.'

'I see.'

The black mare was rearing in the aisle, threatening to crunch Alex's head in as she shouted, 'You go on ahead, Peter, I'll follow you just as soon as I can get this thing pointed in the right direction!'

He led the two horses out and they behaved very well for him, considering he had no experience with horses. He reached the paddock safely and even managed to turn them loose, watching as they cantered off, long legs sailing over the sun bleached grass, fly-bucking and kicking.

Leaning against the fence, he watched as Alex led the other two horses towards him, marvelling at how good she looked in shorts cut up to her backside. Suddenly he slapped his neck as an insect bit deep and, pinching it between his forefinger and thumb, pulled it off his neck and peered at it.

Alex drew level, laughing at his startled expression. 'What's wrong, Peter? Found something that actually likes you enough to bite?'

'Alex?'

'Yes,' she said, still laughing as she watched the other two horses galloping off across the field.

He turned his eyes to look at her, scowling, 'Alex, what's this?'

Her smile died on her lips as he opened his hand and an inch long dart rolled across the palm of his hand and fell to the ground. Her face dropped. 'Shit, Peter, where the hell did you find that?'

He grimaced. 'In my neck. I've just pulled it out. I thought it was a bug of some sort.' He rubbed at his neck, massaging it, trying to stop the numbing feeling that was fast setting in.

'For Christ's sake, Peter, don't rub it,' Alex snapped. 'Get back to the house. GO! She slammed the gate and locked it before running to catch up with him. He was almost running himself.

'Don't run, Peter, it pushes the poison around your blood stream quicker. Slow down.'

He slowed down, almost coming to a complete halt, and turned to look at her through startled eyes. 'Poison? What poison? Shit? Is that what this is? The same poison that killed Kane's ... '

She grabbed his arm before he could finish, towing him along, gathering speed with every stride. 'Forget what I just said, Peter ... *RUN!*'

She slammed the house door and locked it. Screaming at Peter to lie flat out, she tore through the house to the bathroom, wrenching open the cabinet door, scattering tubes, jars and bottles, springing backwards as glass smashed in the sink and showered her. She said a hurried silent prayer for Jodie's insight, in making sure that anti-serum was kept virtually in every available place in the house and out buildings, and flew back along the hall.

She sank to her knees at the side of the sofa and rammed the hypodermic into the glass vial, drawing up the colourless liquid to the top and tapping the syringe until any air bubbles surfaced and popped, as fragile as promises. Then, breathlessly, noticing that he had already broken out in a cold, tacky sweat said, 'Push your sleeve up, Peter, *quickly*, we don't have much time.'

'What's that?' he yelped as the needle pierced deep into his soft muscle.

'Serum.'

He smiled faintly before his face creased into involuntary twitching. 'Thank God. I'm not going to die, am I, Alex? I know I've been an utter shit but I don't deserve to die, do I?'

Before she could answer, his eyes fluttered briefly and he passed out. She launched the syringe at the wall and screamed, then, watched horrified as Peter's colour drained away from his body as surely as if someone had pulled a plug on his blood supply, and he fell into a deep state of unconsciousness. She clamped her hand over her mouth before she started to scream and couldn't stop.

Two minutes later, she released her hand. 'Don't lose it,' she told herself aloud. 'Don't lose it. Peter is probably going to die right here in front of your eyes but it won't achieve anything freaking out and acting like a stupid female. You can cope with this. You can cope. Take deep breaths. Take deep breaths. Breath!'

Peter looked the colour of chalk. His chest wall hardly moved as his breathing rate decreased.

'This is *not* going to beat me,' she told his motionless, cold body, checking his pulse and hardly finding one. She couldn't take her eyes away from his handsome, boyish face. It looked marble white now and felt like ice to her touch. She had no idea what the dart had on it, all she could do was inject him with anti-snake serum and pray to God that it might do some good. It had to be better than doing nothing at all she told herself. She smoothed the hair from his forehead and couldn't help thinking that he looked as if he'd already died and the embalmer had done his best.

As night fell and the house settled with its usual creaks and groans, Alex started to pace the floor. She desperately needed a shower but she didn't dare leave Peter in case he vomited and choked to death while she wasn't there. And another thing – he might be comatose but at least she didn't feel quite so alone and scared with his still body slumped in the middle of the lounge like an island in this sea of madness.

She poured herself a tumbler of brandy and took a good gulp. The last time she'd seen Kane Mitchell *he* was hitting the brandy, angry and cruel, hurt and bitter, questioning his love for her. She drained the glass and poured another. At least if Asak Mulligan came for her tonight she wouldn't feel much. Hadn't they used alcohol in *the old days* as a sedative? Perhaps she'd get so drunk that none of this would matter. No worries about weak, spineless ex-boyfriends, or lying cowboys, or lost babies. She swirled the brandy and stared deeply into the bottom of the glass. She would have to be paralytic for the baby thing not to matter … and then there was the lying cowboy. How drunk would she have to get for *that* not to matter? She glanced across at Peter. Poor Peter. She moved to sit on the floor beside him. He still looked critical, even through what was fast becoming hazy vision. She took his frozen hand and placed it on her heart. 'Take strength from me, Peter,' she whispered. 'Please don't die. I know I said some dreadful things. I'm sorry. You hurt me so much but I promise, if you can just pull through I'll forgive you for everything ... well ... for most of it ... well ... OK, I'll forgive period. Just DO NOT SODDING DIE!' There was no response.

Around two in the morning she fetched the duvet from Kane's room and drifted into a deep, alcohol induced sleep, with the familiar smell of him wrapped around her.

Chapter 17

In the early hours of the morning, when all bright ideas seem perfectly workable, Alex had decided to stay safely locked inside the house until Jodie and Jack got back. In the cold, grey light of day, reality struck and she realised that Jack and Jodie could be away for days, weeks or even months. She had to leave Peter and the security of the house - there was no choice. The horses needed to be brought in from the field, if in fact they were still alive, Mac needed exercising, and the boxes needed mucking out. Mucking out wasn't vital but if she was out there, she figured she might as well do it.

She made a pot of strong, treacle-consistency coffee, downed two cups, and then resolutely pulled on her boots. She rummaged noisily through the cutlery drawer until she found the black handled bread knife and a small, sharp vegetable knife. The inscription on the handle said, *Made to last a lifetime.* 'Yours or mine?' she said sardonically, shoving the small knife into the pocket of her trousers and brandishing the bread knife in front of her as she turned the key in the kitchen door. They had never bothered locking any doors until just recently and it made her angry to think that it was necessary now.

The warm, bright sunshine blinded her temporarily as she stepped out on to the veranda, looking all around her. A slight breeze rustled the potted palms and cordylines and a flock of Rosella's lifted from the house roof and winged their way across the paddock to the nearby Acacias. That was a good sign, she told herself. If any one had been skulking around the house, the birds wouldn't have been there. She made her way nervously to the stables with the knife gripped so tightly that her hand ached. Grabbing head collars, she jogged up to the paddock, caught the horses and ran them back to the stables. For once in her life Do As I Say didn't play the fool and she had them boxed within ten minutes. Locking herself in she set about mucking out and had all the boxes done in just under an hour. Then she tacked up Mac, unlocked the stable door and took him out into the sunshine. He was almost cantering on the spot as she tried to mount him, climbing up onto the fence and jumping across onto his wide back. He was more than ready for the exercise and took off at a hand-canter, bucking and plunging into the bridle. She guided him to the water's edge and let him go, bounding forward into a tireless gallop, splashing and jumping the waves as they broke on the sand.

She knew as she reigned in the horse and her brain went into overdrive that she had to face the facts. Kane had gone. Peter was, in all probability, going to die. She couldn't get off the island, because Kane had stolen the speedboat and she couldn't get help onto the island because the phones were dead. She had in her possession a small knife and a large knife, tucked precariously into the waistband of her trousers. If Asak Mulligan appeared, she would take one of them and thrust it into his evil, wicked heart. And *they* were the cold hard facts as Alex saw them.

Peter was exactly where she had left him. His condition hadn't improved, if anything it appeared to have worsened slightly. He seemed colder – if it was possible to be colder than ice and still be alive? She pulled the duvet around him and pumped another full syringe of serum into his arm, not knowing if it would kill or cure him. It wasn't so long ago that she would have felt some kind of masochistic pleasure sticking needles into the man that had been responsible for the last six, painful years of her life. But things had now moved on from there. Alex was slowly coming to terms with the fact that there was absolutely nothing that she, or anyone else for that matter, could do to change the past. She filled another syringe and pumped it into his other arm. 'Sorry Peter. It's for your own good and at this moment in time it's all I can think of. We have to hang on somehow until Jodie and Jack get back. They're our only chance of getting out of this alive.' Peter remained impervious. She envied him. At least he was out of it.

She busied herself preparing fresh fruit for her breakfast, slicing, cubing and chopping until she had a small mountain of the stuff sitting on the chopping board in front of her. She popped a piece of fruit into her mouth but it was all she could do to swallow it, so she swept it all into a bowl and put it in the fridge. She stood with the door open, taking several deep breaths and letting the icy air coat her skin. Words were beginning to form in her brain, making a sentence that she didn't want to acknowledge. She closed the fridge door and stepped away, as the thought manifested. *What if you aren't strong enough for this?*

Convincing herself that keeping busy was the way to go, she set about vacuuming the whole house, dusting and bleaching everything in sight, popping back to check on Peter every fifteen minutes or so. At lunchtime, she locked the door and ran to the stables with the bread knife clutched tightly in her right hand, to check on the horses.

After a fish lunch, that she really didn't want but had convinced herself she should eat, if only to keep up her strength, she blitzed Kane's bedroom. She tore the sheets from his bed, shaking them in case he'd left a note and it had slipped from view. She checked beneath the bed. Double checked the drawers and triple checked the wardrobe but there was nothing. She looked around the room and tears pricked her eyes. 'It's like you were never here,' she whispered. 'Like I imagined the whole thing.' Her gaze fell across the bed. Kane's bed. The bed he had carried her naked body to and …

Around four in the afternoon the sunny sky darkened and a gusting wind blew up off the sea. The radio warned of an approaching storm, estimated to hit the small group of islands east of the mainland around early evening.

Peter's condition was unchanged as she locked him in, grabbed the bread knife and ran to the stables to set the horses fare for the night. By the time she had fed them, skipped out and ran a general check, it was six-thirty and the wind had increased to near hurricane proportions.

As she mounted the veranda, a mini whirlwind snatched up a potted palm, rolling it sideways until it fell from the pot and took off like a witch's vacant broomstick, leaving compost and smashed leaves in its wake. The door flew out of her hand as she turned the key, sending gusts into the living room, blowing Peter's hair across his face as he lay motionless and cold on the sofa. Leaning against the door with all her weight, she managed to close and lock it. She almost leapt out of her skin as thunder peeled, followed ten seconds later by a whiplash streak of lightning. 'Ten miles,' she said, counting. 'And knowing my luck, approaching fast!'

The sky darkened to the colour of black treacle as she ran through the house switching on every light and lamp. She didn't want any dark, black corners where Asak Mulligan could lurk or where he could hide like a crazy animal about to pounce on its defenceless pray. Her common sense told her it wasn't possible, but her mind was capable of playing nasty little tricks and she really didn't need it.

Miraculously, the centre of the storm seemed to miss the island and veered away out to sea, leaving behind it a strong blustering wind that hurled itself against the house like a screaming banshee, intent on exposing and destroying anything that was weak and vulnerable.

She tended to Peter, washing his face and pushing his hair back out of his eyes. He didn't look any better. She considered giving him another shot of serum but doubted it would do any good. For all she knew she could have already sealed his fate by giving him what she had. If by some miracle she survived this, she would probably be imprisoned for murder. She sat by his side, holding his lifeless hand, remembering the times they had spent together in the past. She had thought then that they were the happiest, most precious times of her life, filled with love and laughter. But that was before Kane Mitchell had ridden roughshod into her life, shattering all that had gone before like the proverbial 'bull in a china shop.' Why had he had to come along, making all others pale into insignificance? Why hadn't anyone even come close to taking her to the heady heights his loving had? She tried to keep such thoughts from her head but it was hopeless. She only had to think about the man and her body responded, wanting to throw off its clothes and lay down before him in unashamed surrender. How was she going to live the rest of her life without him? She really didn't need to be thinking like that right now.

Turning her attention back to Peter, looking into his childlike, innocent face, she couldn't help but wonder if there might be a possibility of taking him back into her life – if he survived. So, what if he did only want her for her money? Money wasn't everything, was it? Kane hadn't wanted her for her money, had he? What *had* he wanted her for? Where was he now? Shacked up in some hotel somewhere, driving some other poor, sad woman to the point of sexual insanity; kissing her mouth, touching her breasts, sliding his experienced hands between her hot, waiting thighs? The thoughts made her want to cry - but she wouldn't.

Around midnight two things happened. The storm that had obligingly side stepped the island earlier, doubled back, hitting the island with a renewed frenzy. And the generator blew, plunging the house into total darkness. She sat perfectly still for a full five minutes talking to Peter, telling him everything was going to be fine, while she crossed the fingers of her left hand behind her back. The generator had never given any trouble in the past and she couldn't stop her brain from telling her that someone was out there tampering with it. And, that she knew who that someone was.

Her heart revved into overdrive, sitting there in the pitch black, lit only intermittently by blinding lightning that zigzagged across the room, sending menacing shadows dancing from wall to wall. As the next shaft of lightning crossed Peter's face, she thought she saw him twitch. He looked like Frankenstein's monster, plugged in and rigged up for recharging.

Thunder crashed on the roof, barely split in time by white, flashing spears of lightning. Cold sweat glistened on her skin as the base-drum roll of the thunder shook the house's very foundations. She dropped her face into shaking hands, praying it would go away. She had always hated thunder, ever since she had seen lightning strike an old oak, running down it and along the barbed wire fence, killing twenty heifers that stood sheltering from the storm. They had dropped dead where they had stood, their noses burned and charred, grass still in their mouths. Another blast hit the house head on; this time there was no split second delay before the lightning forked through the windows. It felt as if the storm was sitting on the roof, as crash after crash bore down, followed immediately by lightning.

As the light gutted the room, a shadow crossed the outside door. Another crash, another flash and the silhouette was still there. Grabbing the bread knife she scrambled to Peter's side as a strangled sound came from his chest. She had never heard a death rumble, but to her it sounded like it might be just that. 'Don't die Peter, please, for Christ's sake, don't die,' she begged, against his cold mouth. 'I'll keep my promise. I'll forgive you for absolutely everything.' Her eyes, wider than saucers, were glued to the door as the handle turned, twisting to the right and pausing before twisting in the opposite direction. In one blinding second she knew – Asak Mulligan was outside the door and he had come for her.

Adrenaline and fear flooded through her body, tearing along her veins, each fighting the other, screaming at her to run for her life but holding her grounded as fear conquered and paralysed her. The handle turned again and in the brief break from the storm, from the stables, she heard a horse scream. Another crash, a flash, and again the horse whinnied. She was shaking so badly she was in real danger of cutting her own throat with the knife clasped rigidly against her breasts. Again, the sound of a squealing horse cut across the thunder. She sat shaking, rocking, with her heart thudding in her ears, staring at the door, waiting for Asak Mulligan to gain access and kill her.

She didn't feel it happen. There was no thought in her head that told her to do it but some inexplicable emotion dragged her to her feet and carried her across the room to the door. The silhouette had gone. The horse still screamed across the thunder. Alex raised her head and took a long, steadying breath and then took another. Whatever was out there wasn't going to kill anything else. No bastard was ever going to take anything else away from her again. Kane Mitchell was the last loss she would ever have to get over. Lightning struck.

Slowly she turned the key, letting herself out onto the veranda, awash, looking like something from the Titanic, before it upended and sank slowly into the freezing waters of the North Atlantic. She wouldn't let her head consider how many people had died that day. Splashing through it, shielding her eyes against the sleeting rain, she leapt down the steps and ran for the stables.

The lock was still in place as she fumbled with dripping, shaking hands to get the key in and turn it. It wouldn't turn. Frantically, with water pouring off her nose, she peered at the key. It was the wrong one! She had risked her life-threatening dash with the wrong key!

With eyes flitting from side to side, like a ventriloquist's manic doll, she spun to run back to the house – and stopped dead.

There, less than ten metres away, stood a cloaked and hooded figure.

Alex's fingers tightened around the handle of the knife as she slowly raised it against her thudding heart. There was no introduction necessary. Before her stood the man that had killed Arthur, who had maliciously darted and killed Kane's horse, who had, in all probability, killed Peter and the man who would now kill her. Seconds seemed to turn into minutes as they stared at each other, silently deciding who would be the cat and who would be the mouse. Who would run first and who would give chase? Alex raised her head, narrowing her eyes against the beating rain. She had never run away from anything in her life and she didn't intend to start now, even though her common sense told her that the odds were not stacked in her favour. The wind lifted an odour of bad meat, wet animal and all things horrid and bore it towards her, causing her to take a backward step. She felt the barn door, cold and wet against her spine. Thunder cracked. Lightning forked. Alex turned her head away from the flash. When she looked back, Asak Mulligan was walking away.

She stood rooted to the spot, watching him go. Watching as he swirled the animal-skin cloak and nonchalantly, chose to leave her standing there, shaking and terrified. Anger bubbled up from inside her and surfaced as a renting scream that cut through the thunder and the rain. The very sound of it shook her, and her feet, seemingly of their own accord, moved forwards. She had survived being burnt alive. She had survived the vast South Pacific. What had Kane said? *This crazy woman has more grit than anyone else I've ever known.* She raised the knife defiantly, the blade flashing in the blue light thrown by the lightning and took a deep, deep breath. She could do this. She could definitely, positively, do this. She had survived everything else. She could and would survive this. Her free hand slid up to her shoulder and she closed her eyes. 'I've never needed you as much as I need you now,' she whispered. 'Please help me. I don't think I can do this without you.' She opened her eyes. There had to be an angel sitting on her shoulder – there just had to be.

Suddenly, as if unseen celestial wings had lifted her, she was running, following Asak Mulligan's bare footprints along the beach and towards The Reach, before the shifting sand filled them in and there was no longer any proof that he existed. He was moving fast, now and then barely in sight as he hurried beneath the storm. Alex threw her weight into the butting wind, stronger on the exposed beach, rubbing at her eyes, blinking against the stinging sand, determined to keep him in sight. She couldn't lose him now or he'd disappear back into the depths of the inner terrain, regroup his thoughts and strike when she least expected it. 'Dear God,' she said aloud, risking a furtive glance at the black sky. 'Please don't let me lose him. Please don't let me lose him.' As she lowered her eyes, she stumbled, dropping the knife. Frantically, she fell to her knees, hands flailing through the sand until they closed around the blade. When she stood up, he'd gone.

'No!' she screamed into the wind, as it whipped her voice away along the beach and turned it into nothing. A break in the clouds gave her a chance to scout ahead but he was nowhere to be seen. She spun a full circle as panic overtook her. Where was he? She didn't understand how he could just disappear like that. She deviated towards the rolling sea. If he appeared out of the undergrowth, at least she would see him coming before he killed her. At least there would be a choice. She could run into the sea and this time she wouldn't swim for shore. This time she would let the waves claim her – but only if there was no other choice.

The storm was turning now, moving out to sea, peripheral flashes lighting the horizon in shades of grey and silver. Black clouds, determined to follow the storm, scuttled across the moon, intermittently releasing shafts of light along the beach. The knife glinted in her hand as she walked on. '*This crazy woman has more grit than anyone I've ever known. This crazy woman has more grit than anyone I've ever known,*' she chanted, through trembling lips, ramming positivity into her brain. Her eyes were glued on the rock mass as she turned the point and came face to face with the Reach. Furious waves reared and plunged, their foam-flecked backs hitting with such ferocity that they bounced up fifteen metres high. It had never looked more terrifying. Her hand tightened around the knife just as the wind lifted her off her feet, spun her around and dropped her where she stood. She scrambled to her feet before the knife was snatched from her hands and the dark night turned even blacker.

Chapter 18

The threatening roar of the sea filled her ears as she slowly regained consciousness and sat up rubbing her head. Water swelled all around her in angry drifts and under-currents. The storm had gone, taking away the thunderclouds, allowing the moon to shine through. She struggled to her feet, trying to get her bearings. Then it hit her. She was on the Reach and there was no way off. Inching to the rock edge she peered down into the rushing, indigo water. Something touched her shoulder and she spun, to come face to face with her knife – and Asak Mulligan.

He towered above her, his eyes hidden beneath the hood of the pungent cloak, making stabbing gestures with the knife, slashing and grinning, following her as she jumped back to avoid the blade.

'Stay away from me you murdering bastard,' she threatened. 'I know who you are and I know what you've done.' She heard him chuckle and she knew then that she was of no consequence to him. He was as insane as she had always known he would be. When she couldn't back any further he grabbed her, his bony fingers fastening around her arms like vices, forcing her to her knees. Effortlessly, he threw her onto her back and climbed across her drenched body before grabbing her vest and ripping it open. His black eyes fed on her flesh as he raised the knife above his head. Alex screamed and lashed out, knocking the knife out of his hand and watching as it winged its way across the plateau and into the sea. He growled and fell on top of her, clawing at her body while she struggled beneath him, her hand trying to free the knife she'd put into her trouser pocket. Her fingers closed around it and as his hands circled her throat, she drove it down hard into the back of his sinewy neck. She heard him gasp and saw blood spurt. She drove it in again and again, screaming each time it crunched into bone. 'That's for Arthur. And that's for Walker. And that's for Peter.' He grabbed her hand, wrenched the knife from it and cast it into the sea.

'You crazy, murdering bastard!' she screamed, striking out with her fists, punching at anything she could contact. 'You crazy, murdering bastard!' He fell off her and she scrambled to her feet, staggering and splashing across the flooding platform towards the sea. At the edge, she hesitated, scanning the water, desperately seeking an area that wasn't interjected by rock. There was no such place. As he closed the distance between them, she turned, saw him approaching, and prepared to jump. As she lifted from the rock, he caught her, dragging her back by her hair, shaking her like a mad dog with a rag doll, before forcing her to kneel before him. Alex stared as the hood lifted in the wind and slipped from his head. For the first time she saw Asak Mulligan and she felt her thudding heart miss a beat. This was no man. This was an animal. An animal that used to be a man. 'Don't you have any remorse?' she screamed at the wizened face. 'Don't you feel the slightest bit sorry for killing everything in sight?'

Asak Mulligan threw back his head and emitted a terrifying howl before reaching down and placing his hands around her neck. She grabbed his wrists, pulling at them, digging her nails into his flesh, trying to free them but he was too strong. She closed her eyes, feeling her blood pulsing beneath his bony fingers. She was going to die. Her whole life had led to this moment and in a moment it would all be over. She wouldn't get the chance to put right all the things that she'd got so wrong. She wouldn't leave this world unburdened and pure. She silently prayed that God would take her to him and that the first face she might see would be Arthur's and that he would tell her he forgave her. And that Jack would look after Jodie and hold her close when she cried for her friend who had died and left her.

As Asak Mulligan's scrawny fingers closed tighter over her larynx and she could no longer feel the pulse in her veins, a deafening blast filled her ears. Louder than the booming waves. Louder than the thunder. Warm, sticky fluid splattered against her face, running into her eyes, and suddenly she was falling backwards, blown away by the blast. She hit the ground rolling, until jutting rock stopped her. She dragged herself onto her knees and back onto her heels, coughing, spitting, rubbing at her face, trying to clear her eyes. She stared, firstly at her hands covered in blood and then through her opened fingers and to the sight of Asak Mulligan's body floating away. Blood gushed from what used to be his head. A wave broke over him and took him under. She couldn't scream. She was way beyond that now. She had to get off the Reach – away from his body that was somewhere beneath the water. You could never trust these situations. The evil murderer always reared his head for another onslaught. They always launched a final attack. They were never *quite* dead. She wasn't going to fall for that. She turned towards the horizon, took a deep breath and in the split second before jumping, a voice rang out.

'Don't jump, Alex! Not that way!'

It hit her full on, more powerful than any wave and she reeled away from the edge, splashing and falling through the water. Again the voice rang out, 'Turn around, Alex! Come this way! Come to the edge! Reach out your hand to me!'

She spun blindly, three full circles, to face the voice and burst into tears. 'Kane?'

The moon drifted out from behind the last straggling storm cloud, lighting up the rock, as surely as if someone had turned on a spotlight and there, standing centre stage, on the other side of the water he stood. She had never in all her life seen anything that looked half so good.

'Alex, come on honey, we haven't got any time left,' he called across the whirlpool. 'Come to the edge. Reach out for my hand. You have to jump, now!'

She stared across at him. In his right hand he carried a gun. As she watched, his fingers lost their hold and the gun slipped from his hand and into the water.

'Reach across, Alex. We have to get you out of here *now*!'

She stared across the churning water. 'Where have you been?' she sobbed. 'Where the *hell* have you been? How dare you leave me here like this? You said you'd never leave me.'

'First things first, honey. Reach out your hand.'

'I can't,' she cried. 'It's too far.'

'No it isn't. You can do it. Try.'

'I can't do it!' she screamed against the rush of water. 'It's too far, Kane. I can't do it'

'No it isn't, honey. Try harder.'

'No! Isla and Kitty Mulligan couldn't make it and I can't. It's too far.'

'I've got longer arms than Isla,' he chided, watching the wave about to break behind her. 'Come on, honey, reach out. Trust me. I swear to God I'll never ask you do another thing as long as I live, but you've got to do it *now*.'

She stretched out her hand until every muscle screamed, and then, as the wave broke behind her, she jumped.

Their fingers touched, grabbed and held. Kane caught her, pulling her into his body with such ferocity that he almost broke her ribs.

'Where the hell have you been?' she sobbed again, flattened against his pounding chest. 'Where the hell have you been?'

'Anger's good,' he said straight-faced, the breaking wave mirrored in his eyes. 'You'll need that to get us through this. Take a deep breath, Alex.'

'What?'

'Take a deep breath.'

As the wave hit them, he cursed. It bounced them off the rock with an unstoppable force, hurling them into the sea, before it closed over them and they hit the reef. Thrashing out against the spinning turbulence, deafened by the water's apocalyptic roar, they kicked out for the light above. Together they shot through the surface, bobbing up and down in the swell of the waves. Blood trickled from Alex's forehead where she'd hit the reef. She attempted to wipe it away, but missed her aim, disorientated from the blow. Kane turned to look at the next oncoming wave. Alex followed his gaze.

As the waved rolled over them, Kane slipped his fingers under Alex's belt and pulled her under before the spin hit them. This time they didn't hit the reef and they surfaced in the wake of the wave. Kane tightened his hold on Alex's belt, pulling her away from jutting rock. He lifted a hand and gently wiped the blood from her head. She closed her eyes at his touch and didn't open them.

'Alex? Alex!'

She couldn't answer him; couldn't open her eyes. Her body had been running on pure adrenaline since leaving the house. The supply had finally run out. A great tiredness, like she had never known, swept over her and before Kane could catch her, she slipped beneath the water.

'No!' he yelled, beating the water with his fist. 'For Christ's sake!' He dived, grabbing her sinking body and pulled her to the surface, where he closed his mouth over hers and forced air into her lungs. For two minutes, nothing happened, then she spluttered, coughed up seawater and opened her eyes.

'C'mon, Alex. You have to stay awake.'

She didn't want to stay awake. It was all, finally, too much. She couldn't play the heroine any longer. The desire to conquer all was gone. She would dismiss her angel and someone else could have it. It had served her well.

Kane shook her until she opened her eyes and looked at him. 'I'm not losing you now, for Christ's sake. Wake up woman! Fight!'

'I'm sick of fighting,' she mumbled, the words barely coherent.

Kane shook her again. 'You'll never be sick of fighting. That's what you do. That's what you're all about. That's the one thing you were put on this earth to do.'

'People can change.'

'Not you.' He pushed a hand through her wet hair until it stood erect, then he placed a finger beneath her chin and tilted her face, his eyes boring deep into hers. 'We're going to make it, Alex, believe me.'

'You don't have to say that, Kane,' she said through chattering teeth. 'We've had it, and we both know it.'

'You're wrong, Alex. We'll make it.'

They weren't going to make it – she knew that. She couldn't use her legs anymore and she just wanted to sleep. There was a limit to how much she could take and she'd passed the finishing line way back. *She* was holding him back. He would stand a better chance without her. He didn't deserve to die. She'd been wrong at every step of the way about Kane Mitchell and there was only one way she could show her remorse and that was by giving him a chance to survive this.

As the next wave broke, with her remaining strength, she pushed free of him and as the roll took her down and she sank, it didn't hurt at all. In fact, it felt strangely comforting. Visions raced through her head: her mother, her father, Arthur, Holly, Mac, Jodie, Kane. The last two visions might have been worth living for if only she didn't feel so tired. The illusions faded, clouds swirled, a light shone, beckoning, pulling her towards it. Music played – soft, wordless. She touched clouds, felt sunshine on her face, smelled roses and honeysuckle. No, it didn't hurt at all. She dragged open her eyes to take a closer look - and screamed. It escaped her mouth in bubbles that rushed upwards towards the surface as if they too were fleeing from the hideous sight. Ahead of her, trapped in the reef, was Asak Mulligan's body. His head bobbed back and forth in the movement of the water, while black scavenger fish ripped and picked at his flesh in a feeding frenzy. His sodden cloak, torn below his breastbone, flapped in the swell like the giant wings of a huge bird of prey. Beneath it, ribs protruded, white and dull, exposed by the fish. Above, a black shape, like an aeroplane coming in to land, loomed, attracted by the blood that still flowed from his broken head. She hit the reef reeling backwards, hands flailing at her sides, backing along the seabed, away from the horrendous sight. Something hit her from behind, a hand closed on her shoulder and suddenly he was there, dragging her to the surface, his mouth clamped over hers, breathing air into her. She clung to him like a limpet, accepting the breath that he forced into her. Suddenly death didn't seem such an inspiring option. Suddenly, doing the right thing and giving Kane a chance to make it on his own didn't seem so magnanimous. Asak Mulligan was dead and travelling somewhere. Today wasn't a good day to die. What if their paths crossed? What if they both ended up in the same place? No. Best to let him make the journey alone. She could always travel another day, when the road to heaven or hell wasn't quite so busy. She knew her thinking had shot it. A sharp sound rang out and she felt a slight irritation on her cheek. Another shot and the irritation felt more like a bee sting. Another slap and the pain of it bit through to her senses and she regained consciousness to see Kane, his hand raised about to strike her again.

'That won't be necessary,' she slurred, sounding drunk. 'I'm back.'

His face was as dark as the night sky. 'Stupid bloody woman! Are you trying to kill me?' he gasped, sucking in air to replenish his depleted supply. 'What the hell were you playing at?'

Her head still lolled as she said, 'I thought you'd make it better without me.'

'Yeah, today maybe,' he said, placing a hand at the side of her head, steadying it. 'But what about the rest of my life? How do I make it through the rest of my life without you, Alex?'

She watched the flecking dancing in his concerned eyes, saw the sincerity buried there and knew that he meant it. Wasn't a man like this worth fighting for? 'I'm sorry,' she whispered. 'I just thought …'

'Best not to, eh? As I remember it's not one of your strongest attributes.'

She trod water, forcing her legs to work, as Kane spun her round away from the horizon and struck out across the water dragging her with him. After ten minutes, swimming against the turning tide, he stopped. They had made little impression and the retreating tide was becoming stronger with each wave. Soon it would carry them away and the distance would be too great. They would never get back. Perhaps the answer was to try to get back onto The Reach. Surely, the water, now that the tide was turning, wouldn't be too fractious there. He pushed himself higher in the water trying to get his bearings and estimate how far away they were from the mass. He could just make out the outline through the sea spray. Waves still bounced. It was pointless trying to get any nearer. They would never get out of the water. Alex clung to him, eyes closed again. Her body felt like ice. Perhaps now was the time to admit defeat? Just stop swimming and hold her until the inevitable happened. He'd seen the shark circling Asak Mulligan's broken body and didn't fancy ending up as shark bait or, worse still, to see Alex dragged from his arms and taken piece by piece. Again, he struck out, pushing across the top of oncoming waves, spearing through them with an outstretched arm, towing Alex in his wake. Another ten minutes and he stopped swimming and trod water. Alex clung to him, shaking, almost blue. It was a wonder to him that she wasn't dead already. How much more could she take? Christ! Why had he been such a damn fool? It had seemed a good idea at the time. Come back from burying Walker, start a row with Alex, get her to believe that he'd changed his mind, pack every last hair and disappear into the night; steal the boat, pretend to leave and wait for Asak Mulligan to appear, confident that Alex was alone - except for Peter. But Peter was a recent arrival and Kane was putting money on the fact that Mulligan didn't even know that he was on the island. He knew he was placing Alex in extreme danger but his plan was to creep back onto the island, unseen, under the cover of night and wait and watch over Alex, until Mulligan put in an appearance. The plan had backfired when Peter showed himself at the field gate and Mulligan shot him. Kane had followed him as he'd retreated into the jungle but lost him. Unable to give away his whereabouts, Kane had waited for Mulligan to reappear. It wasn't until the storm struck that he saw him again. He had him in his sights and was about to pull the trigger, wounding him, stopping him in his tracks, when Alex appeared from the house and ran to the stables, obscuring his line of fire. He'd watched whilst she struggled with the wrong key, saw her turn and come face to face with Mulligan; he'd waited for her to bolt for the security of the house. It was then that a warning bell clanged. This was Alex. Alex wasn't going to bolt for the house. He'd watched, horrified, as she'd taken off after Mulligan along the beach, disappearing into the storm before he could get to her. He'd left it all too late. By the time he'd reached the beach, Mulligan and she were out of sight. When he finally caught up with them, Mulligan had Alex by the throat and was about to kill her. He'd had no choice but to put a bullet through his brain.

Kane rubbed saltwater from his eyes and peered across the waves. He didn't know if he was hallucinating or if it was just wishful thinking, as his eyes focused on two small lights moving along the shoreline. He watched them, as they bounced and rolled, stopping and starting, stopping and starting, until they came to a halt at the Reach.

'Alex, open your eyes. Look.'

Slowly she opened her eyes.

'Look,' he said, spinning her around in the water until she could also see the lights searching. Now they were shining out across the sea directly at them.

A man was stumbling along the Reach, rising and falling time after time, shouting and waving his arms. His progress was slow, coming to an abrupt halt where the sea still churned between the rocks. He was shouting and gesticulating with his arm.

'Peter?' they questioned in unison.

He was throwing out a lifebelt attached to a rope. The lifebelt made little distance from the rocks and they watched wide-eyed as the man, who had been knocking on death's door, sank to his knees.

'I take it all back,' Kane said, spitting out salt water. 'That man does have some endearing qualities.'

'But ... Peter's dead,' Alex stammered. 'I heard a death rattle. He was barely breathing ... I was sure he was dead.'

'Obviously not. Unless it's his ghost.'

'It'll never reach us. He's too far away... too weak to throw it far enough.'

Kane released his hold on her. 'Stay here, keep kicking.' He dived and with the ability of a seasoned cross channel swimmer, sliced through the outgoing tide until she could barely see him. In that moment she knew, categorically, that he could have saved himself at any time, had he chosen to? He had only stayed, and risked his own precious life because of her.

He reached the life belt easily, grabbed it, turned and swam back to her before her legs gave up.

'Hold on, Alex. I reckon Peter has this sussed,' he said dropping the belt over her head. Attached to it was a rope.

Peter was back at the Land Rover, horn blasting, lights glaring on full beam, lighting the invisible road home across the heaving sea. He slammed the winch into drive. The rope lifted from the water, tightened and towed them across the receding waves. As they hit the beach, Alex collapsed on the sand. Peter struggled towards them and fell by her side, rolling over onto his back, breathing hard – but breathing!

'I don't know how the hell you found us, Gregson, but thank you,' Kane said, meaning it, as he rose to his feet. 'We wouldn't have made it without you.'

Peter raised a hand in acknowledgment but didn't speak – he couldn't. He still looked like death.

Kane pulled off his shirt and wrapped it around Alex. She buttoned it with shaking fingers, her eyes staring out to sea. 'He is dead, isn't he?' she croaked. Her throat felt like it had been ripped out.

Kane nodded.

She knew he was dead. She'd seen him – or what was left of him. But what if he really did have supernatural abilities? What if he was so much a part of the land that, like the land, he would always be? She shivered. 'It still feels like he's here,' she said, shakily, turning up the wet collar of Kane's shirt.

Kane looked out to sea briefly, before tossing the life belt into the back of the vehicle. 'He's gone, Alex. Asak Mulligan is resting peacefully in the gut of a shark. Trust me.' He pulled her to her feet, then helped Peter up before saying, 'We're finished here. Let's go home.'

Alex dragged herself into the Land Rover and Kane half carried and half shoved Peter until he was sitting by her side. His head lolled forward and his chin touched his chest. Alex took his hand in hers and squeezed it, noting that finally it held some warmth. Kane turned the key and the Land Rover belched into life, giving Alex a much-needed feeling of normality. He pointed a finger through the windscreen and towards the horizon. 'Look at that,' he said. 'How can anything be wrong on a morning like this?'

Peter raised his head and they followed Kane's finger. The storm had gone to some other place. The wind had dropped and pink, candy-floss clouds lined up on the eastern horizon, as another beautiful day broke.

Peter tried to speak and after several failed attempts to control his facial muscles said. 'G ... Good job old Asak M ... Mulligan wasn't really a twin, or we'd really have something to worry about.'

Alex and Kane swung round to face him.

Peter shrugged and attempted a grin. 'Just joking,' he said through wobbly lips 'Just ... something I heard on the ... m ... mainland. I didn't believe it, so there's no reason why you should, is there?'

'Oh shit! You don't think that's possible, do you? The mainlanders were right about Asak Mulligan. Could they be right about that as well?' Alex said, holding her throat, still croaking

Kane placed a hand on her shoulder and gently turned her to face him. His eyes sought hers. His mouth smiled. 'There was only one Asak Mulligan just like there's only one Alex McBride.' He gently kissed her mouth before adding, 'And for that, on both counts, we can only be grateful.'

Alex frowned. 'I'm not sure that's a compliment … and don't go thinking you are forgiven for running out on me like that, because you're not. You still haven't explained yourself and another thing …'

Kane placed his hand over her mouth, stopping her words. 'You see what I mean? 'That little episode out there -' he nodded to The Reach '- was just a normal, average day in Alex's world, wasn't it?'

Alex reached up and gently removed his hand from her mouth, coughed a couple of times and said, 'Well, I wouldn't go as far as to say normal but … well … yeah, I guess stuff does happen.'

Kane shook his head, and took hold of her hand. 'Well, *stuff* won't be happening anymore because I'm here and quite frankly I don't see you having much time on your hands. There's a feisty little girl to think about.'

Peter tried to waft a fly from his nose and missed. 'Much as I'd love to sit here all day feeling like death and listening to your foreplay, Kane, do you t … think there's any chance we could go now? I think I've had enough excitement f … for *one* life time.'

Alex gave his hand another little squeeze and kindly removed the persistent insect from his nose. Peter, that useless waste of space, that spineless baby-hating jerk had saved their lives. Kane was right, without Peter they wouldn't have made it. The old rules no longer applied, he had paid fully for his past mistakes and callousness. They would never be lovers but they could be friends. He could stay on the island until he was fully recovered and ready to leave. Perhaps she would set him up in business, after all, what price did you put on two lives? Or she might even introduce him to Ruth, the delivery lady, she was nice.

She turned to look at Kane and rasped, 'This is going to be one crazy story to tell Jodie. She'll never believe you left me all alone and went walkabout while Asak Mulligan was choking the life out of me on the Reach.'

Kane's expression changed instantly. 'Yeah, well, I think I might go walkabout again and leave that *little* thing for *you* to do.'

Alex couldn't laugh, it hurt too much, but she managed a smile and said, 'Any one would think you're scared of our little Jodie.'

Kane grimaced and slipped the Land Rover into gear.

'Don't worry,' Alex said, pulling the shirt tighter round her shivering body. 'I'll do it. After all, I am the bravest woman you've ever known.'

Kane suppressed a smile, rammed his wet, booted foot down on the accelerator and the Land Rover headed for home.

With heartfelt thanks to Amanda S. John for her invaluable help and guidance.

Also available by Jennie Orbell:

Starfish

Eternal: A Collection of Short Stories